Once Around the Sun

To Stephanie, Enjoy!

Once Around the Sun

Sweet, Funny, and Strange Tales for All Seasons

Edited by
A. E. Decker and Marianne H. Donley

Carol L. Wright

Jeff Baird

BWG

Bethlehem Writers Group, LLC
Bethlehem, Pennsylvania

ONCE AROUND THE SUN

First edition: November 2013
ISBN 978-0-9892650-0-3
Library of Congress Control Number applied for

Cover image © Fotosearch.com
Cover design © 2013 Carol L. Wright
Layout by Ruth Heil

Printed in the United States of America

With continued gratitude
to our families and friends,
to our teachers, editors, and readers,
and to each other

Also from the Bethlehem Writers Group:

A Christmas Sampler:
Sweet, Funny, and Strange Holiday Tales
Winner of two 2010 Next Generation Indie Book Awards:
Best Short Fiction and *Best Anthology*

Bethlehem Writers Roundtable
A monthly journal of
quality short fiction, interviews, and more
bwgwritersroundtable.com

Bethlehem Writers Roundtable
Annual Short Story Award
For information see:
bwgwritersroundtable.com

The Bethlehem Writers Daily
paper.li/BethlehemWriter/1325670670

The Daily Wryter
paper.li/BettysTips/1325667986

The Bethlehem Writers Group is a community of mutually-supportive fiction and nonfiction authors based in Bethlehem, Pennsylvania. The members are as different from each other as their stories, spanning a range of genres including: children's, fantasy, humor, inspirational, literary fiction, memoir, mystery, paranormal, romance, science fiction, women's fiction, and young adult. They meet regularly to help each other refine their craft. Learn more at their website: bethlehemwritersgroup.com.

Table of Contents

WINTER

Singers for Heaven.. 7
Bernadette De Courcey

Ninety-Four Winters 17
Paul Weidknecht

The Ice Prince.. 19
A. E. Decker

If Daylight Ever Comes.. 41
Jo Ann Schaffer

Ave Maria 47
Katherine Fast
Winner of the 2013 Bethlehem Writers Roundtable Short Story Award

Cold Turkey.. 51
Jo Ann Schaffer

Bittersweet 59
A. E. Decker

SPRING

Butterfly Wings.................................... 71
Courtney Annicchiarico

The Call.. 73
Paul Weidknecht

A Spouse's Guide to March Madness........................... 81
Headley Hauser

Seven Seconds.. 85
Ralph Hieb

Felicity and Fortune.................................... 89
Emily P. W. Murphy

Timothy Worthy Teddybear and Spring Cleaning......... 105
Will Wright

The River 113
Ralph Hieb

The Muse.. 123
Emily P. W. Murphy

SUMMER

The Farmer's Daughter 129
Jerome W. McFadden

Sandal Season 139
Emily P. W. Murphy

My First Red Sox Game 145
Carol L. Wright

Tomato Blight 153
Marianne H. Donley

First Impressions, Second Chances 171
Diane Sismour

Redheads by the Cement Pond 201
Jeff Baird

Keeping Promises 207
Sally W. Paradysz

La Quebrada 225
Paul Weidknecht

FALL

Only a Game 235
Jerome W. McFadden

Prisons and the Digital Age 241
Jeff Baird

Gramma, How Could You? 247
Carol A. Hanzl Birkas

The Little Ghost Who Couldn't Say Boo 253
Courtney Annicchiarico

Mortified 255
Will Wright

The Banshee 263
Bernadette De Courcey

Autumn Pursuit 269
David Chesney
Winner of the 2012 Bethlehem Writers Roundtable Short Story Award

This Business of Wood 275
Sally W. Paradysz

ABOUT THE AUTHORS 285

ACKNOWLEDGEMENTS 291

WINTER

Singers for Heaven

Bernadette De Courcey

The glass in front of me is full of water. The condensation is leaving a ring on the coaster protecting the fine mahogany wood. I look up and meet the stare of the man facing me. His eyes are brown and steady. He gave me the option of leaving if the questioning is too much for me; I glance at the glass door and think about it. Then I look back at the man and the woman sitting next to him, her silver pen poised above a blank notepad. He asks again.

"What do you remember about school?" The question twists, flickers, and then slides foremost in my memory, to take a firm hold there, like a concertgoer standing his ground in the front row. Following it is my sister. She always hugged me, squeezing the breath out of me, before taking the little bag from our mam, and looking down at her bare feet, she would leave. School was where she was going, a magical place where everyone had little bags. "Don't you run after her," mam would scold me daily, or sometimes she would use her best Irish and say, "*Ná dul i ndiadh di.*"

Most people remember their first day of school. Not me. What I do recall is my little bag, maroon patent leather with a buckle, a pink skirt with a white flower in the corner, and a cream sweater with a hole in the sleeve tucked into it. The hair on my head was pulled tight and banded. Loose hair was only worn by *stripachs*. My sister, in her grey pinafore and worn purple sweater, walked with me. "Hush now it's just a little bit farther," she would say, always carrying my little bag once we passed Fitzs' haystacks on the corner. On the darker days, there were the duffel coats with buttons that were too big for my fingers.

Once Around the Sun

There were mornings, slow and dark, when the moon reflected off the rain puddles outside the window. These days began with both a boiled egg and some homemade brown bread, with jam or milk sprinkled on the bread, with sugar shook on top. Then came the journey to the place where every child must go. On dry fine days, my sister and I took a shortcut through Donahue's fields. The wheat was golden and as tall as me. We picked and shelled it between our fingers, developing the fine art of blowing the shell away before sucking each morsel out of the palms of our hands. The path we left behind was the width of ourselves and was easily spotted by a curious passerby's eye. The farmer we called Big Tom never complained. Farmers are kind souls as those paths took a lot of walking off our journey.

Our school, a three-room building with an outside lavatory, was whitewashed and smelled of damp. I would put down my little maroon bag next to my chair. In it was my jotter, pencil, and a small bottle of milk, or in the winter, cocoa sometimes, and two slices of homemade bread with butter and jam. From baby infants to third class, Mrs. Logue taught us. Her grey bun sat on top of her head, a black shawl around her shoulders, and plump wide arms that could wrap all the way around you in a hug. She never missed a day or left early, not even the days she came in with purple and blue bruises on her cheeks.

There were days we all came in squelching in our clothes, our bare feet brown and slick; soaked to the bone by a shower from God. She did her best to dry our coats or at least take a lot of the wet out of them. That way we could wear them for the evening journey. They all lay steaming atop the fireguard, and, sitting in my chair dripping onto the floor, I would keep watch on the fire, staring into the redness praying for it to stay lit until we left to go home. It seldom did.

There were days when the two windows were frozen shut, and our feet were blue, and she would take our milk bottles or cocoa bottles and line them up around the fireguard. The red fire would reach out and touch the bottles warming them. I hated warm milk then and still do.

Mrs. Logue was the only teacher who told us we were like Moses' children, for all the walking we did to get to school. She did everything right, except light the fire. The fire was her nemesis. There were no such things as newfangled fire-lighters, and the turf was not always dry; with all the showers from God how could it be? To start the fire one almost had to possess a sort of inherited skill. Once she tried to light the fire with kerosene. She lit the paper, the chimney, the rug in front, and with the school almost about to go up in flames, the turf still wasn't lit. From that day on she relied solely on some paraffin oil. The result was more smoke than heat that dwindled to ashes and went out.

Her skills as a teacher were less challenged. She taught us all how to read, write, say our prayers, do our tables, and spell properly. Homework consisted of half a page of our English book, and a few lines of Irish which she said was difficult to learn when no one spoke it at home. We also had some tables and at least four words of spelling in both English and Irish. Prayers were cited and recited at the start, middle, and end of the day. As we got older, she would bring out the big sewing box and the basket of knitting wool. The boys didn't have to learn how to turn a heel of a sock, or close the toe. They weren't expected to practice the running stitch, top sewing, tacking stitch, and the blanket stitch. The girls all did the very best with this for Mrs. Logue, as it was all put in a book for the inspector when he came to school.

That visitor arrived once a year with a briefcase, brown hat, and umbrella. He sat cross-legged in the back of the class, and you were tempted to turn and look, but you didn't dare. Mrs. Logue wore a blue dress on those days. "Be on your best behavior tomorrow, class; the inspector is coming," she would say. Everyone was at school the days the inspector came, and no one ever said anything. The small room in the back of the school was always empty that day.

Singing class was every Friday morning. My sister and I would skip to school those days. Everyone said I had a voice like a Linnet. I didn't know what a Linnet was as I'd never met one. There, I would stand in front of the others, and as I got older I sang the parts that were underlined in black. I thought I would sing in a band when I left school; that never happened and is unlikely now. The boys would be let out to run amok when we were singing, but, in the attempt of fairness, they got jobs to do we didn't. Drawing water from a well near the school for the teachers' tea, cleaning out the turf box, emptying the bucket from the outside toilet, and making sure that no one ever went in the third room locked in the back. Whitewash buckets, kerosene, and other such dangerous things for children were kept there. Such were the jobs to be done each day by the boys and only the boys.

First Holy Communion was made in second class, and that was a lot of learning. Prayers had to be quoted word for word, and then there was the big visit from the priest, Father O'Brien. He came to ask us our catechism. His black robe had a gold knotted belt around the middle; his glasses always fogged from the rain, and he would pant out of breath as if he'd been running. "Who made the world?" was always the first question. Dutiful as children could be, we chanted loudly in unison. "God made the world." As a reward for our chanting the answers correctly, Mrs. Logue would bring in a big bag of sweets the next day: black jacks, red suckers, bulls eyes, flogs, and butterscotch. All the preparation was then worthwhile as far as we were concerned. Plus it meant no one would be sent to the Master's room.

We had play time in the yard, where we usually played catch, or if the boys had a ball, we would kick that around, doing our best to avoid mucking our clothes up as that was a sin. Skip rope was popular, but someone had to bring in a piece of rope, and two would have to turn it. Then we took turns running in to jump. It kept us warm, and fit too I guess, but warm was the goal in our skirts and jumpers, or dresses. No tracksuits or pants for girls in those days.

When I left Mrs. Logue's classroom and moved out to the Master's room, the good times ended. For starters, no more drying of coats or warming milk bottles or anything nice. He came to school equipped with a leather strap which he carried in a black bag. This strap was worn smooth; I know because I felt the whip of it, many times. Math was to blame for that. Try as I might I could not get it right, well rarely ever. Ivan Payne was his name, that Master. Once a boy came in to school without his school bag, and the Master took the strap to him with such vigor that the boy fell down. We all sat stared thinking he was dead. But he only wished he was. After that, he was brought out to the room at the back.

Our biggest concern was always who would be the first to miss a question. That poor lad or lass got it. He kept the strap in his pocket while he was in class, and you'd be watching his hands all day to see if they were reaching into the pocket. I was so afraid of having my sums wrong I would walk to a neighbor's house where a very smart man named Mikey Deady would be visiting, and he would help me with my sums. It was often dark on the walk home, and every noise in the bushes raised alarm in me. But as long as I had my sums done, I was happy to face the darkness.

On days I didn't have them done, I just wouldn't go to school. I would head out from home and then not go. The kid next door, who hadn't his sums done either, and I spent one day *mitching* school in a bog. We stayed until we thought it was time to go home, having no watch to go by. He hated school as much as I did. I asked him if he had ever been in the room in the back. It was forbidden to talk about it, but the question just jumped out of me. He looked at me with his blue eyes and nodded, then turned and ran off home.

I endured third to sixth class, struggling along one day at a time. Some days the Master beat me; some days he beat the others. In the evening, my sister and I were always together. She would put a salve on my red blisters, and I would put some on hers. Sometimes when our dad saw our sores he would take the belt to us as well, telling us we had better start behaving better in school.

Once Around the Sun

In the winter, we had to do our homework by lamplight, and our jobs at home—like drawing water, bringing in the turf for the fire, and feeding the animals—were all done in the dark.

In the summer, we ran barefoot all of the time, even going to the bog to foot the turf with my sister and our neighbors, and making up the hay with the rest of my family. The cows were milked, and we had fresh milk. Then not only did we have our own homemade bread, but homemade butter as well. The cream we kept off the milk each day, until we had enough to make a churn. We all had to have a turn winding the handle until it was butter. My arms would ache the next day. The butter milk made the most delicious bread and griddle cakes, which my mother made regularly for us. My father worked in the town and had little time for the work being done at home. He would organize people to cut the turf, and he would cut the hay himself with us doing most of the saving of that, with our neighbors help. The days rolled along, and we tried not to think the summer would have to come to an end. It did, but we told ourselves that school wouldn't last forever either.

Finally, the end of sixth class came along, and our class had our first big exam known as the Primary Cert. Coming up to the big exam we really got beat up with learning. Each time I heard the strap zip through the air I started, and the hair on the back of my neck would stand up. Thank God I passed mine; he must have heard all my prayers, because those who did not really got the black strap when the results came back.

After the exam was behind me, I was off to the convent school. I was so excited in my uniform, carrying my big bag of books on my new bike. Boy was I ever in for a shock; the excitement didn't last past the school gates. The first nun I met told me to take the smile off my face and get on my knees in front of the class to say the rosary. Her gold band on her left hand glinted as she slapped me across the head for not having my rosary beads in my pocket. This was the first of many days like it at the convent.

On the nice evenings walking home, we would talk about who was the first to get slapped that day and why. What was the question they didn't answer properly, and what was the correct answer. We would try to memorize it for the next time in case we were asked it. This was just like the Master's class except for the room. The rest of the time, we played our favorite games. We loved to play soldiers. Soldiers are long tall stemmed weeds that grew and still grow along the hedge row. They have a weedy top on them. You pull them from the ground close to the root as you can, to get as long a soldier as possible. Then you hold out your soldier and the other person holds out theirs. With one slap of your soldier, you try to take the head off his or her soldier. Whichever one is strongest and beheads the other has the best soldier. "Off with the heads of the Sisters of Mercy," I would say sometimes, looking around to make sure I couldn't be heard.

We would wind our way home doing things like that. Sometimes we picked sloes in Clifford's field and then ate them on the way home, our starter before dinner, so to speak. I didn't know then that sloes are great and are the main ingredient for gin. If only we could have become rich and famous making gin at an early age. Ha, that would have been something. Those nuns would have been sorry then.

At other times when the apples were ripe, we would rob them. That was a big challenge as the best orchard that we knew of was Stacks, and we rarely went there. The old lady would hear us and come out shouting, "Get the gun, get the gun," but sure we knew she had no gun, and for all the apples we only took a few. Wrong I know, but devilment will win out at times. Taught by the nuns, saints we were not.

Being at the convent school was very different to the primary school, apart from the beatings which were even worse by the nuns. The uniform of a maroon gymslip and a lemon blouse was nice, but I only had one due to shortage of money, and there were many like me I'm sure, except for the well off as we called them.

Once Around the Sun

The sisters had rosary beads that were as long as a belt and hung down along their habits to the ground. Some of them were not too bad, but if Sister Concillio got a set on you, your life was made hell. She taught mathematics. That not being my best subject, I was the one who came under fire. "You are stupid," she would say after she had me up at the board to do the exercise. She would try to explain it to me, but very soon ran out of patience. My nerves would prevent my brain from thinking anything other than, "She's going to hit me, and I'm up here in front of the class." Then she would say, "Oh for God's sake and your own, just go and sit down. You are a hopeless case, and you will never learn anything. You and your whole family are as thick as bricks." I believed her.

The Reverend Mother taught Geometry. Her bent frame was about five-foot-one, and her white hair was pulled tight beneath the old style habit. Rumor had it that she was one hundred and two. Her class was my worst nightmare. I could never get the gist of Geometry no matter what I did, and she had no patience to teach me. Who knows, maybe I was never going to be able to do Geometry anyway. My friend Carmel Ashe would say, "Oh don't mind them old nuns and their sums, sure we'll get by without them anyway. Sure they aren't right in the head." Carmel lived in the town, and I envied anyone who lived in town. I never got to see her outside of the convent, and then only in class, as she could go home for lunch and I had mine in school. Sometimes during lunch, Sandra and I would walk downtown to Woolworth's, which was our favorite place to try on the lipsticks. Back in class, Carmel would ask me did we go to Woolworth's, and of course I filled her in on all the glitter. The nuns were very nice to the townies, especially if their dads had big jobs. Carmel never got slapped.

One day as I was filling in Carmel about all the new colors at Woolworth's, Sister Concillio overheard me and brought me up to the board. Knees weak, I did as I was told. The problem on the board was nothing I'd ever seen before. "Go on, take the chalk," she said, half smirking. I picked it up and stared at the board. Minutes passed by, and no one in the room moved. The first belt I felt was on my right ear; the second came on my cheek. I tried to block the third blow with my hand, but that just enraged her even more.

When I woke up, I could not see. I reached around me and felt a broom handle and some dusters. The closet by the back door maybe, I thought. I stood and tried to find the door handle. Feeling up and around from one corner to the other, there was none, only cobwebs. Hours must have passed. I screamed, "Let me out. Let me out." I banged the door with the broom. I listened. Nothing. I sat on the floor weeping. Later Carmel told me that Sister Concillio dragged me out of the room and told them not to stir an inch. It wasn't a closet; it was a small storage room. There were cans of paint, and on the floor were a few old towels. I laid down on them holding my head in my hands. My face was sticky, and my hair was knotted. I felt around in the dark for my hair band, but couldn't find it. I heard men's voices, and I remember begging to be let go; I was sorry for my sins. I prayed and I prayed.

Time passed slowly, and I thought about my friend Sheila Flaherty from the primary school. She was from the country like me, and we both struggled with our sums. We knew the sting of the leather strap well. The trouble was you were only friends in class, and she could only walk half way home with me to her house. Me and my school *mitching* friend, Timmy McMahon, lived the furthest away. He lived just beside me on the *bohereen*. This must have happened to them, too. They were both sent to that room at the back of the school.

Sister Rosario came and took me to Dr. Gannon the next day. She told him I'd been found *mitching* with the McMahon lad. "Her dad must have given her a beating for being with that lad, and right he was, too. She's nothing but a tart this one, a *stripach*," she said. My protests fell on deaf ears. Dr. Gannon was half drunk on whiskey, and, after stitching my face, told me to run along home. Timmy never laid a hand on me, but someone had, that part was true.

Once Around the Sun

I tell them everything but nothing at the same time. My name will be released in the official government report. Their names will be withheld. "To protect them," they say. I half run half walk back to my car and climb into the driver's seat. To think that I endured two years in hell with those nuns before I left and joined my sister at the Technical school, which turned out to be the best thing I ever did. I look in the rearview mirror and touch the scar on the side of my face. "Do I remember my school days?" they asked me, sitting in their dry-clean-only polyester suits.

Ninety-Four Winters

Paul Weidknecht

Every winter as a teenager, she'd find herself standing at the pond. She remembered her fascination at how the shelves of wafer ice, more fragile than bulb glass, would grow and knit over the wilted pickerelweed, eventually thickening enough to support her father's tractor. Though the years had bundled themselves into decades, she recalled, with the clarity of someone much younger, the last time she had been to that edge. Now her view came from the parlor chair, past mother's yellowed lace curtains: a dozen children skating and sledding, laughing and shouting.

She turned toward the phone. One call to the sheriff would end their trespass. His four-wheel drive would appear at the crest of a hill a quarter-mile away, bump over the cattle guard at the end of her frozen road, and come to rest near the dock. He'd talk a moment before gesturing vaguely for them to leave, probably half-embarrassed he was breaking up their fun. As the group slumped away, they'd glance at the house, knowing who had called: the bitter old woman who lived in stale shadows, whose youth was so ancient as to be alien.

And they'd be right, she thought. At least a little. Yet there would be no call today. They didn't need to know that ice sometimes breaks, shattering lives and dreams with it. So she stood, pulling the chair close to the window, hoping the ice would hold, and that they would never leave.

The Ice Prince

A. E. Decker

At some point, Daphne knew she would have to go home. Just . . . not yet. Better to prolong her evening walk, despite the chill December wind, than face her empty apartment. Stopping under one of the lampposts that illuminated campus center, she tried to rub some warmth back into her numb ears. She always forgot her hat.

A small noise drew her gaze down the flight of concrete stairs leading to the campus green. There, a young man stood on the white-dappled square of grass, trying to catch snowflakes on his tongue. Lost in a private moment.

I should look away, thought Daphne, staring at this endearingly—and incongruously—childlike figure in a long tailored coat and tartan scarf, his head thrown back, and his tongue stuck out as far as it would go. A sympathetic laugh escaped her.

He heard it.

"Oh, sorry," she said as he whipped around, so fast that his silver-rimmed glasses nearly flew off his face. She was, too. In an instant, he'd transformed from a happy child into a solemn man.

The wind tugged his auburn hair back as he stared up at her. Half-moon reflections off his glasses' round lenses obscured the color of his eyes. A silence lay between them, heavy and awkward. All at once he nodded, thrust his hands in his pockets, and walked towards the steps.

He meant to brush past her and exit her life, Daphne guessed. To spare herself a lifetime of self-reproach, she waited until he'd drawn level with her before speaking. "When I was eighteen, my parents caught me dancing around the living room in my underwear singing 'Like a Virgin.'"

As she'd hoped, he paused. A soft laugh huffed out of his throat.

"Why were you doing that?" he asked, and a little part of her squirmed with delight upon hearing his British accent. She couldn't help it; she watched Alan Rickman movies just to listen to his voice.

"I don't remember," she said. "Silliness." He tilted his head, and a shaft of light from the lamppost struck his face. "Hey, I know you. You're Mr. Serraun, right?"

"Yes." He blinked. "I'm so sorry, I've forgotten your name."

"We've never actually met. My friend Melissa Garth is in the music department. She TAs for Professor Wright, too. She's mentioned you." She extended her hand. "Daphne Cooper."

He clasped her fingers. "Pleased to meet you."

Then, one of those dreadful pauses ensued, a long silence where each waited for the other to speak. Daphne knew she'd break first; she always did. So she shrugged and went for it. "How about I buy you a cup of cocoa at Emily's as an apology?"

He laughed again, a bit louder this time. "You have nothing to apologize for."

"Sure I do. I intruded on a special moment there, didn't I?"

A blush came into his cheeks, but he shrugged it off. "It's only snow."

"The first snow of the season. Maybe we'll have a white Christmas this year." It was coming down thicker now, big lacy flakes, like doilies drifting out of the dark sky. Some settled in his hair. Another landed on the tip of Daphne's nose and sat there, not melting. Laughing, she brushed it away and took his arm. "Please say yes."

He pursed his lips. "Very well. But I'll buy the pastries."

"Deal."

They passed the university center in friendly silence. Ahead, the lights of downtown twinkled in red and green. "Are you going home for the holidays?" asked Daphne.

"No, I'll probably spend it doing research. And you?"

The question was perfectly fair, utterly innocent. He couldn't know that her stomach had clenched and a lump formed in her throat. *Brett, you jerk. Who breaks up with someone three weeks before Christmas?* Swallowing the lump, she forced cheer into her tone. "My plans got canceled at the last minute, so I guess I'll just hang around town."

She'd already bought tickets for the play, made the restaurant reservations, booked the hotel—everything—when Brett announced that he wasn't ready for this level of commitment, and vanished.

They rounded the corner onto Main Street. Emily's pastry shop, with its mouth-watering displays of cupcakes and éclairs beckoned, its windows outlined in twinkling lights and holly. The bell over the door rang as Daphne pushed it open. Warm, buttery scents wreathed her face. Her ears prickled, beginning the process of unfreezing. She really needed to stop forgetting her hat.

Her companion drummed his fingertips against the pastry case as they waited in line. Not impatience; he seemed to be tapping out some complicated rhythm. "What kind of music are you studying?" asked Daphne.

He looked down at his fingers as if only now noticing what they were up to. "Cognitive musicology," he said, folding them self-consciously.

"Uh, okay." She laughed. "I'll pretend I understood that."

Smiling, he tucked his hands into his pockets. "Basically, I study how the brain interprets music. I convert songs into algorithms. Bores the piss out of most people. What's your field?"

"I'm working on my MA. Art and history. I want to be a costume designer. I love your coat, by the way."

His shoulders tightened beneath the blue fabric. "A gift from my father."

The solemn man was back. Although she would've loved to ask about the coat, Daphne just nodded. After a moment, he relaxed.

Once Around the Sun

They snagged one of the small round tables just as another couple left. He wiped off the crumbs while she grabbed a cinnamon sprinkler. They sat, her with an éclair, him with a brioche, sipping their cocoa and listening to the carols piping over the speakers.

"So," said Daphne, dusting cinnamon into her cocoa, "is your name really Angel? Melissa said some guys in your department call you that."

A look of pain crossed his face. "No, they bequeathed me that nickname because my first two initials are L A."

"So what's your real name?"

"Something more ghastly than Angel." He bit into his brioche.

"Lloyd? Lemuel?" said Daphne, picking the worst L names she could think of on the spot.

He sipped cocoa.

"Oh, come on. My name's Daphne. The kids at school used to call me Daffy Duck."

"Daphne: a nymph pursued by Apollo and turned into a laurel by Gaia, mother of the Earth," he said, then colored, as if only just realizing he'd spoken aloud. "I took a classics course," he said. His gaze flicked out the window. "Why not call me L?"

Daphne shook off her amazement. "No way. You don't look a thing like L." He gave her a blank look. "I take it you haven't read *Death Note*?" She licked cream off a finger. "It's a manga. One of the character's a detective named L."

"What's it about?" he asked, and that led to a conversation about the books each was reading. Snowflakes flitted past the window like white butterflies as their cocoa vanished sip by sip. When nothing remained of their pastries but crumbs, Daphne reluctantly suggested they let someone else have their table.

"You could go by your middle name," she said, buttoning her coat.

Holding the door open for her, he shook his head. "It's just as appalling."

"Your parents really had bad taste in names, huh?"

Again that faint air of distaste. "That's a polite way of putting it."

"Lester."

"No." He sighed. "I should restrict you to three guesses."

They were strolling along Main Street, pausing every so often to admire a window display. Snow continued to fall, settling over the grass and trees. Daphne wasn't ready to return to her apartment, still populated with memories of Brett. At least once a day she'd stumbled across one of his books or CDs or even a tube of toothpaste, and all the bad feelings would flood over her again. At least she'd stopped crying herself to sleep while hugging his old green sweatshirt.

"Linus," she said.

"Linus is a perfectly respectable name."

"Linus sucks his thumb and obsesses over a blanket. Ludovic."

"Yes."

"Really?"

"No, of course not. Is 'Ludovic' actually a name?"

"I think so." She stopped to look in the window of *Riddle Me This*, one of her favorite shops. Games, brain-teasers, and mystery books were all laid out against a background of gold foil. Daphne's gaze went to the puzzle in the center of the display. It portrayed a knight in battered silver armor standing ankle-deep in the snow. Sword drawn, he watched a wolf emerge from wintry woods. Something about his posture and the wolf's expression suggested mutual respect rather than impending violence. A cardinal observed the pair from a tree stump, its crimson feathers a brilliant contrast to the subtle white, lavenders, and grays of the winter landscape.

"That's a nice picture," said L, as she was forced to think of him.

"Must be the contest winner," said Daphne. "Twice a year, Mr. Hartman holds a competition for the local artists, and the winner gets their picture made into a puzzle."

"It's quite good."

Once Around the Sun

Several times during the evening, to forestall returning to her apartment, Daphne had considered suggesting a movie. But this night, this meeting, called for something more imaginative. Now, an idea crept into her head. As usual, she went for it. "Let's buy it."

"It's two thousand pieces, did you see?" he called from the kitchen.

"Hmm?" asked Daphne, gazing around his apartment. She'd expected something fussier, smelling of disinfectant, swept free of dust, all the covers on the furniture hanging perfectly straight. The reality was something more agreeably raffish: a neat, square room with a wooden floor, a worn two-seater couch, and a stained coffee table. A keyboard sat in the corner amid piles of notebooks and paper.

"Two thousand pieces," he repeated, coming back from the kitchen with two glasses of water. "It could take months."

"Murf?" demanded a new voice. Spinning around, Daphne found herself eye-to-eye with a tabby cat, perched on the back of the sofa. "Murf?" it asked again.

"Hi there," she said, her pulse returning to normal. She stroked the cat's head, and it arched its back, a purr rumbling in its throat.

"That's Blondie," said L. He set the puzzle on the coffee table. "I suppose I'll have to cover this when we're not working on it, or he'll scatter the pieces."

"He?" Daphne straightened. "Isn't Blondie a girl's name?"

"Not if you're Clint Eastwood. I take it you've never seen *The Good, the Bad, and the Ugly*."

"No." She spotted the DVD on a shelf by the TV, alongside a dozen others. *Tombstone. Unforgiven. High Noon. True Grit.* An Englishman who loved Westerns. She smiled at the odd juxtaposition.

"Right, then." He lifted the lid off the box. "Shall we make a start?"

Daphne gathered all the red pieces and began assembling the cardinal. He, more methodical, picked out the corners and side pieces and fitted them together. Blondie kept jumping onto the coffee table and had to be scolded away. Daphne discovered she was smiling more frequently than she would have believed possible when she set out for her walk. This wasn't what she'd call a lively evening, yet she felt perfectly content to pick through the irregular, colorful pieces, like bits of candy, in the company of this quiet man. She was sorry when she looked at her watch and saw that midnight was drawing near.

"I still have one more final before the break," she said, petting Blondie, who lay purring on the sofa.

"And I have papers to grade." He accompanied her to the door, where she hesitated, winding her purple scarf around her throat. The puzzle thing had been, like many of her whims, a spur-of-the-moment idea. It wasn't until now that she began questioning if she really wanted to commit her holiday to working on a puzzle with a relative stranger.

Commit. That reminded her of Brett. Again.

"You needn't feel obliged to continue," said L. Daphne flushed; he'd read her thoughts as easily as if she'd spoken aloud. His faint smile said he hadn't expected much to begin with.

"No, I want to finish it," she replied, surprising herself. "Are you free tomorrow afternoon?"

He hesitated before nodding. "Say, one o'clock?"

"One o'clock." She opened the door. "See you then, Lionel."

"Hang on." He touched her arm, stopping her. "Three guesses a day."

"Oh? And what do I win if I guess right?"

"You get to know my name."

She snorted and folded her arms.

"Not good enough?" He stared at the ceiling, pondering. "All right, if you guess my name before we finish the puzzle, you get . . ."

"Should I offer my firstborn?" she asked when the pause dragged on.

"Not unless I manage to spin straw into gold first. I think we're going to have to lower the stakes." He thought a moment longer. "How about my coat, since you like it so much? Hand-tailored in London."

The coat hung on a peg by the door. Daphne lifted one dark blue sleeve and let the fabric slide through her fingers. Heavy. Soft. Obvious quality. He wasn't that much taller than her, and he had a slight build. It would probably fit her. "All right. And if I lose?"

"You're a costumer, right? You'll have to construct a real Western duster for me."

"It's a deal," she said, holding out her hand. "But you can't work on the puzzle without me."

He shook it. "And you're not allowed to look my name up on the internet or ask one of my colleagues."

"Fair enough. Good-night, L. It isn't Lionel, is it?"

"No. Good-night, Ms. Cooper."

"Lampon," said Melissa with an air of finality. "It has to be Lampon."

Daphne nearly choked on a peanut. "What kind of a name is that?" She gasped, grabbing her ale.

"Greek. Awful isn't it? If my name rhymed with tampon, I wouldn't admit it either." Melissa cracked a peanut and threw its shell on the pub's floor. "I dated this Greek guy once, and it was his dad's name."

"L's British."

"Doesn't mean anything."

"I'll add it to the list," said Daphne. She'd already guessed Lot, Luther, Lars, and Legolas, on the chance his parents were Tolkien fans, over their last three meetings. *Three puzzle sessions. Melissa's going to think we're dating.*

On cue, Melissa leaned back in the wooden booth and took a sip of her lager. "So, what's he like in bed?"

"Melissa." Daphne let her forehead thunk onto the table. "We're friends. As in 'not sleeping together.'"

"Why not?" asked Melissa. Daphne sighed and fell back against her own side of the booth. She hoped the waiter brought their pizza before they stuffed themselves on peanuts. She always did when she came to the Oldworld Alehouse. It was such fun to throw the shells on the floor.

"Maybe he's gay," persisted Melissa.

"No. I asked."

"You did?" Melissa's eyes rounded. "Cool." She extended her hand. Smiling even as she blushed, Daphne slapped her a high five.

Melissa snatched more peanuts. "You like him, don't you? Why else ask if he's gay?"

"I was just curious."

"Yeah, right. I have met him, remember? A little skinny, but his voice is to die for. If I hadn't been with Daniel at the time, I might have nailed him. Actually, I probably should have. It would have saved me two weeks of Daniel's clinging jealousy."

"Yeah, and saved the rest of us two weeks of your complaints." Giving in, Daphne took another peanut. "I don't think L's the type to hook up."

Melissa started to protest, then shut her mouth and nodded. "Yeah, I kind of got that impression from him. He's not exactly shy, but . . ."

"Aloof," said Daphne. She'd come up with the word after their second puzzle session. Every time she showed up at his place he seemed slightly surprised. Not displeased, but she occasionally wondered if he were simply humoring her with the puzzle and the name game. Sometimes when they talked, she felt like she was trying to reach someone encased in a layer of ice.

Their pizza arrived, gooey cheese bubbling around toppings of fresh spinach, tomatoes, and sweet bay scallops. Both she and Melissa contemplated it in reverential silence as the waiter set it in the middle of the table. "Enjoy," he said, before whisking off to refill someone's beer. Daphne and Melissa paid another few seconds homage to the pizza, then dove for the first slice. Daphne got there first.

"Maybe it's you," said Melissa some blissful time later, after the first slices had been savored. "Maybe you're not over Brett yet."

Even though Daphne had suspected it was coming, Brett's name soured the delicious food. She sipped ale to wash the taste away. "Of course I'm not over Brett. It's only been twenty days."

"Oh, God, you're still counting days." Melissa rolled her eyes. "Look, doll, Brett is so not worth it. He's one of those funfor guys."

"Funfor guys?"

"Yeah. Fun for a while, and then they become tiresome. He only moved in with you because he wanted to see what it was like to play house."

"I thought you liked Brett."

"Sure. He's a big toddler. Endearing so long as you know he's gonna take a nap sooner or later." Melissa cut herself another slice of pizza while Daphne digested this new perspective on Brett. She'd always told herself she admired his free-and-easy take on life.

"He could've waited until after Christmas to break up," she admitted. "Do you know how much Broadway tickets cost these days?"

"He didn't want to go. While you were squeeing about getting to see Clive Owen in *Macbeth*, he stood behind you making faces."

Ten different emotions fought for control of Daphne's vocal cords. "He didn't!" she finally blurted.

"He did." Melissa chewed complacently. "Why don't you ask L to go instead?"

"I already sold the tickets to Julia." Which was the truth, but it also masked a deeper thought; that inviting L to New York with her was too much. Too soon. Too . . . something.

"Shit." Dropping her half-eaten slice onto her plate, Melissa folded her arms. "You were so looking forward to the show. I'd be hunting Brett down and kicking in his balls, not pining for him."

"It's running until April." Daphne forced a smile. "Maybe I can get tickets for spring break."

"Yeah." Melissa retrieved her slice. "Maybe you and L will have finished the puzzle by then and moved on to better things."

"Mel, we're just friends. Get it? Capital F, R . . ."

"So go as friends." A wicked gleam came into Melissa's eyes. "You can move onto the better stuff in New York."

Daphne picked up her ale. No point arguing; Melissa was single-minded. And incorrigible.

"You should at least buy him a present," said Melissa.

She's right, thought Daphne kicking herself for her own selfishness.

So, after dinner—a celebration of the end of exams—she dragged Melissa out shopping. Three days before Christmas, the streets were crammed with people with a similar goal in mind. A bookstore looked promising, but—

"Damn, they don't have any *Death Note*," said Daphne. She pawed through the music section, frustrated. She didn't know what L already owned.

Melissa stuck a Sondheim libretto back on the shelf. "Why don't you give him whatever you were going to give Brett?"

"That would be a trip to New York." Again, not the entire truth. Tucked away in the back of her sock drawer was an antique pocket watch. Brett never arrived on time. She could almost hear him chirping "I'm late, I'm late," in that bogus British accent

He *did* like to show off, didn't he?

She brought her mind back to her current dilemma. "What do you buy guys you're not dating?"

"I haven't the faintest idea. Unless they're brothers, in which case you buy a gift card for the nearest video game store."

"Not helpful." Daphne pushed her way out of the bookstore. The December wind blew sharp as if about to break and spray her with fine fragments. A layer of snow from the other night turned the grass into a white carpet. *The night I met L*, she thought. Him with his tongue sticking out. The memory seemed all the more ridiculous, now that she knew him.

Melissa joined her outside. "Clothes?" she suggested, pulling her knit cap around her ears. Daphne had forgotten hers again.

Once Around the Sun

"No way. He's got great clothes. Yesterday he was wearing this hand-knit black wool sweater—or jumper as he called it—like it was nothing. Apparently his father takes him to some tailor in London when he visits."

Melissa stopped dead in the middle of the sidewalk, much to the annoyance of a pair of heavyset women, their arms loaded with bags. They stepped around her, glaring, but Melissa ignored them. "His clothes are tailor-made?"

Daphne nodded, tugging on her arm. "Some of them. I think his dad's rich."

Melissa wouldn't budge. "And you haven't jumped him yet? Damn, girl, what's your problem?"

"Didn't anyone ever tell you it's wrong to sleep with someone for their money?"

"How would Donald Trump ever get married if it was?" Melissa retorted, but at last her feet came unglued from the sidewalk. "Where are we going now?"

"I got an idea," said Daphne, stopping in front of *Riddle Me This.*

Melissa peered in the window. "Another puzzle? Shouldn't you finish this one first?"

"That might not take much longer." It amazed Daphne how quickly L could match up pieces; he had a real eye for patterns.

"Oh," Melissa's disapproving tone changed to one of enlightenment. "So this is a backup plan in case he finishes this one too soon. I approve." She pushed open the door. Sighing, Daphne followed. What would it take to convince Melissa they were just friends?

The right present sat on a shelf opposite the door, all but coughing politely to attract her attention. "This," said Daphne, reaching up to take the box down.

The box's front bore a picture of a castle. All the three-dimensional puzzle's pieces were made of clear plastic, so when it was assembled, it would look as if it were constructed of glass. Or ice.

"Pretty," said Melissa, looking over her shoulder. "But are you sure it's not too childish for him?"

"No." Daphne patted the box. "It's perfect."

Outside the shop, Melissa hugged her. "I'd better go pack for Boston. Have a good Christmas."

Lucky Melissa, going off to enjoy the holiday with her loyal boyfriend, Sam. Tamping down her jealousy, Daphne returned the hug. "You too. Merry Christmas."

Melissa gave her a final squeeze. "I'll call," she said and hurried away.

"Tomorrow's Christmas Eve," said L. Then grimaced. "Sorry. I hate obvious statements, especially when I make them myself."

Daphne leaned back against his sofa. Blondie took this as an invitation to tangle his claws in her hair. It had only struck her recently that she was really, truly going to be alone for Christmas. "Were you asking me if I want to come over tomorrow, or telling me to stay away because you have other plans?" she asked, tickling Blondie.

He picked his teacup off the coffee table where it sat among a scattering of puzzle pieces, and turned it in his hands. She'd rarely seen him lose composure, even for a second. "I suppose I was testing the waters. Traditionally, you spend Christmas Eve with family."

"Mine's in Jamaica by now."

His brows rose. "Weren't you invited?" They hadn't talked about their families, mostly because she'd sensed an aversion to the subject on his side.

"Yeah, but I'd made other plans. Then those fell through, and it was too late to accept." She shrugged, although missing a trip to Jamaica was another disappointment she could blame on Brett. "What about yours?"

"My father's in Edinburgh, my mother's in Paris. I don't have any siblings." He spoke in a clipped way as if he wanted to marshal the words out as quickly as possible.

"I wouldn't pass up a trip to France or Scotland."

A long silence, during which he stared at the cup between his hands. Then he lifted his head, flashing an unhappy smile. "Sorry. I brought it up, didn't I? You've probably deduced by now that I don't get on with my parents."

Once Around the Sun

"What did they do to you?"

He shrugged, his shoulders bunched up around his ears. "Actually, nothing. I was raised by nannies and tutors while they jetted around the world giving lectures, or locked themselves in their studies. Hardly ever saw them. Had a bout of pneumonia when I was eleven, and it was three days before either of them came to hospital to visit."

"Three days?"

"My mother came after three days. It took my father a week." He tried to smile as if it were funny, but the expression slid away. "When I was born, they realized they didn't like children. Now that I'm grown, they throw money at me, trying to win my affection."

Daphne cast about for something to say. "Are their jobs really important? Is that why they were gone so often?"

"Hardly. My father's an expert on Sir Walter Scott, my mother an authority on Alexandre Dumas. They met at a literary convention twenty-five years ago and fell madly in love. It lasted maybe three months, but I was already on the way by then. Strangely enough," at last he relaxed enough to smile a genuine smile, "I have little taste for literature."

"Yeah, that's a big surprise." She smiled back. "So, no trip to Paris this year."

"No. Which brings me back to my original question, or whatever it was. Would you like to come over tomorrow?"

She pushed some pieces around the table. The border was all in place, the cardinal finished, the wolf half done, and the knight shaping up. She wanted a break from the puzzle, she realized, but not from him. Not when some genuine intimacy had entered the conversation.

Another one of her ideas popped into her head. "How about I come over, and we watch *The Good, the Bad, and the Ugly*? I'll bring the eggnog and gingerbread."

"Don't you mean the sherry and mince pie?"

"Hey, bub, this is America. You'll drink eggnog and like it." She yawned then bounced to her feet. She'd have to buy treacle if she was going to make gingerbread.

"I'll drink it, but I won't promise to like it." He helped her on with her coat.

"See you tomorrow around seven, Lancelot."

"Wrong again."

"Too bad. That would be a neat name."

She left his apartment humming, bought treacle at the corner grocery, then walked down Sloane Avenue trying to remember where she'd stashed her gingerbread recipe. Her feet danced along the sidewalk, and her mind felt as clean as the crisp winter wind buffing her cheeks.

She turned the corner, and there was Brett, waiting on the steps to her apartment.

Daphne drummed her fingernails against her water glass. Perhaps she should repaint them. She wasn't sure she liked the color. It was too dark a green, not the rich holly shade the bottle promised. Maybe she should try red instead.

Inconsequential thoughts. They kept her heart from pounding out of her throat. Kept her from asking Brett if he intended to stay. Kept her from watching her future, which had seemed to be coming together this evening, shatter like a puzzle dropped onto a floor.

"I guess you're wondering why I'm here," said Brett, lounging on the squishy yellow sofa. A lock of hair fell boyishly over his face.

"Well, yeah, since last time we spoke you said you weren't ready to settle down." He'd actually used the old "it's not you it's me" excuse. And she'd bought it.

"I know. I'm sorry." He smiled up at her through his eyelashes. "I was an idiot."

Daphne bit her lip. She'd imagined him saying the words a hundred times, so why was the reality so unsatisfying? Still, part of her wanted to believe them. She folded her arms. "So, why?"

"Why did I leave?" He leaned forward, looking into her eyes. "Hey, Daf, this is the most serious relationship I've ever been in, you know? And then, just a few weeks ago, Bob told me he intended to propose to Sheryl. That shook me. It's like, we've really grown up. Maybe this is the real deal. I wasn't sure I was ready for that."

Once Around the Sun

"You could have talked to me," said Daphne. Her thoughts whirled. *The real deal? Us? Could it be?*

"Yeah. That's where me being an idiot comes in." Grinning, Brett leaned back, brushing a hand through his hair. "So what d'you say, Daf? Give me another chance?"

Someone always lost out. Hugging the wrapped castle puzzle and the plate of gingerbread to her chest, Daphne trudged down Sloane Ave. It wasn't fair, but that was life.

In front of L's door, she hesitated. *I could still ask if he minds if I brought a guest along tonight.*

But she'd already suggested it to Brett that morning. "I don't want to share you on Christmas Eve," he'd said, laughing. "Besides, that's just a dumb buddy Western, you know? John Wayne shoots the bad guy and saves the girl."

She rang L's doorbell. She'd thought of and discarded a hundred excuses, and still didn't know what she was going to say. The truth sounded even more miserable: "Hey, my ex-boyfriend returned, and I decided to give him another shot. Sorry for dumping you."

I'm not dumping him, she reminded herself, ringing the bell again. *We're not dating.*

No answer. He'd probably gone out; not expecting her for a few hours. It made everything easier and yet so much worse.

She set the puzzle and the gingerbread by the door along with a hastily scribbled note:

> *Dear Leslie? Llewellyn? Lyle?*
>
> *Some personal business came up. I won't be able to come tonight. Sorry. I hope we can get back to the puzzle soon.*
>
> *Merry Christmas,*
>
> *Daphne*

Then she turned away, rubbing her prickling eyes and feeling like a traitor.

Brett loved the pocket watch. He amused her with his White Rabbit impression while he cooked brunch. He'd bought her a lovely silk blouse, but when she tried it on, she found it was too tight. Plus, the silvery green color turned her skin sallow.

"Sorry, hon," said Brett, giving her a kiss as he set down the plate of French toast.

"It's all right. I can alter it."

So she didn't have anything new for Bob's party that night. She wore her purple dress with a fringed black shawl tied around her waist instead. Brett insisted on going. Daphne had always found Bob a trifle annoying. In fact, when they'd received the invitation a month ago, she'd felt a profound relief that their New York trip meant that she wouldn't have to endure Bob's company until New Year's.

If Brett hadn't left, I would have seen Clive Owen play Macbeth last night, she thought as Bob recounted his tale of a botched fishing expedition in Montana for seemingly the hundredth time. *We could be strolling down Fifth Avenue this very moment.*

And if he hadn't come back—

No, she wouldn't think about that. He'd come back; that was what was important, and maybe they could see *Macbeth* over spring break. Surely he owed her that much. So she laughed at Bob's jokes, played the obligatory charades, and drank more wine than she really cared for. Midnight passed before she managed to drag Brett away. The air cleared her head a little. It hadn't snowed after all. No white Christmas this year.

A package wrapped in silver paper sat on her doorstep. Brett scooped it up and examined the tag before handing it over. "Who's L?" he asked.

Daphne read the note attached:

> *Dear Ms. Cooper,*
>
> *I'm sorry you couldn't come. Happy holidays*
>
> *L.*
>
> *P.S. Wrong on all three counts, I'm afraid.*

Daphne opened the package. Inside was a pale violet cap and matching scarf knitted out of the softest yarn she'd ever touched. Alpaca, her educated fingers guessed. She put on the cap and instantly her ears began to warm. She'd forgotten hers, of course. "Purple. He noticed my favorite color."

Brett flicked the scarf's fringe. "Who's L?"

Daphne wadded the scarf into a soft ball against her chest. "Just a friend."

She saw him the Wednesday after Christmas as she and Brett strolled through the campus square. "That's L," she said to Brett. "I must thank him for the present."

They angled across the square to cut him off before he vanished. Daphne thought of apologies, expressions of gratitude, words of pleasure at seeing him again. But when they stopped in front of him, and he cocked his head in expectation, Brett spoke first.

"Howdy, partner," he said, using his look-at-me-aren't-I-cute voice. Daphne's face burned.

"Thank you for the hat and the scarf," she murmured. "They're lovely." She was wearing them now.

L looked from her to Brett, and she knew he'd deduced the reason why she hadn't come Christmas Eve. She braced herself for the hurt, the look of recrimination.

But he just nodded. "Thank you for the puzzle, Ms. Cooper," he said. "I trust you had a good Christmas."

She nodded. "Say hi to Blondie for me," she said.

Then he was walking away, off towards the library, his coat fluttering, and his head held high, as if the winter air lacked the power to chill him. Daphne followed him with her eyes.

She hadn't disappointed him. She'd met his expectations. And that was worse.

"What a stiff," said Brett.

Blondie. Why did that name suddenly bother her?

Later, she went for a walk around town to clear her head. She found herself staring in the window of *Riddle Me This*, not really seeing anything, not really thinking anything, when a voice called her name.

"Hey, Daf, out shopping for a new puzzle?" It was Melissa.

Daphne embraced her. "Hi, Mel. Did you have a good Christmas? You never called."

Melissa's cheerful expression fell. "Oh, shit."

"What?"

Melissa sucked in a breath. "You'll need fortification to hear this," she said, and offered no more until she'd dragged Daphne to Emily's and set her down with a thick cup of cocoa in a bright pink mug.

"So what is it?" asked Daphne, taking a sip. "And how was your Christmas?"

"My Christmas was fine. Listen, Daphne, I did call. Twice. Once on the afternoon of Christmas Eve. I left messages both times."

"Huh. My answering service must not be working."

"Oh, I bet it's working just fine." Melissa's cocoa sat cooling before her, untouched. "The serpent's returned to the Garden of Eden, hasn't he?"

"What?"

"Brett. He's come crawling back, hasn't he? The reason you didn't get the messages is because he erased them."

Slowly Daphne set down her cup. Meeting her eyes, Melissa nodded.

"He didn't leave you because he feared commitment. He was trying to get into Jessica Talbot's pants. Sam and I met her in Boston. She told us she'd been stringing him along for months. He finally wised up a few days before Christmas, threw a tantrum, and left. I knew he'd run straight back to you."

Daphne stared into her cup. The whipped cream was slowly melting across the dark brown surface. Melissa touched her hand. "I'm sorry."

"I could have figured it out," said Daphne. A tear trickled down her cheek; angry, she scrubbed an arm across her face. "That blouse he gave me . . ." That silvery-green silk blouse would suit willowy blonde Jessica very well. "Why am I so stupid?"

"You're not stupid," said Melissa.

Once Around the Sun

"Maybe not." Daphne took several breaths, allowing the consolation to sink in. "But I need to start thinking before I act." She pushed her chair back. "Thanks for the cocoa, Mel. You're a good friend."

She was typing on her laptop when Brett came in. She'd had ample time to fill the cardboard box sitting by the side of her desk. "There're your things," she told him, not looking up.

"You packed my belongings? Why?"

She swung the laptop around so he could read the Wikipedia entry. "John Wayne isn't in *The Good, the Bad, and the Ugly*. It's a Clint Eastwood movie. That 'dumb buddy Western' is considered one of the best films ever made."

"You're mad about that?" He laughed, and this time, because she was listening for it, she heard the careless condescension in the sound. "I must've got it confused with something else." Coming over, he tried to put his arm around her. She pushed him away.

"Like you got Jessica Talbot confused with me?"

The smile dropped off his face, and she knew, knew down to her bones, that Melissa was right. An instant later it returned. "What are you talking about, Daf?" he asked, and she could almost smell the lies brewing in his head.

She pulled the laptop back towards her. "Just go, Brett. I'm tired of your games. Tired of your ruining my plans so you can have your way."

He made excuses, but she ignored them. He blustered, but she read the Wikipedia entry on Alexandre Dumas, paying him no heed. By the time he'd shifted the blame for everything wrong with their relationship onto her and picked up the box, she'd clicked on the page for Sir Walter Scott.

"Leave your keys on the table," she said as he opened the door. "You're not coming back. I kept the pocket watch, but you can have that green blouse. Make sure it fits your next victim before you give it to her."

The keys clanked onto the table with a hostile thunk. The door slammed. Daphne returned to scanning the page.

The Ice Prince

Sir Walter Scott had written fifteen novels. *I guess I'll have to read all the entries*, she thought. Sighing, she scrolled further down, to the section on his poetry.

And she found the name.

Snow, great white puffs of it, had begun falling by the time she reached L's apartment. He didn't answer when she rang the bell, so she waited in the front yard, catching flakes on her tongue. This one was sure to settle; already the roads were turning white. Nearly an hour passed before he came slogging up Sloane Ave, a violin case under one arm and snowflakes settling in his auburn hair, but her ears stayed warm under her violet cap.

Spotting her, he stopped. For the first time since their original meeting, genuine surprise showed on his face.

"Daphne," he said. Then, "Good evening."

She smiled. *"Oh, young Lochinvar is come out of the west. Through all the wide Border . . ."*

He held up a hand. "Please don't. My father had me memorize it." He looked down at his feet, already sinking in the snow. "I suppose I should take off my coat now."

"You can wait until you're inside. It's cold, if you haven't noticed."

"Lately I've felt the cold more than I used to." His breath misted the air. "I never imagined you'd guess."

"I didn't guess. I figured it out. Your parents named you after their literary obsessions. Is your middle name Athos or Aramis?"

"Aramis." At last, he smiled. "You're good. You should win an extra prize for that."

Daphne took a step towards him. "We can discuss my reward while we work on the puzzle."

"I dismantled it." He looked away. "I didn't think you'd be coming by anymore." She saw him swallow. When he spoke again, his voice was hoarse. "I always expect people to let me down. So I don't make a lot of effort to keep . . . friends. But . . ." Now he looked at her. Behind his lenses, his eyes shone the brown of fresh gingerbread. ". . . I confess I was a little lonely this Christmas."

39

Once Around the Sun

The ice prince in his frozen castle is melting, she reflected. "I did let you down. And I'm so sorry. I was lonely too, even though I wasn't alone."

A gust of wind blew a load of fresh snow off the limbs of a fir tree. Lochinvar shivered. "I suppose we could start the puzzle again."

Smiling, Daphne took his offered hand. "Starting over sounds like a good idea."

He opened the door. "Come inside. It's warm."

If Daylight Ever Comes

Jo Ann Schaffer

Dave's head jerked from the pillow. Tired to the bone, he turned to the bedside clock and groaned: 1:38 a.m. First one foot, then the other found the floor, as he rolled his body into an upright position. They'd moved up the time of the meeting, and, thanks to a delay at LaGuardia, he was late getting into Chicago. The presentation still needed some fine tuning, but he could wing it. Better to call it a night.

Stuck somewhere between sleep and awake, he reached for the remote to switch off the TV. Something about a tsunami and the Atlantic made him look up. The newscaster seemed agitated. Dave turned up the volume; ". . . a major earthquake." As he listened, his knees grew weak, and he sat down hard on the edge of the bed. *This can't be happening!*

Grabbing his cell phone, he punched in Jan's number and stared in horror at the screen.

Jan's heart raced as she fought to cast off the net of terror the dream had flung over her. She awakened to a dizzying vortex of sound: shrieking sirens and the insistent tinkling of the 1812 Overture. Her cell phone. Jolted into consciousness, she groped around the nightstand and latched onto it. Squinting through one eye to check the caller's ID, then noticing the time, she groaned. *Why is Dave calling at this hour?*

The maniacal mooing of emergency sirens assaulted her from every direction. Must be some fire, she thought.

Once Around the Sun

"Honey, you won't believe the racket going on here," she said as she switched on the bedside lamp. "But your timing is impeccable. You dragged me out of a doozy of a nightmare." The clock radio glowed 2:38. She took a few deep breaths to calm her racing pulse. "Dave, don't tell me you're still working on that project."

"Janet Joy, get out of bed," he shouted, each syllable a sleek, pointed projectile tearing through the phone. "Get in the car, and get the hell out of there, *now.*"

"What the . . ." she stared at the cell phone. "It's the middle of the night!"

"Christ, Jan, I can barely hear you over the sirens."

She got up and closed the bedroom door. The blinds were a useless barrier to sound, so she drew the curtains across the windows.

"Okay, tell me what you've heard," she shouted, pressing the phone tightly to her ear. In the back of her mind, a thought coalesced: *odd that there were no pauses in the siren to indicate the type of emergency.*

"I was just turning off the TV when they announced a humongous earthquake in the Atlantic. They're pretty sure it's triggered a tsunami, and that it's heading for Long Island."

She suddenly remembered that the sirens never go off before five a.m.

"All right, Mr. Unflappable, even if there is a tsunami, how big could it be? Hell, there was barely an extra ripple in the tide after that big quake in Haiti."

"They're saying this is bigger than the one that hit Japan in March." She could hear the tremor in his voice. "Look, Jan, I know it's the middle of the night. I know there aren't any monitoring devices in the Atlantic, but the experts I'm watching look like they're about to lose it." As rapidly as he spoke, she could tell the words were getting stuck in his throat. "Jesus, Jan, the quake happened a couple of hours ago. Maybe it won't get that far inland. Maybe it will only strip the sand away on Jones Beach. For god's sake, just humor me and get in the car."

Her breath came in ever quickening spurts. "Okay, you win. I'm getting outta here."

Scrambling off the bed, she cupped the cell phone between her ear and shoulder, and jabbed at a sneaker with her bare foot. The phone slipped free, but she managed to grab it before it hit the floor. "Look, Dave, I'm going to put the phone down for a second so I can throw on some clothes." Grabbing a sweatshirt from the pile of laundry, she yanked it over her head and stuffed her arms through the sleeves. Her pajama bottoms would suffice.

False alarm, false alarm, false alarm. No matter how many times she said it, she couldn't stem the flow of adrenaline pulsing through her body.

Retrieving the phone, she threw her handbag over her shoulder and fished around for the car keys. "Hold on, hon, I'm trying to remember where I left my keys." *Think, dammit, what did you do when you got home yesterday?* Retracing her steps as best she could, she found them next to the kitchen sink.

"Got 'em!" she shouted. Racing to the garage, she karate-chopped the door opener. The door lifted as if it were being forced open by a swollen torrent of sound. Jumping in the car and slamming the door shut, she took a couple of deep breaths, then turned the key in the ignition.

"Dave, do you have any idea how far I need to get from the South Shore? I mean we're already three miles inland." Before she'd even cleared the garage, she stomped on the brakes. Cars were stopped at the foot of her driveway. Craning her head left and right, she could see that, at the cross streets, traffic was bumper to bumper.

Never had she seen this great an exodus, even for a category four hurricane. *There really is a giant wall of water racing towards us!*

"Good, you're in the car." She heard the relief in Dave's voice. "You should be okay if you can make it to the Long Island Expressway."

"Will do," she said, but inside, a switch flicked. *Who are you kidding, Jan? It will take an hour to go even a few blocks.*

Once Around the Sun

An unexpected calmness enveloped her; muscles unclenched, and her heart rate began returning to normal. *So this is how it ends.* She pulled back into the garage and cut the engine. Cupping her hand over the mouthpiece, she got out of the car and walked into the house.

Placing her purse on the hall table, she made her way upstairs, one step at a time.

"Jan, what kind of progress are you making?"

"The street is jammed, but Fred and Cheryl let me pull in front of them." She feigned an exasperated sigh.

"They've only gotten as far as our house?"

"Well, hon, who pays attention to the sirens if they're not a volunteer firefighter?" She looked out the window and watched the cars still stalled in front of the house. "But I've got to admit, paint dries faster than we're moving."

"I'm just thankful that you're on the road." *Is he really buying my upbeat mood?* "Let me know when you get to the Wantagh Highway."

"Roger that, control tower." She laughed, hoping it didn't sound too forced. *Please, don't let him think he somehow let me down.* Walking to the dresser in the master bedroom, she bent down and unplugged the cell phone charger. Although the sirens hadn't lessened one decibel, she was finding it easier to tune them out. As she passed the laundry basket, she reached in and pulled out one of Dave's shirts. Tears welled in her eyes as she held it to her nose.

Standing beneath the opening to the attic, she placed the phone to her ear. "Okay, I'm making the turn onto Washington Avenue."

Dave's eyes kept flicking back to the time at the bottom of the screen. He knew what Jan was up against: tens of thousands of drivers, all desperate to find an escape route that wasn't already clogged shut. The Island was her turf, he reminded himself. She could navigate it better than he.

They'd been on the phone seventeen minutes. *God, I wish I could keep it together as well as she seems to be.* His fingers brushed through his hair as he watched the announcement slide past; what data they'd been able to verify indicated that a large wave would hit the sandbar islands off Long Island within eight minutes.

"Jan, are you up to Jerusalem Avenue yet?"

"Just about, Dave." She muffled the phone against her chest as she eased open the door in the ceiling and let down the attic stairs. Softly, she began to climb, and raised the phone to her mouth. "I can see the Southern State. Doesn't look like they're letting anyone on."

"I guess there's no point letting anyone head west toward Staten Island," Dave said, the hope in his voice fading.

The space under the eaves was unfinished, but it did have a plywood floor. Gripping the shirt under her arm, she plugged the charger into the outlet on the overhead light and inserted the other end into the phone. Moving containers of Christmas decorations aside, she sat down. There were no windows, but the sirens had been replaced by a crescendo of noise. It was as if she were hunkered down in a railway tunnel with ten massive locomotives rushing towards her, their power rattling every nerve and fiber of the house. She held the phone tight against her face, wanting desperately to hear and be heard.

He sensed that something had changed; he couldn't tell what. Maybe it was just the connection going bad. The spike in call volume must be overloading the system. *Please, God, keep the line open.*

"What's the mood like out there, babe?"

It was the background noise; it had changed, grown louder. He caught the hesitation before she spoke. "Whenever you meet someone's eyes, you can see the panic. But we nod encouragement to each other, and somehow, for a split second, it helps."

"Jan?" It was growing harder to force words past the lump lodged in his throat.

"Yeah, Dave?"

"You're not in the car, are you?" There was a long pause.

Once Around the Sun

"I'm in the attic."

He slumped to the floor at the foot of the bed and stared at the TV. It was switched to mute, but his eyes followed the updates scrolling across the screen. It felt as if his soul were slowly seeping through the carpet to the room below. All he could hear was a thunderous static.

"Tell me what's going on," he shouted into the phone. Someone in the room next door pounded on the wall.

"Dave . . . can't hear . . . anymore . . . sitting . . . holding your shirt . . . never change . . . aftershave . . . it's the scent . . . taking with me . . . love you . . ."

Getting up, he made his way to the window, he looked at the skyline, but nothing would come into focus. He kept the phone pressed to his ear, and let the tears flow.

Ave Maria

Katherine Fast

Winner of the 2013 Bethlehem Writers Roundtable Short Story Award

"C'mon, Joey. Stand up like a man!" Chuck packed snow around the base of the statue, working quickly in the sub-zero temperature. Six in the morning, and he was wrestling with the Nativity scene.

Oh joy! Life on Candy Cane Lane. As with so many things—his marriage being a case in point—the early days were the best. The newlywed years when life and Christmas decorations were simpler.

He, his wife, and their neighbors bought into the development the year it was finished. They grew together like one large family, sharing recipes and ice skates, dreams and disappointments. Every holiday was an excuse for a party and decorations—cupids, Easter bunnies, ghouls and goblins, turkeys—but their specialty was Christmas.

Soon the neighborhood blazed with holiday lights.

Chuck couldn't remember whose bright idea it was to post six-foot tall, lighted candy canes along the street. Shortly thereafter, Channel Seven dubbed their street Candy Cane Lane. As children left for college, marriage, and careers, the empty nesters built ever more spectacular displays.

Earlier in the week, Chuck had mounted Santa, sleigh, and reindeer on the roof. Then he crowded four immense toy soldiers, five carolers, and three giant nutcrackers on the lawn, and circled them with an animated train set with a five-car LED light display. Because of the wattage required, he'd had to jury-rig electrical connections and was way behind schedule with the Nativity.

He surveyed his work. Baby Jesus lay in the manger next to Joseph. Outside, three wise men bearing gifts approached from the east, guided by a star tacked to a pole. A shepherd knelt before the stable, surrounded by a donkey, a cow, two sheep, a lamb, a camel, and a goat.

The scene, "perfect for institutions and churches," was built to human scale. Newer fiberglass animals were easy to carry, but the full-sized plaster figures of the Holy Family were heavy and surprisingly fragile.

After packing each figure with snow, he sprayed it with a fine mist that instantly bonded snow to statue with a layer of ice. He continued spraying until each figure was encased in ice thick enough to last until spring.

His wife, Maria, hadn't liked his surprise. He'd knelt before her as he'd done years ago, but this time he offered tickets to Martinique, hoping time in the sun would spice up their fading marriage.

"Actually, I have other plans," she'd said. She jiggled ice cubes in her glass.

He topped off her drink and waited.

"I want a divorce."

He should've seen it coming. She'd become colder and colder in the past year. Their sex life was nonexistent. She blamed her lack of libido, and general bitchiness, on "the change."

No, she insisted. She wasn't unhappy. Or dissatisfied. Or angry. She was in love—with another man.

He yelled. Threw a few things. Yelled some more. She wouldn't give him a name.

"Doesn't really matter who, does it?"

He pleaded, hollered, and cried.

"I hope these are refundable," she said. "Will you be able to finish the Nativity by the time Channel Seven arrives tomorrow?"

"You really are the Ice Queen." He stormed from the house and vented his fury on the nearest statues. "One divorce coming up, chop chop! Finish the decorations, chop . . ." The last chop sent King Balthazar's hand sailing.

He'd had a problem reattaching it. Glue couldn't hold the weight. Looking for duct tape, he tripped over one of his wife's Christmas baskets. She'd stuff them with fruit, wrap them in heavy plastic film, and then blast them with a hair dryer to shrink the film to an airtight fit.

Using a dowel as a splint, he'd wrapped film around Balthazar's hand and arm. Three layers made a snug, invisible repair. Fixing up Mary had been a bigger challenge. He'd had to wrap film around the praying hands and the lower part of the head.

He placed her gently beside Joseph and gave a sigh of relief. The invisible film clung like a second skin. He packed snow around her and turned on the hose.

A hand clamped his shoulder.

"Jesus!" Chuck whipped about.

Chuck's neighbor and best friend, Jerry, jumped aside to avoid the spray.

"What are you doin' out at this ungodly hour?"

Jerry waved a leash toward a black lab sniffing around the sheep. He rubbed his bare hands and shoved them into his pockets. "Bitchin' cold. Cutting it close this year, Chuckles."

"I'll finish before we leave."

Jerry raised his eyebrows. "Where're you going?"

"Martinique. I sprang it on the wife last night. Boy, was she surprised!"

"Huh." Jerry shivered.

"Shoulda seen the look on her face! You know we've had problems, but somehow last night everything clicked." Snowflakes melted on their faces. "I don't expect honeymoon passion. Probably kill me." He gave Jerry a playful rabbit punch. "These days I gotta take it slow."

Jerry's dog trotted to the manger.

"Get away!" Chuck lunged, grabbed his collar and jerked.

"Easy!" Jerry snapped on the leash and backed off.

"Sorry. I don't want Our Lady kneeling in yellow snow."

"Our Lady?" Jerry cocked his head. "When did you get religion?"

"I haven't. Powerful story, though." Chuck nodded toward Joseph. "He worshiped his wife. Believed everything she said." He shrugged, turned to Jerry, and grinned. "I'll think of you freezing your cajones up here. Don't expect postcards."

"Better keep moving. Catch my death out here."

"Jeez, I almost forgot," Chuck called after Jerry. "I asked Audrey to water the plants. Maria said to use the key she gave you."

Jerry stopped but didn't turn. "Sure. Hi to the wife."

Chuck waved and watched his friend go and then knelt before Mary. He wished he hadn't lost faith and could believe again. "So beautiful," he murmured studying her porcelain complexion. "Ave Maria. Pray for us sinners, now . . . and at the hour of your death."

Chuck adjusted the spray to a fine mist.

Mary blinked.

Cold Turkey

Jo Ann Schaffer

Something kept poking at me as I lay cocooned in a mound of blankets and quilts. Moaning my annoyance, I burrowed deeper. There was no denying he deserved points for subtlety. Turkey doesn't winge or whine, doesn't bark a doggy S.O.S. when he needs to go outside. As I freed my head from the covers, he trotted around the bed and rested his muzzle next to my nose.

"You know, Turkey," I said, my voice rising as he padded towards the back door, "if I didn't have the inner resolve of a marshmallow, you'd be swapping homes with a cat!"

Unknotting myself from the covers, I quickly remembered why I had tossed a wool blanket atop the two comforters I'd added the night before. Every cell in my body scrambled to get its standard-issue heat shield up and running. The image of Luke Skywalker suspended from the ceiling of an ice cave kept popping into my mind as I pulled on clothes as fast as I could.

It was while searching for a second pair of socks that I noticed the insistent rattle of the windows and the shrill whistle of the wind. *Right, the dog's got ten seconds to do his business, or he's on his own.* I did a fast-forward trot through the kitchen and yanked Turkey's leash off the hook in the mud room.

Twirling open the mud room blinds, I didn't like what I saw; there was something mean-spirited in the low-slung clouds brooding overhead. After barely a twist of the knob, a gust of Arctic wind blew open the door. My body now a mass of goose bumps, I shouldered the door closed and unlocked the doggy hatch.

Once Around the Sun

"Turkey," I commanded in my best alpha-dog voice, "door flap." His head turned toward where I was pointing, then swiveled back.

"Oh, don't be such a wuss," I said as I rehung the leash. "Think of it as training for the Iditarod. Picture it, the first black lab in the history of the race. I'm talking Guinness Book of World Records!"

He gave me a *yeah, whatever* look, and was out and in before I reached the coffee pot.

With a steaming cup in hand, I went into the living room and picked up the remote. Turkey's cupboard was now bare, so there was no getting out of a trip to the super-market. The Saturday crowds would be a nightmare. *But, I pondered, if the weather turns nasty, might I not avoid a check-out queue as long as the Great Wall of China?*

The weatherman assured his isobar-challenged audience that, while thickening clouds might linger, there was little likelihood of precipitation. My eyes panned from the TV set to the black lab staring out the living room window at the nickel-sized flakes sashaying in the wind. I reached down to scratch his head. "Well, Turkey, if that's not snow, God's got one serious case of dandruff."

A wet nose pressed against cold glass was all the meteorological equipment Turkey needed to forecast his next move: a nice warm cushion by the radiator. Bowing to the sagacity of such an intelligent breed, I returned to my bedroom and re-inserted myself into the warmth of my quilt-strewn bed with a P.D. James mystery. How much worse could the weather get in two hours?

By mid-afternoon, I'd finished the book, and the weather seemed to be taking a breather. The snowfall had been light and fluffy, the kind you could brush easily off the car with your hand. Although a dusting of white coated the ground, the roads remained clear. I picked up the phone and called my friend, Dina. According to the station she'd listened to, the storm wouldn't hit our area before three a.m. Hoping she hadn't been tuned to the same channel

I'd watched earlier, I told her I would pick up dinner, and we could spend the evening wallowing in our spinsterhood.

"Great!" Dina said. "I've just picked up a few bottles of ice wine, and what a perfect day for a tasting."

"*Ice* wine?" I sniffed. "Sounds like a plot by an underground temperance league to blunt the alcohol content." During college, Dina had done a stint of bartending, graduating with a degree in Chemistry and a wicked aptitude for the oenological arts. But much like pigeons and windshields, her offerings always hit the mark.

"Philistine!" she groaned. "Leaving the grapes on the vine to freeze concentrates the grape's sugars and intensifies the flavor. Have a little faith."

Inserting a pregnant pause in the conversation, I waited.

"Yeeees." She sighed. "It does have a lower alcohol content."

"Yeah, well, when I stop at the Food Emporium, I'll ask which of their take-out entrees would be a suitable accompaniment."

"Sushi—or meatloaf—whatever." Neither of us was much use in the kitchen. We gladly made obeisance to the culinary talents of others, especially those who offered meals to go.

As I hung up the phone, I slapped a palm to my forehead and thought, *remember to pick up dog food!*

Hearing me rummaging through cabinets, a yawning Turkey walked into the kitchen and watched as I cranked open a can of tuna fish and dumped it into his bowl. Sniffing at the contents, he looked at me as if I'd lost my mind.

"Granted, it looks as though I've confused you with some other quadruped," I said, hugging his neck, "but I just want to be sure you don't keel over from hunger if I get home late."

Grabbing my purse and car keys, I raced out the door. "I promise I'll never run out of dog food again," I shouted as the door slammed shut behind me. I heard Turkey barking a familiar reply: I've heard *that* before.

As they say, man makes plans, and God laughs.

Once Around the Sun

Dina had been right about the ice wine, which we paired with a couple of tilapia fillets. I relaxed knowing there was a nice supply of dog food chilling in the car. When I finally looked at the clock, it was six, and the flakes were falling thick and fast. There were a good five inches on the ground when I got ready to leave Dina's apartment.

She'd offered her sofa for the night, but I was feeling guilty about my woeful performance that morning; I kept remembering those big, chocolate-drop eyes begging me not to send him outside. *Why hadn't I splurged on that down-filled doggy vest?* And that "you're kidding, right?" look as I spooned tuna fish into his dish. How deep a karmic hole could I dig?

To be honest, I'd never wanted a pet. It's a control thing; as soon as I let anyone or anything into my life, they start to take over, be it a houseplant, a pet, or a man. Turkey was a Thanksgiving Day surprise from another big mistake. Brad might have been the love of my life, except for the wife and two kids in New Jersey he'd forgotten to mention. But that's another story.

A thirteen-year-old Volkswagen Beetle, five inches of snow growing deeper every minute, an equation for disaster? Math was never my strong suit. It had occurred to me, when news of the approaching storm was first broadcast that I really needed a snow brush and ice scraper. But with one thing and another, as they say at the Pentagon, I failed to achieve my objective. Fortunately, Dina had a spare.

As I turned on the ignition, the heater gave a low rattle and sent out a blast of cold air. My feet were soaked, but I knew that at least a modicum of warmth could be achieved by the time I pulled into my garage.

Waving to her standing in her doorway, I could see the furrowed lines on Dina's brow. She suddenly held up her hand for me to wait, and went back inside. As she came running over to the car with a paper bag in her hand, I rolled down the window.

"Here, you may need this before you get home," she said as she handed me a half empty bottle of ice wine.

"Good idea, Dina. Thanks," I said, and slipped it under the seat.

"You know, Ernest Shackleton you're not."

"Look, it's only a few inches." I sighed. "And anyway, they must have plowed the main roads by now. I'll be fine." She reached in and squeezed my hand. She wasn't buying my bravado.

"Okay," my parent-self said aloud to my quaking inner child, "we'll just take this nice and slow."

The wipers flicked flakes as fast as they could, but the condensation on the windshield had me squinting to see the road.

I was quite chuffed at making it the three blocks to the main road without mishap. Beech Street was usually pretty busy, so I expected an easier time once I made the turn. From there, plows willing, it would be smooth sailing for the rest of the trip.

Then I noticed that the traffic light at Beech wasn't working; not a good sign. A handful of cars, all big SUVs, were crawling along. Knots looped over each other in my stomach as I saw how quickly the snow was deepening. Where were those benighted road crews?

As I made a right turn, the Bug glided, graceful as an Olympic skater, to the opposite side of the road. An oncoming car was far enough away to avoid an accident, but my heart started flailing around inside my chest.

Why hadn't I brought Turkey with me? If we died together, at least I wouldn't have to worry about someone finding his starved carcass on the kitchen floor.

So much for the main roads, and the snow seemed to be thoroughly enjoying its free fall. My other option was the highway. Surely that would have been the plows' first priority. Hands clutching the steering wheel in a death grip, I crept another five blocks and made a left turn without incident. But as I raised my eyes from the roadway, my stomach lurched; it looked like Las Vegas night at the church hall. Half-a-dozen police and emergency vehicles, strobic lights flashing, were blocking the entrance ramp.

As I eased my foot onto the brake, my tires lost their grip, and I swerved to a stop inches from the rather imposing figure of a policeman in a neon-striped down jacket. In spite of the rising tide of panic washing over me, I managed to plaster a smile on my face as I lowered the window.

"Sorry, ma'am, there's a thirty-car pileup two exits down and the highway is closed."

"Closed!" I sputtered. "Oh my god, how awful." And yet, in an adjacent fold of my frontal lobe, I thought, *nice eyes*.

"It's not as bad as it sounds," he said, stepping back and shaking his head as he eyed my baby buggy ride. "More dented fenders and bumpers than anything serious, but damn lucky you stuck to the streets, or you'd have been joining the queue."

Pursing my lips, I blew out a gale-force wind of frustration. "What do I do now?" I moaned as my head slumped to the steering wheel.

"You feeding a mastiff?"

"Huh?"

He nodded at the industrial-size bag on the seat beside me. "That's one huge supply of dog food."

"Turkey."

"Excuse me?"

"Sorry, officer, that's the name of my black lab. Oh, God, oh, God," I groaned. "All I had to leave with him was a can of tuna fish."

He exploded with a laugh like a cannon shot.

"Man, I didn't see that one coming!" he said, wiping the tears from his eyes.

And a sense of humor—maybe things weren't as dire as they looked.

"Where are you headed in that tin cup?" he said, leaning closer.

Stifling the whimper of helplessness rising in my gut, I straightened my back and looked him square in the eyes. "There're just two-and-a-half miles between me and a starving dog, and I'll drive as far as I can, then walk the rest of the way if I have to."

He took a step back and looked at the surrounding roads, then at my micro car.

"Wait a minute. I'll be right back." He walked toward the group of vehicles, then abruptly turned back.

"By the way, my name's Frank," he said, extending his hand through the open window.

"Sandra. Nice to meet you, Frank," I said, feeling the strength of his grip.

Instead of getting into one of the patrol cars, Frank opened the door of an SUV with a small plow in front. Maneuvering it in front of me, he waved his hand out the window for me to follow.

Hmm, I wonder if he likes ice wine, I thought as I eased my foot off the brake.

Bittersweet

A. E. Decker

Only half past noon, and there went the last pound of brandied rose creams. *I must make more for the evening rush,* thought Marcel, watching the satisfied customer walk out the door, gift-wrapped box under his arm. *Do I still have all the necessary ingredients in the kitchen, or must I—*

Then the next customer in line bore down on him, and his train of thought shattered like a sugar sculpture dropped onto a hard floor. "What do you mean, you sold the last rose creams?" the man demanded, his loud, aggressive voice carrying over the noise of the small crowd that filled *Doux-Amer.* "I came here specifically to buy them."

Zut alors, monsieur, Quelle tragidie. Quick—tackle that last customer before he reaches Bleecker Street. Marcel bit his tongue. Why did men of this ilk—self-important, business-suited types—never think to call ahead and reserve what they wanted? He stole a look around the shop, hoping to foist this particular pest off on one of his subordinates. Both George and Amanda quickly busied themselves with other customers. They'd heard that bellow and knew the aggravation it portended.

I'll give them hell later, Marcel promised himself. "If you return this evening, I will have made fresh ones," he told the seething businessman. "Perhaps you could reserve—"

"Return?" The businessman swelled up. Even his striped power tie looked belligerent. "I took a train to get here. This is coming out of my lunch hour, you know."

Marcel rubbed his brow. In an aisle to his right, two customers squabbled over a box of mixed creams. A little girl threw herself onto the floor, transforming into a screaming bundle of arms and legs over her mother's refusal to buy her cocoa. The checkout line began shifting like an angry centipede as those waiting grew impatient at the delay. Three hundred matters pressed for his attention, and this man acted like taking a subway from Wall Street to Greenwich Village was comparable to traversing the Sahara. *Try being a chocolatier on Valentine's Day, monsieur.*

"You have more in the back, don't you?" the businessman accused.

"I assure you we do not."

"I'll pay extra."

"There won't be more until this evening."

The businessman drummed an angry staccato on the counter top. "Let me speak to the manager."

Marcel wrenched his attention from a woman who wandered the shelves near the window, picking up boxes of chocolate and turning them over in her hands before setting them down again. Her cap's brilliant crimson-red color had drawn his attention when she'd first entered the shop, at least half an hour ago. "Pardon?" he asked.

"I want," said the businessman with insulting distinction, "to speak to the manager."

"I am the owner, monsieur, and I tell you I cannot magic brandied rose creams into existence. Come back this evening." *Or keep hassling me and discover what I can magic into existence,* he added silently.

The businessman gaped. "You, the owner?" read the almost-visible thought balloon hanging over his head. "Barely old enough to shave and not even American?"

Twenty-two is old enough to shave, merci beaucoup. Blond beards just grow more slowly. And what did you expect from a shop called Doux-Amer, a Texan?

Taking advantage of the man's no-doubt temporary silence, Marcel signaled to George to ring up the next customer. The constipated line finally moved, much to the relief of his patrons.

The businessman recovered. "Tell you what," he said, checking his watch, a gesture meant to convey both urgency and importance. "I'll give you my address, and you can send the chocolates when they're finished. I need them by six-thirty."

The wandering woman picked up a bag of chocolate-covered raspberries. Her thumbs caressed the foil as she held it, longer than anything else she'd selected. Her eyes squeezed shut a moment, then she put it back on the shelf.

Marcel shook his head. "Sorry, but we don't do deliveries."

The businessman's face tightened. "I can always go elsewhere, you know."

Marcel turned quickly away, feigning a cough. It was either that or let the derisive laugh escape. *Take your business elsewhere? Thank you monsieur, I could use a break.* He couldn't see the checkerboard floor for all the bodies obscuring it. More people kept piling in; the bell over the door hadn't stopped ringing since eleven o'clock. His neck burned, and his legs ached all the way up to his hips. Better to be a sled dog in the Arctic than a *chocolatier* on Valentine's Day. At least after being run off your feet, you'd know you'd gotten somewhere.

"That is your choice, of course," he said, once he trusted himself to speak, "but no other chocolatier makes brandied rose creams. They are one of my signature chocolates." And he'd been a fool to allow *The New Yorker* to write that article about them. Suddenly they'd become the "in" confection to give one's sweetheart on Valentine's Day. Most likely this businessman was looking to impress a fashion-conscious lady friend. And after she'd cooed and swooned, the chocolates would probably end up in a bin, untasted.

A customer left with his purchase tucked in a gold foil bag. Three more promptly surged in, tracking fresh snow over the floor. The smell of hot bodies wrapped in heavy coats, some of them wool, nearly overpowered the aromas of chocolate, butter, and sugar. Still the businessman refused to concede.

"I know you have more in the back," he said. "Sell them to me. You can make fresh ones for the other guy."

Once Around the Sun

Marcel rubbed his temples. Oh, what a beaut of a headache was blossoming there! The worst part was this idiot was right; he did have another half-pound tucked away in back. Maybe he should concede, sell them to this businessman just to be rid of him.

But no; Dan Lucas was a reliable customer who'd had the foresight to place his order the week before. It wouldn't be fair. Besides—Marcel touched the gilded theobroma blossom tucked beneath his shirt—he had another option available, one not open to the average chocolatier. He chewed his lip. Using magic on a customer? Surely the Theobromancer's Guild—the secret organization of chocolate wizards—would object. *But this is an emergency.* He forced his hand to unclench. "Might I suggest an alternative?"

"Are you offering a discount?" asked the businessman, almost before he finished speaking.

Marcel quickly reviewed his vocabulary. True, English was not his first language, but when did "alternative" become synonymous with "discount?" "I'm offering something exclusive," he said with the care of an angler casting into a deep pool.

Ah, he did know his English well. "Exclusive" was the right hook. A covetous expression stole over the man's face.

"Something not available to the general public, you mean?"

"*Exactement, monsieur,* something very special."

"How do I know it's any good?"

Fish landed; Marcel fought back a smile. "Taste for yourself."

Reaching under the counter, he took from the display case a crystal dish containing six chocolates as exquisitely arranged as rare gems. He hesitated a moment, sorely tempted to offer the white chocolate with the sugar-crystal dome. But no; the Guild would be within their rights to discipline him if he put a customer to sleep for the next month. "Try this one," he said, indicating a shiny dark chocolate embellished with a creamy whorl instead.

The waiting customers watched enviously as the businessman took the proffered chocolate off the dish. He lifted it to eye height, studying it as if he expected to find the words "made in China" printed in small letters across the base, then finally, grudgingly, took a small bite. The soft crack as his teeth broke through the chocolate shell shouldn't have been audible over the general babble that filled *Doux-Amer*, but it was.

The tight lines bracketing his mouth softened. His cheekbones stopped straining against his skin as if about to burst through. He took another bite of the chocolate and the hard squint around his eyes vanished.

Marcel set the dish back inside the display. The filling now melting on the businessman's tongue was as light as a snowflake settling on the tip of one's nose. It tasted—subtle, more hinting at flavors than actually declaring itself. A suggestion of burnt caramel gave way to the perfumey lushness of sugared violets only to be replaced by vanilla's bourbon-sweet bitterness.

But the taste mattered less than the effect. These were Zephyr Creams, his own invention. One bite and the eater surrendered to the most blissful inner tranquility.

Again Marcel touched the gilded theobroma. *I've done no harm,* he assured himself. Indeed, knots of tension in the man's neck and shoulders were melting like the trickles of dirty snow tracked across the shop's tiles. He'd probably sleep better tonight than he had in weeks, and whomever he intended to buy the rose creams for would find him pleasantly agreeable at their dinner this evening.

Marcel's conscience quieted, not without a few final grumbles. He released the theobroma. "The fresh rose creams should be ready by six o'clock," he said. "Surely you can leave work a little early on Valentine's Day."

"Of course," the businessman nodded, smiling at nothing. "Those files can wait."

"*Absolument.*" Marcel took up a notepad and pen. "Now, would you prefer dark or milk chocolate?"

He jotted down the information, a process that took far less time and stress than the prior confrontation. As the businessman wandered dreamily out of the shop, Marcel stretched the ache out of his lower back. With the passing of the lunch hour, the crowd thinned. There'd be a lull until late afternoon. *I'd love to sleep in tomorrow*, he thought wistfully. But no, tomorrow customers would come, hoping he'd be offering his chocolates at half price, like some cheap chain—

A flash of red caught the corner of his eye. The woman was at the counter now, peering through the glass at the dark chocolate crème brulees.

He glanced quickly off to the side. Amanda was wrapping up an order while George rang up a purchase. Ah, well. "May I help you?" he asked.

The woman's head shot up, her eyes widening under the red cap. Perhaps she'd only just realized how long she'd been wandering the shop without making a purchase. "Um," she began, then faltered and stared down at her hands. Her pale, cold-looking fingertips poked out of her fingerless gloves. Chewed nails. A pleasant enough face, but tired, shadowed under the eyes.

"Sorry," she said. Her lips curled upwards without achieving a smile. "My . . . someone bought me chocolates from here last year. I was trying to remember what kind they were."

She forgot what his chocolate tasted like? Marcel quashed a surge of indignation. "What did they look like?"

Her gaze wandered to the ceiling. "Um. Round. Red at the top, with little gold beads sprinkled on them."

"Those would be the strawberry champagne truffles." He never forgot a chocolate he invented. "Unfortunately, we're not offering them this year." After last Valentine's Day, he'd decided he wasn't satisfied with their texture and retired them, vowing to perfect them later. A vow he'd forgotten until now.

"Oh," she said. She studied her hands again. "I really liked them."

Why did I forget? Picking up a cloth, he polished an already clean section of the counter. "Perhaps I could interest you in something else?" he suggested, flicking his gaze at her.

"No, thank you. I probably wouldn't have bought them even if . . ." She folded her hands into balls. "Sorry. I don't even know why I came in." Lifting her head, she bent her mouth into another of those terrible not-smiles. This time Marcel noticed the redness in her shadowed eyes, the rawness of her nose. And he remembered. Remembered whom Valentine's Day was hardest on, after all. Not the chocolatiers.

Valentine's Day? Might as well call it "Shame the Singles Day." For every happy couple holding hands and looking into one another's eyes over a candlelight dinner, a lonely soul sat at home or meandered the streets, resigned to their solitude or bitterly envious of their happily mated friends.

But as depressing as the holiday could be for those people, there were others for whom it was nothing less than a paean to pain. He'd bet every last chocolate in *Doux-Amer* that sometime over the last year, this woman had lost her beloved. Death, divorce, infidelity—in the end, what did the *how* matter?

He really should get to making more brandied rose creams. The floor needed mopping, and he needed to reorganize some displays and bring more stock out of the back.

"Have a cup of cocoa," he suggested, coming from behind the counter. Taking her arm, he tried to draw her towards one of the tall tables by the window, where she could perhaps find peace watching the light snowfall trickle down out of the gray sky.

"Oh, no." She sounded almost alarmed by the prospect. "I couldn't."

"Certainly you can. On the house. A Valentine's Day gift."

A prodigy. That's what his teachers called him. He'd spent his adolescence studying chocolate in all its aspects, rarely looking up from his grater and tempering bowl. And he'd risen rapidly through the Theobromancers' ranks. But perhaps if he'd set the cocoa beans aside just once, he'd have known the right words to say now.

Once Around the Sun

She stiffened under his hand. "A Valentine's . . . no. No, thank you." Her chin dipped into her scarf. A muffled sob escaped her, then she twisted away from him, fumbling blindly for the door. In another breath, she'd be through it, lost to the crowded streets.

"Wait, please!" For the second time in less than an hour, Marcel went behind the counter and took out the crystal dish of magical chocolates. His conscience didn't emit so much as a peep as he held it out to her. "Have just one," he pleaded, turning the plate so a crescent-shaped sweet painted with a streak of bright yellow was in the fore.

If she'd only bite into it. The dark chocolate shell would crack, and a bright, tart, citrusy cream would ooze over her tongue. She'd swallow, perhaps noticing no more at first than the taste of lemon mellowed with vanilla and cream, and a slight warm tingling in her stomach. That warm sensation would spread through her torso as she bid adieu and went out the door. By the time she'd walked a block, she'd be warm to the tips of her ears. By the time she reached home, she might even be humming a tune. Perhaps she'd make a cup of tea, call a friend, find something to laugh about, and smile a real smile.

Cheering Moon, he called these chocolates. He'd presented them to the Guild on his graduation. But she turned in the doorway, that awful not-smile trembling on a face that looked ready to crack in half. "I'm sorry," she said. "I don't want chocolate this Valentine's Day."

"Please . . ."

She slipped out the door, so smooth and quick the bell suspended over it didn't as much as chirp. A bitter breeze blew a spray of snow through the gap before it swung silently shut. Through the window, Marcel saw her walking briskly away, her shoulders hunched. Her hand dug into her coat pocket and came up holding a crumpled tissue. She was just pressing it to her nose when a group of three laughing couples passed, blocking her from sight. By the time they cleared the window, she was gone.

Marcel exhaled. He set the crystal dish back in the display, then stood with his palms pressed against the counter a while. The familiar smell of chocolate wreathed his head. The walls of his shop encompassed him, warm shades of burgundy, cream, and gold. George fetched a mop and cleaned the checkerboard floor. Amanda straightened shelves. Over the speakers, audible for the first time since the mad rush began, Ella Fitzgerald crooned: "I cried a river over you."

I should've checked the song list more carefully, Marcel noted in some abstract portion of his mind.

The bell over the door rang. Marcel's head shot up, his heartbeat accelerating. But whatever his wild, inexplicable hopes, it was Dan Lucas who came strolling in, his amiable features pink with cold and alight with good cheer.

"Came for the rose creams," he said, stripping off his gloves. He took a seat at a high table by the window. "But I might as well treat myself to some cocoa while I'm here. Brr! That wind's bitter."

"Very bitter," agreed Marcel. Shaking off his melancholy, he fetched Dan's chocolates plus an extra-large mug of cocoa with whipped cream and sugar sprinkles. He set both on the table, and Dan instantly picked up the mug and took a sip.

"Mm, that's good." He sighed, wiping his lips. One hand reached out to stroke the red foil wrapper on the box of rose creams. "Lindsey will be so happy," he said. "Nothing says 'I love you' like chocolate. Especially your chocolate, Marcel."

"Nothing." Marcel faced the window. Snow was falling heavier now, obscuring the figures of passersby walking the Village streets. "Yes, that's important to know. Be sure you say 'I love you' to Lindsey."

Soon he'd have to get started on the brandied rose creams. Snow or not, the customers would come pouring in after work, eager to find that perfect gift for their loved ones. But just for now, he'd watch the street, sparing a moment of thought for those who would come home to an empty room rather than flowers and kisses.

Once Around the Sun

And to spare a moment of pity for himself as well—
the prodigy, who, for all his talent, all his magic, couldn't
promise his customers love. Only chocolate.

SPRING

Butterfly Wings

Courtney Annicchiarico

I can't stop watching the phone. *Please ring.* I stumble through the apartment searching for chores to redo. I scrub the toilet, feed the dog, and wash the kitchen floor—anything so I don't have to think about the visions of twisted metal that are stalking me. "I'm not dreaming," I chant. "I only have premonitions while I'm dreaming. What I'm seeing can't be real."

I take a deep breath and dial Greg's cell. It doesn't even ring and goes right to his voice mail. I knew it would. It's a piece of melted junk now, mixed with pieces of an engine, carburetor, and a bunch of other car parts I don't have names for. Greg tried so many times to teach me, but I never listened.

I keep seeing Greg's shattered face juxtaposed with the way it looked this morning when he woke me. He was kneeling by my side of the bed. He said he had a few extra minutes to climb back into bed and cuddle. His blue cable-knit sweater was already half off. I laughed, ran my hand over his half-exposed chest, and shooed him away saying his libido was going to get him fired. Why didn't I pull him into bed?

The doorbell rings, and I run to the door, throw it open, and catch myself before I leap. It's not Greg. It's his sister. Did I call her? I can't remember, but I must have because she is crying. We fall into each other's arms and wait.

My stomach lurches as I walk into the church and inhale the stench of incense and grief drowned in vats of cheap cologne. To settle it during the procession, I look past

71

the casket and focus on the pillar candles in front of the altar. Luckily for the mourners, sedatives have turned my thoughts into bobbing apples that disappear from the surface when I try to grab them. The roar of protest in my head dilutes itself to a whimper of submission as my sister-in-law pats my shoulder with the hand that I'm not squeezing. I sit in the first pew and stare at my gloves as the priest who married us seven years earlier prattles on about God's plan and Greg's reward in Heaven. Droplets dapple my lap during the eulogy, turning my black skirt darker, and I suppose I must be crying. My sister-in-law—can I still call her that—stays by my side, and somehow the day ends.

It's been a year, and I'm going on a date. Jason is an adjunct history professor with dimples and a Texas twang he tries to hide. My face in the mirror looks splotchy as I redo my mascara and try to forget that the black wrap around dress I'm wearing used to be Greg's favorite.

My little bump is barely noticeable under all the layers of white organza billowing from the empire waist of my gown. It's my little secret, my fluttering butterfly, and I love it as much as I love Jason. I'm not happier now than I was with Greg. But because Greg could not have children, I'm more completely happy. I pat my chest to feel Greg's wedding band hanging from a necklace beneath my bodice. I take a deep breath as the doors to my dressing room open. Greg's sister runs in to rearrange my skirt and fit my veil. It's time.

"Steph...Steph...wake up."
I feel something wet on my nose.
"Wake up beautiful . . ."
Greg is kneeling at my side of the bed.
"I have a few extra minutes. I can climb back into bed and cuddle."
His blue cable-knit sweater is already half off.
I reach up, run my hand over his half-exposed chest.

But I can still feel the flutter of butterfly wings.

The Call

Paul Weidknecht

When the friendship between Sammy McGill and me fell apart by accident, it did not seem to be irreparably ruined. Rather, the incident resembled something two people could laugh about years later, each claiming with a wink to be the true victim. But feelings hardened immediately, neither of us allowing an apology or the acceptance of such to get in the way of immaturity, stubbornness, or even good old fashioned self-righteousness. It didn't matter that the blood spilled that day—minimal and non-fatal—had been wiped clean, and that the offended nose had healed long ago; his anger simply lingered. Mine too, I suppose. That's just the way thirteen-year-olds sometimes behave.

For years, Sammy and I were the kids neighbors always saw together; where one went, the other was soon to follow. We'd catch crawdads in the nearby creek, standing barefooted in the impossibly cold water, pants rolled up, amazed at the way these creatures propelled themselves back into rock crevices where fingers could never reach. Somebody's mom was always dropping the two of us off at the movies, and it was commonplace to sit on the living room carpet of the other's home for hours watching TV like a born and bred member of the family.

Most athletic talents shook out under fairly even distribution. I was better in football; he had the edge in basketball. I was faster on a track; he could squirt a soccer ball between ready defenders. But in the sport we both loved, both watched on TV, and both went to see at the stadium,

Once Around the Sun

he was always superior. Baseball was the only sport that really mattered, and it mattered to be good.

Sammy could hit. If the ball happened to be anywhere near the black of the plate, Sammy had it rocketing back out with pitchers flinching, shortstops diving, or outfielders galloping during most at-bats. Seeing the ball leave the fingers of the pitcher, he'd turn, hips, shoulders, and wrists in motion, the commitment to damaging that ball irrevocably decided, his bat having more right to it than the catcher's mitt. Even when he didn't get the whole thing, his foul balls were epic, the long far kind that made umpires snatch off their masks, players crane their necks from the dugout, and pitchers toe the dirt on the mound, pretending it didn't bother them. On the other hand, I would begin swinging when the ball had popped the catcher's mitt.

The day I smashed Sammy's nose by accident had not been a good one, as a new torment was spreading around the school. Kids would walk up behind each other in the hallway and step on the heels of their sneakers in midstep, causing the back of the sneaker to fold under the victim's heel, sometimes taking the shoe off entirely. The act was known as giving someone a "flat." It wasn't painful, but depending on the number of witnesses, occasionally embarrassing. Inevitably, the shoe then would have to be untied, removed, replaced on the foot, and retied. I had gotten two flats that day.

During that past year, Sammy had changed. Youthful tomfoolery had turned to adolescent contempt. Laughing at people, instead of with them, had become his way. In truth, some of these changes probably weren't his fault. Rumor had it that his father left a note for his mother saying the past fifteen years or so with her had been a waste. Back then, I couldn't tell if the changes in Sammy were his father's doings or his own. I also had no idea he was the one giving me flat number three.

Spinning around with my elbow up, I caught him. He bent forward, hands cupped under his nose, the blood forming a syrupy pool in his palms. Only then did I realize who he was. His nose wasn't broken; my intention had been to make this unknown person back off, never to injure. My apologies went unheard, and I tried to help. He shrugged my hand from his shoulder. Instead of laughing, the small group with him faded back and stared.

Our friendship ended that day. Later, after school, I went over to his house to speak with his mother. She closed the door in my face. It didn't help that the incident was the talk of the school for a week, that from Monday to Friday Sammy had to make it through the halls with people cupping their hands under their noses and whimpering. In the neighborhood, scowls between our families passed unconcealed. We were like feuding clans tucked into a backwoods hollow, forced to look at each other, keeping watch on every move, ready for any misstep that could give us advantage over our rivals.

The winter passed uneventfully. My goal that spring was to make a Senior League team, any of them, it didn't matter. Last year's last place team was fine. Thirteen, fourteen, and fifteen-year-olds yearned to be in this senior division of Little League, especially if they had no chance of making the high school team. And this year was special. A larger than usual crop of fifteen-year-olds was leaving the league, meaning a larger than usual number of thirteen-year-olds would be picked to replace them.

The day of the tryouts was raw and gray, the kind of weather even millionaire professionals hate to play in. Hit a ball in that weather and your fingers felt like they'd cracked, fingertip, nail, and knuckle right down the center. Fog hung in the morning air as dozens of teenagers formed a long column down the third base line, chattering from the chill and their own nerves. I felt this temptation to look up and down the line in an attempt identify the real baseball players from the pretenders, but this was useless; hitting a baseball is about skill and finesse, not muscle or physique. The coaches of every team watched as each kid took several swings and fielded a couple of grounders.

Sammy was the fourth or fifth kid to hit. Everyone murmured as he drove his allotted pitches into the outfield, each one a solid line drive. On one of the drives, the outfielder assigned to retrieve the balls slipped on the slick grass and fell down, allowing the ball to roll to the fence, giving the tryouts a moment of real-game drama as everyone imagined a double turning into a triple. Coaches scribbled on their clipboards.

My own tryout was less stellar. Of my five pitches, I fouled off one in a long looping arc over the backstop, dribbled one back to the mound, and missed three completely. On the last pitch, hit or miss, the player was to leg it out to first, then on to second base. I made the most of my lone sprinting talent, and on my way back from second I looked up to see several coaches writing on clipboards. Near the dugout, Sammy and one of the coaches chuckled easily to each other as if speaking peer to peer. Evidently he wouldn't have to wait until Wednesday to find out if he'd made a team.

The Wednesday following tryouts was the day of notification, the day when everyone found out if they had been chosen by a team. The coach would call the players in the evening at their homes to tell them when and where practice was taking place. No call meant no team.

When we left school that afternoon, everyone promised to call each other, wanting to know if they had gone from being classmates to teammates. That evening, seven-thirty came and went without a phone call. Then my cousins, the twins, Keith and Kyle, called at seven forty-four notifying me they were going to the Red Sox and Phillies, respectively. Doug Moweski called at eight-nineteen bragging that his new team, the Tigers, were last year's champs. Then the phone did not ring for the next fifteen minutes. I quickly lifted it up to check for a dial tone. It was working.

At eight thirty-nine, I walked past the kitchen and saw my Mom hand-drying the dinner plates with a dish towel. She looked in my direction, her face a little too sad, the gaze a moment too long.

At nine-twelve, my Mom walked into the living room where I was watching TV.

"Honey, I don't think they're going to call," she said gently.

The Call

"Mom, they've got a lot of people to call. Maybe one of the coaches got off to a late start, or maybe he forgot about it and just now remembered."

"All right then," she said patting my shoulder and walking back out into the kitchen.

Nine fifty-six, and still no call.

Ten-twelve. No call.

Ten-sixteen. The phone rang, and I bolted from the living room chair, not letting it ring a second time.

"Hello."

"Hello, is this Richard Walker?"

An adult voice. My head swam. "Yes, this is Richie. Richard."

"Hi, sorry to be calling so late. This is Coach Hollins, of the Pirates. I lost my list and am just now getting to everyone. I wanted to call to tell you about our practice tomorrow. We'll be using field two at the middle school at four thirty. Do you know where that is?"

"Sure. Uh, I'm on the team, the Pirates," I said, more as a question than a statement.

"Yeah. Well, see you tomorrow."

"I'll be there. Middle school. Field two at four thirty. Thanks."

Mom smiled as she dropped me off for practice. I could tell she was happy about being wrong. As she drove away, I started across field one. My teammates on field two had already paired off, soft-tossing, limbering up their arms. Some guy who was probably a coach emptied two canvas bags onto the ground, one filled with bats, the other containing the catcher's equipment, then he carried a bucket of balls toward the pitcher's mound. Some other man who had to be Coach Hollins walked over, taking his clipboard off the roof of the dugout.

"Can I help you?" he asked.

"Yeah, I'm Richie. Richard Walker. We talked last night." He stared for a moment.

"You're here for baseball? This is the Pirates," he said.

"Yeah, the Pirates," I said.

Once Around the Sun

"I'm not sure I'm the one you were talking to. Maybe you're looking for another team. The Red Sox are playing on field two at the *high* school."

"You're Coach Hollins, right?"

"I'm Hollins, but I don't think I called you. Everyone set for this team is already here."

"But you called me last night. It was late, past ten. You said you'd lost your list, and that was the reason you were calling so late."

Hollins shook his head. "Wasn't me. Sorry. I had all my calls in by eight."

"Eight? But you said . . . Can I see that?" I asked, pointing to the clipboard.

Coach Hollins blew out a breath and handed me the clipboard. "It's all yours."

For some reason, I had expected the list to be less formal, maybe handwritten with scrawled notations about the tryouts on it, who had struck out, who had gotten a hit, who had run the bases well. But this was simply a roster, name, age, address, and phone number. Neatly printed from a computer, the list's only notations were checkmarks from a blue ballpoint pen next to each name:

Alvarez.

Armeto.

Burnett.

Dunnfield.

Fellman.

Letort.

McGill—

I stared at the name, forgetting momentarily that the purpose was to find *Walker*. Sammy had made the team. Sammy was on this team. *This* team.

I scanned the rest of the list just to be sure. No Walkers, of course.

When I looked up, the coach had his hand out waiting for the clipboard.

"I'm sorry," he said. "Maybe there was a mix-up. Maybe you're looking for another team. Like I said, the Red S . . ."

"No, there's no other team."

The Call

Anyone could have made the call for Sammy. An uncle, his mother's new boyfriend, anyone. Maybe it was his brother, Gavin, the one ten years older, with the beard, who was always getting locked up. Might be something he'd do. Then I noticed him. Sammy had stopped soft-tossing to smile, and I began the walk home.

A Spouse's Guide to March Madness

Headley Hauser

Relating to a spouse during March Madness isn't all that complicated, really. It's all about laundry and Tic Tack Toe.

I'm not exactly Dr. Phil. The closest I've come to a long-term relationship was with a hardy Swedish ivy. It died after seven years of accidental neglect. So how I am qualified to write a spouse's guide to anything?

Well . . . I'm a guy. I know how guys think, and when I say spouse, I'm not talking about husbands, I'm talking about women, or as we single men call them . . . We never really learned what to call them. That's why we're single men.

I know, there are women out there saying, "I know a lot more about basketball than my husband/boyfriend/Swedish ivy." Perhaps so, but do you have the capacity to lie on a couch for three successive extended weekends, and do nothing but ignore women, watch television, and build teetering towers of dishes and beer cans?

Yup, there are some things we guys will always do better.

"So, Headley," asks my fictitious female interrogator, "why does my normally active and moderately interesting man vegetate for an entire month listening to Dick Vitale?"

"It's simple," I say while squirting my underarms with breath spray (can't be too careful). "It's about laundry."

My best friend growing up was Paul Sender (not to be confused with Paul Westphal, Chris Paul, or the nineteen sixty-two Elvis hit, *Return to Sender*.) Paul had a large open laundry hamper in his room. This hamper was the primary reason Paul consistently beat me at horse, pig, or any other barnyard-animal-themed basketball shooting game. It was also why his room was neater than mine—an excuse I'm sticking to.

Every night before going to bed, Paul got into his PJs and lined up his dirty socks, underwear, pants, GI Joe T-shirt, and even his PF flyers (sneakers that made him run faster and jump higher). Then, he launched each item into his laundry hamper from the foul line (roughly defined by a line of Legos.) If he went seven for seven, he tossed his little brother in to celebrate.

Big brothers are supposed to do such things.

Now, my mother is a fine woman, but she understood nothing about the formative, therapeutic value of an open laundry hamper, nor did she understand its relationship to subsequent multi-million dollar NBA contracts. She had me put my laundry in a bag, much like those you might see a merchant marine carry, except for the Wild West pictures and the printed words encouraging me to "Ride 'em Buckaroo."

The thing about a duffel-type laundry bag is that, when hung from a hook, it has only a tiny opening at its mouth —not big enough to throw a sock in, much less a pair of dungarees, and certainly not Paul Sender's little brother. With careful aim, you could toss in a marble, as long as it wasn't a shooter.

Mom didn't much like marbles in her washing machine.

So you see, basketball is all about our obsession with laundry tossing; that's why we watch March Madness. If we didn't, we might chip in and clean up around the house— something men just don't do.

But if you live with a man, I don't have to tell you that.

"So," says my simulated female questioner, "what does Tic Tack Toe, have to do with it?"

Isn't she great? I never would have been able to make this segue without her.

Each young boy's obsession with Tic Tack Toe is well documented. All you have to do is look at any elementary school lunch table to see the familiar four-line grid,

A Spouse's Guide to March Madness

complete with Xs and Os. It's as ubiquitously present as that lovely limerick about scenic Nantucket. But it disappears in middle school. Why?

Somewhere around sixth grade comes the great disillusionment. When played by two enlightened players, Tic Tack Toe always ends up in a draw. All you need to do after your opponent X's a corner square, is put your O in the . . . Well, I'm not really sure, but it always comes out a draw.

That's why men created the March Madness bracket. All those lovely lines reappear in a format that we know will never result in a draw.

If you wish to relate to your significant male in the month of March, all you have to do is fill out your own bracket—and it helps if you know nothing about basketball. Choose the teams numbered one and two in each quarter grid to make it all the way to their respective regional finals.

Men are too proud and stubborn to recognize how often that happens. Then choose the underdog in every other match-up. Who cares if you lose twenty of your first thirty-two games, you'll have all the upsets on your grid.

When your man is on the phone with his man-buddy asking what genius predicted the Fighting Sarah Palins of Alaska Moose-skinning Tech to beat Florida State in the first round, you can show him your bracket. Suddenly you're a savant, a hero, one of the guys, with promising hours of conversation about the 2/3 Zone and set shots off the screen for the rest of the month of March.

Hey, at least he'll be talking to you. If you want to foster a meaningful relationship during March, read someone else's article.

Seven Seconds

Ralph Hieb

John parked on the gravel shoulder at the end of the bridge. He got out of the car and looked at the expanse of concrete and asphalt, then turned, walked to the back of his vehicle, and opened the trunk. He removed the pack and put it on, checking several times to ensure the straps holding it to his body were tight.

He took a deep breath, then walked the half mile to the center point of the structure. While waiting for the traffic to pass, he noted that the majority was heavy trucks that didn't even cause a vibration; only the wind from their speeding movement indicated their passing. He rechecked the straps to make sure of a tight fit before proceeding. He looked both ways before he crossed the four lanes to the side he had chosen to jump from.

John climbed the guardrail then leaned forward. Peering into the chasm below, his arms outstretched behind him, his hands firmly gripped on the guardrail of the bridge, and the tips of his shoes protruding over the edge of the bridge, he saw the river over eight hundred feet below. Sweat collected on his brow as he contemplated what he was about to do.

But as he watched the water, it mesmerized him into wanting to let go. To finally jump. If he didn't do it now, he never would get up the courage to go through with what he planned.

Taking a last gulp of air, he leaned as far out as possible. Saying a quick prayer, he released the rail.

One one-thousand.

Once Around the Sun

The feeling was exhilarating. As he picked up speed, the wind made his hair flutter, a delightful caressing sensation. The river seemed to fly towards him like a waiting lover.

His mind registered every detail. The bright green spring colors of the trees sparkled and glistened with the early morning dew. John wished he had a camera to share with the world the beauty of nature he was witnessing.

Two one-thousand.

He cleared the bridge. Time to throw out the small chute that would pull the main parachute out of his pack.

As he let the small one sail out, his heart raced with the thrill of the moment.

He looked up smiling, expecting to see the main chute blossom overhead as it pulled from the pack. In a millisecond, his smile turned to horror. The chute had not opened. The beauty of the scenery transformed into a horrifying spectacle . . . his last sight.

Three one-thousand.

A tale sprang into his mind, of a young man who committed suicide by jumping off this bridge. John didn't recall why the guy jumped, but he knew it had happened, and the man's father had arrived at the bridge to stop him.

The father reached out trying to grab his son, overextending himself; he not only missed his son, but also lost his own footing. Both plummeted to their deaths.

Many people claimed to have seen the father's image in the clouds of the early morning mist that gathered over the rapids.

John gave up tugging uselessly at the ripcord. Everything that concerned him or his life would be in the hands of his family.

Four one-thousand.

Blurs of green, yellow, white, with streaks of brown; flashed by his face. He shut his eyes. The sound of breakage assaulted his ears; he assumed it was the carnage of his bones shattering as he crashed.

He expected to feel the brief sensation of cold water running over his body then, after a second or two, oblivion. But instead, something tore at his skin. The cold, the river's wetness, was not there. Just a gentle breeze as he felt the sudden jerk of stopping.

Five one-thousand.

Perhaps he wasn't dead, but he was surely in shock. He felt as if he had run through a thorn bush. He'd shut his eyes; now he dared to open them.

Looking down, John saw that he was dangling only feet above the water. The rapids below allowed a gentle spray of mist to reach up and dampen his boots. Surprised, he looked up.

Six one-thousand.

He hung from one of the trees that lined the edge of the river. He'd drifted well right of the central location he picked for his jump. He was scratched and bruised from falling through the trees. But those same trees he'd admired earlier had caught the remnants of his parachute, holding him fast, preventing the impact.

Above the river's roar, John could hear the wail of distant sirens. Someone must have watched him jump and called the police. As he hung there, he looked out towards the river.

Seven one-thousand.

Wondering how he was going to get out of this predicament, he let his eyes slowly drift up towards the sky. John sensed a person staring at him.

It was the face of an older man. His eyes stared blankly. Etched into the face were the lines of someone who worked long and hard in the sun. He could see the trees through the man's features.

Am I hallucinating? wondered John. He reached out towards the face. As he moved, the vacant eyes focused. A slow smile spread across the weathered visage staring down at him. The image nodded at him. Before John could say anything, the face faded.

Felicity and Fortune

Emily P. W. Murphy

Laura Charles, charming, accomplished, and pretty, with indulgent parents and a substantial fortune, seemed to unite the best blessings of existence, and until the age of nineteen had done very little to vex her parents. Mr. and Mrs. Charles prided themselves in raising their daughter to expect her wishes to be realized, and taught her from a young age to form her own opinions. It was a lesson they did not regret—until she fancied herself in love.

The second son of a York jeweler, Mr. George Bingley was certainly not the sort of man any gentleman would choose as a son-in-law. His mean upbringing and lack of fortune, fashion, or standing were enough that Mrs. Charles likely never thought to warn her daughter against his charms. If Mrs. Charles gave any consideration to the jeweler's son, it was only as that child who delivered parcels.

But to Laura, George was much more than a delivery boy. From a young age, she admired his easy manners and welcoming smile when she entered the shop with her mother. She often found herself in George's company as his father and older brother tended to her mother's needs. As the children grew older, their friendship unfolded into a greater admiration of each by the other, and before Laura entered her first season, she knew Mr. George Bingley was the only man she could ever marry.

This certainty grew over her months in York, and Laura dreaded returning to town for the social season when her parents would expect her to find a suitable husband from among the sons of their friends and social equals. She and her governess, Mrs. Holmes, were out enjoying their last days in the country when her worries came to an end. It was unseasonably warm for early spring, and the two ladies were reclined upon a blanket each with a book. Noting Mrs. Holmes had fallen asleep, Laura rose from the blanket to take a short stroll around a nearby pond. She had stepped no more than ten paces away when she encountered Mr. George Bingley coming down the path towards her.

"Miss Charles," he said, removing his hat. "I had hoped to encounter you here." He hesitated, looking past her shoulder.

Laura turned and followed his gaze to the sleeping Mrs. Holmes. "Let us walk this way." She indicated the path around the pond. They moved off a short distance so their conversation could not be overheard even should Mrs. Holmes awaken. "Are you here to deliver my mother's pearls? I had thought they would not be ready until Friday."

George shook his head. "You thought correctly. My father is at work on her necklace even now. No. I came here to speak with you for I find I cannot delay any longer my wish of asking you a particular question."

Laura felt a flutter of hope within her breast, but knew not what to say.

"Forgive me, Miss Charles," he said, looking down. "I should have written, but I daren't put on paper my feelings for you, on the chance they not be reciprocated. That is, if you do not care for me." He turned his hat in his hands. "I wish to ask you, but perhaps I am too bold." He scowled. "I should not have come. I am sorry for bothering you." He took a step away, returning his hat to his head.

"Wait, Mr. Bingley," Laura said, holding out a hand as if to touch his arm, but withdrawing it before doing so. "I do wish you would tell me what you have come to ask."

His eyes met hers, and she detected within them the slightest glimpse of hope. He stepped closer to her and took her hand. "My friend," he said, looking first at her hand, and then into her eyes. "I do not believe myself worthy of your attention, and yet I seem somehow to have received it. If I did not believe you felt for me some fraction of the affection I feel for you, then I should never ask, but . . ." He hesitated again.

"Go on." Laura gave his hand a small squeeze.

He drew a deep breath. "Someday, when I have established myself in business and can provide for a wife, would you ever think you could be the lady to fill that role?"

Laura could not help but laugh at the awkward proposal, but nodded. "Of course, my dear George," she said. "I should think it obvious that I would never allow another lady to take the position I have longed for since my girlhood." Holding his hand, she pulled him back in the direction from which they had come. "Let us go tell Papa right now."

George's position did not yield. "No, my darling—for now I may call you so—I do not wish to approach your father on the subject until I can present to him evidence that I should be able to provide for you. At present, I am merely the younger son of a jeweler. I have nothing to my name, and what little my father has will go to my elder brother. To ask for your hand now would surely lead to rejection, and perhaps a bar to our seeing each other again. That is a fate I cannot risk. But I have aspirations, and soon I shall make them reality. And when I do, your father might think more kindly towards my plight."

"I do not need aspirations or dreams," Laura said, pouting. "I need only you, and I wish to be married at once. What difference can a few years mean to your business that is more important than what those years will mean to us?"

"I have a plan," George said, pulling her towards him and wrapping his arms around her. "Through my father's business I have made many acquaintances and have found there is a need for a man who can facilitate connections. I wish to become a matchmaker of sorts for suppliers and shops. The need is there, and with but a year or so in operation, I know I shall be able to demonstrate to your father the level of success I will one day achieve. Be patient, my love." He planted a small kiss on her upturned forehead. "The wait shall prove worthy."

Once Around the Sun

* * *

Reluctantly, Laura returned to town with her family. She kept to herself when possible, not wishing to expose her secret, but on the eve of Laura's presentation at court, her mother summoned her.

"You are about to embark upon a glorious adventure, my dear," Mrs. Charles said when they were alone. "Tomorrow you shall at last be able to venture into society."

Laura smiled, but did not speak, not wishing to tell her mother more than she ought.

"You seem nervous," Mrs. Charles said, peering at her daughter through her spectacles. "Do not be afraid. You shall be quite every gentleman's favourite tomorrow and every day until you are wed. Fortune and family such as yours are rarely found in one lady united, and your sweet temper and pretty smiles will be sure to make you welcome in even the best circles."

"Thank you, Mama," Laura said, feeling her cheeks warming at her mother's praise. "I shall endeavour to contain my nerves."

Mrs. Charles nodded. "It is essential that you maintain your composure at court. I wish you to marry the son of an earl, at the very least, and nobility always prefers young ladies who know their place and are confident in their entitlement."

"An earl, Mama?" Laura took the tiniest of steps back. She had known her mother's wishes for her future husband were high but she had thought she would be contented with a gentleman.

"Oh yes, indeed." Mrs. Charles sat back, raising her eyebrows. "I should see you marry the son of an earl, or even a marquess or duke. Eldest sons only, of course. It is my wish that your children inherit not only your wealth and beauty, but also your husband's title."

Laura returned to her room at the first opportunity. She perched on the edge of her bed in the flickering candlelight, breathing slowly to calm her nerves. Until this conversation, her largest concern had been to not unduly encourage any future suitors. She knew Mr. George Bingley to be a talented and charming man, but despite his ambitions, a title was beyond his reach. If her mother wished her married to the son of an earl, there was nothing George could possibly do to meet with her parents' approval.

She lay in bed considering her options. Perhaps she ought to sneak away in the night, find George, and elope to Gretna Green. But if she did, both she and George would be banned from her parents' house for all time. It pained her to think of bringing shame to her family, and she did so wish to maintain a friendly relationship with her parents. No. Nothing had changed. She must go through the motions of seeking a husband to appease her parents, and wait for her beloved to come for her.

Though Laura entered society with the finest education, manners, and gowns a grand fortune could procure, she did not attract many admirers. She knew her parents spoke of the matter when they believed she could not hear them. Her lack of suitors was a mystery to them, for they could not know how she subtly discouraged the young men who approached her. She smiled at them, but did not feign interest in their stories, or volunteer much in the way of conversation. When asked to dance, she always accepted, but never laughed or threw flirtatious glances over her fan to encourage a second set.

Despite her mother's desires, Laura ended her first season without acquiring an offer of marriage from so much as a baronet, let alone a duke. Still, Mrs. Charles maintained her hope that her daughter would marry into nobility, and only reassured Laura that her second season would yield more positive results.

The Charles family returned to the country on a hot August day. Heedless of the temperature, Laura hurried to the jeweler's in the hope of seeing her love. Alas, when she arrived she found only his older brother tending the shop. Since no one, not even George's brother, knew of their arrangement, she could not ask after him. That night, she wrote him a letter, posting it before her parents awoke.

Once Around the Sun

George's reply came later that day. His business, he wrote, was progressing better than anticipated and would take him to town that evening. He closed his letter assuring her he would return to York in a fortnight, at which point he would be prepared to speak to her father.

Laura danced through the first se'night, but as George's return to York approached, apprehension replaced her elation. She feared her father would oppose the match, but could imagine no future happiness if she could not become Mrs. Bingley.

She knew not when exactly Mr. Bingley should call, so she stayed near the house in the hope of seeing him. For days, when she accompanied her mother to the drawing room, she contrived to sit near the window to practice her needlework.

She was thus arranged when he arrived, but from her position at the window she did not at once recognize him. Never before had she seen him dressed in his finest with a powdered wig atop his head. Once she knew him, it took every bit of her strength to keep herself from running downstairs.

She listened as he was escorted into the house, his voice barely audible at such a distance. She heard footsteps as he and the butler crossed the foyer. Her father's library door opened and closed. She felt faint from nerves as she imagined what conversation must be taking place in the room below. Several minutes later, she heard the library door open again, and footsteps cross the foyer. She looked out the window in time to see Mr. Bingley leave the house. He glanced up, saw her in the window, and shook his head.

Laura's hand flew to her mouth. George gestured towards the grove, and she understood he wished her to meet him there.

"Excuse me," she said to her mother who was unaware of the drama unfolding below. "I feel a headache coming on, and believe I should lie down."

Her mother's forehead creased in concern, but she agreed that Laura should go to bed.

Laura slipped out of the drawing room, but rather than going to her chamber, she crept down the stairs and out the front door. She dashed across the lawn and into the grove of trees where she found George awaiting her arrival. He was pacing among the trees, wig in hand, but when he saw her approach he grew very still and solemn.

"What did he say?" Laura asked when she was before him. "It is not good, I can tell."

"Not at all favourable." He threw his wig to the ground. "I will spare you the choice words he had for me and summarize his meaning. He assured me that he does not, and shall never, consider me a suitable match for his daughter, nor even, or so he claimed, for any young woman under his employ."

Laura's hands flew to her face. "Did you tell him of your business? Of your great success and plans?"

George nodded. "I told him, but he remained unmoved. I even showed him my accounting books." He gestured to a satchel she had not until that moment noticed he was carrying. "He cares nothing for my business nor aspirations. He requires a title, and a high one at that."

He stepped away from her and resumed his pacing. "There is nothing, nothing at all, that I can do to convince him to alter his opinion, of that I am certain."

"So we shall elope," Laura said, hurrying after him. He stopped at her words, and they nearly collided as he turned to face her.

"I could never ask you . . ."

Laura pressed her fingers to his lips. "And you have no need to. I have already agreed to be your wife, and if my father cannot be persuaded to see the merit in my keeping my word, then I shall have to do so without his blessing." She moved her hand from his lips to his cheek. "Worry not, my love. One way or another, I shall be your bride ere long."

Mr. Bingley seemed uncertain.

"Give me until tonight." Laura bent to pick up the wig, removed a dried leaf from it, and handed it back to him. "If I have not persuaded him, I shall leave with you then."

Once Around the Sun

Bidding Mr. Bingley adieu, Laura hurried back into the house, praying she could convince her father to approve of her marriage.

Laura expected her father to speak to her of Mr. Bingley's visit sometime that evening, but he said nothing. However, when the ladies withdrew to the drawing room after dinner, Mrs. Charles beckoned her daughter to sit beside her.

"How is your head feeling?" she asked, as Laura arranged her skirts over her knees.

For a moment, Laura was confused by the question, but then she remembered the excuse she had given to escape her mother's company. "Much better, Mama, thank you."

Mrs. Charles nodded. "You missed quite an event this morning," she said with a smirk. "After you went to your chamber, your father informed me that a young man from the village came to ask for your hand in marriage." She laughed. "You cannot imagine which young man it was."

"Mr. George Bingley," Laura said, meeting her mother's eyes.

"Why . . ." Mrs. Charles hesitated, a look of surprise upon her features. "Yes. How could you have known?"

"Because he asked me to marry him last March. And I accepted his offer."

The colour drained from Mrs. Charles' face, and for a moment Laura thought she would need to call for her mother's smelling salts.

"What can you . . . how . . . " She flipped open her fan and waved it before her face. "It is not possible."

"And yet it is so." Laura reached for her mother's empty hand. "He is a good man, Mama. He has excellent prospects in the world, and we love each other. I so dearly hope you and Papa will give the match your blessing."

"Our blessing?" Mrs. Charles shook her head. "No, indeed. He is a highly unsuitable match. He has not title, nor fortune, nor breeding. He will never do as the father of my future grandchildren."

"Mama, I love you and respect your wishes, but I must be very clear on this subject. I am quite determined to marry him."

"Marry whom?"

Laura jumped as her father's voice boomed across the room.

She turned to see him standing by the drawing room door, arms crossed before his chest.

"Mr. George Bingley." Laura rose to her feet and willed her voice to stay strong. "I know he came to speak to you today, and I would like for you to bless the match." She braced herself for an outburst of temper, but her father's voice, when it came, was so low she had to hold her breath to hear him.

"Never will I consent to throwing my daughter away in such a manner." His face grew red. "You are never to speak of that man again." He turned to leave the room.

"No, Papa," Laura called after him. "I shall marry Mr. Bingley."

That night, Laura packed a small bag. She left behind all but her favourite gowns, knowing she could purchase new ones. She packed only items of great sentimental importance: the emerald ring her mother gave her, her grandmother's book of sonnets, and the writing desk her father built when he was a boy. She crept from the house and met George who, having no carriage of his own, drove the cart he used to do business. They eloped to Gretna Green, spent their wedding night in a Scottish inn and returned to York within the week.

Not wishing to cause her parents more grief than they had already endured, Laura implored her husband to bring them into town at night to limit the neighborhood gossip. George agreed on the condition that, when they concluded their journey, she wait outside while he lit candles so her first glimpse of her new home would not be disappointing. She agreed readily and waited in the cart as he ran inside. She looked up at the brick face of the townhouse and watched as, one by one, the dark windows came alight.

Once Around the Sun

"Why, I wonder," she mused aloud, "does Mr. Bingley not have his staff light the candles before he arrives home?"

"Who'd that be, Miss?" the man holding the horses asked.

Laura jumped in surprise. She had not noticed the man was there, and certainly had not been addressing him.

"Mrs. Bingley," she corrected, smiling at her new name. "You may call me Ma'am."

"Begging your pardon, Ma'am." He touched his cap and patted the horse's neck.

At that moment, Mr. Bingley emerged from the house.

"Are you ready, my love?" He held up a hand to assist her from the cart. "Thank you, Smith," he said, handing something to the man who held the horses. "If you would just see that our baggage is set inside the front door before you leave, I should be most grateful."

"Why should you be grateful?" Laura asked as they ascended the stairs to the front door.

"It is late," Geroge said, patting her hand. "And he is only contracted to see to my horses, not our luggage. He is doing us a favour."

"What do you mean, contracted?" Laura frowned in the darkness.

"Smith does not work for us alone," George said, opening the door and placing his hand on her back to usher her through. Laura froze. "For whom else does he work?"

George shrugged. "For whomever he likes. I board my horses at his stable, and he sees to their care. Ordinarily I would walk the distance from the stables to the house, but I did not think you should walk on your first night at home." He moved her through the door, leaned down to kiss her, then closed the door behind them. "Welcome, Mrs. Bingley," he said, extending his arm into the hall. "May I give you the grand tour?"

The grand tour consisted of four rooms: one bedroom, a dining room, a drawing room, and a kitchen. Laura could not even pretend to be impressed by her surroundings, but hoping to keep her horror to herself, she merely nodded and bit her lip. When the tour came to an end, she endeavored not to cry.

"Of course, this is just for now." He seemed to recognize her disappointment and wrapped his arms around her. "This was plentiful when I was living alone, but soon we shall need more space, I am certain of it. I assure you, when that time comes, we shall have something larger."

"Oh yes, of course." Laura smiled up at her husband. "This is only temporary. Soon we shall have someplace nicer."

"Yes, my dear. Very soon."

The next morning, Laura awoke to her husband stirring the fire. "My love." She sat up in bed. "Whatever are you doing?"

George stood, brushing his hands together. "I did not want you to be cold when you awoke." He smiled. "If you like, you may stay here while I fix breakfast." He did not wait for an answer but turned and left the room.

Laura sat in bed, frowning. Until that moment, she had not realized there were no servants to greet her husband upon his arrival home, no one to help them out of their travel clothes, or offer them tea. No one but each other. How was it possible that a successful businessman did not keep a manservant? That he did not have a cook? That she, his wife, had no lady's maid? Her breathing accelerated, and she began to feel lightheaded.

The door opened, and George entered, balancing a tray. "My love." He set the tray on the small table by the door and hurried to her. "Are you unwell?"

Laura shook her head. "I am only just realizing . . ." She let her voice drop off. She could not hurt him by telling him of her disappointment. She forced a smile. "That I am your wife at last."

Laura grew very practiced at pretending to be happy in the next weeks as she discovered the hardships of living without her father's wealth. When she asked about hiring a cook, George explained that most of his money was tied up in investments. He assured her that soon, very soon, they would be able to afford such luxuries, but that day would come sooner if they could save money by cooking for themselves. So Laura watched as her husband prepared their meals, and learned to do the same. She learned to tidy their rooms and keep the house clean. New gowns were so far out of the question that she did not even ask for them. She had to manage with the few possessions she had brought with her when she left her father's house.

She found that despite having many accomplishments that were valued in her former society, in the skills she needed to be a proper wife to George she was sorely lacking. She stumbled through her days, despairing over ever being the wife George had hoped for, her spirits clouded by her disappointment in her married life. When she had dreamed of becoming Mrs. Bingley, it had not occurred to her that doing so would mean leaving behind not only family, but comfort. Now she lived in small, cold, sparsely-furnished rooms without the assistance or company of the servants upon whom she had always depended. In her nighttime dreams, she wandered their tiny house, opening secret doors to find previously undiscovered rooms filled with rich furnishings, tables laden with food, and more servants than even her father's household could contain. "Look, my dear," she would say. "Things are not so very bad." And George would embrace her and say, "Oh yes, I forgot about these rooms. This is why I felt I could marry you." The sense of relief she felt in those dreams was not nearly so great as the sense of despair she felt upon waking.

In spite of her hard work and their meager meals, Laura soon found that new gowns would be necessary, for she was with child. She worried what her husband would say, for she understood enough of their finances to know that they were not yet ready to move to a larger home. She delayed telling George of their expected addition for as long as she could, but eventually she had to share with him her news. He heard her with the same mixed emotions she felt upon learning of her condition—joy, yes, but also sadness. They agreed they could not relocate as yet, but must continue to save and invest in the hope that the Bingley business would prosper.

Felicity and Fortune

The babe, a girl, arrived on schedule, and they settled her into a basket near their bed. George chose her name, Louisa, after his mother, and hired a neighboring widow to help take care of both mother and daughter until Laura was sufficiently recovered to do so on her own.

Laura lay awake at night, listening to her husband's and baby's steady breathing, and wondering if such a day would ever come. She was never intended for a life of such hardship, and now she had a small baby to care for. How could she possibly give Louisa the life she deserved?

It was with some shame that Laura finally realized why her parents had withheld their blessing of her marriage. They had understood the full consequences of the match. Although George's business was an inspired idea, he lacked the social connections necessary to bring it to fruition. Mr. Charles had understood this; Laura had not. If she had realized she would be living in poverty, if she had truly understood what that meant, surely she never would have married Mr. Bingley.

But, even in her despair, the thought of not being married to George, of not having darling Louisa, caused her pain. Each time she thought with longing of fine furniture and rich food, she inevitably pictured George by her side. In all her spoiled childhood, no one had brought her more real joy than he. She sat up in bed. Surely she need not resign herself to misery for the remainder of her days. All her life she had gotten what she wanted; why should this be any different?

Louisa cooed, and Laura lifted her out of the basket. "You, my dear, shall marry very well. Perhaps not the son of a duke, but . . ." Laura thought through her daughter's options. She wanted for two things at present: fortune and fashion. The Bingleys could never become a fashionable family without a substantial fortune. But, after all, George did have the potential to move up in the world; all he needed was some help in society. "We shall make Papa's business a success," she whispered to Louisa. "You shall have a dowry to attract the most fashionable of husbands."

Once Around the Sun

With renewed resolve, Laura dismissed the widow and took over the care of her baby. She cooked and cleaned to the best of her ability. George, to his credit, complained neither when the floor was streaked, nor when the food was burned. Laura observed how hard he was working and endeavored to do the same. With practice, she improved. At meals, Laura inquired of her husband about his day. She made a study of the particulars of his business and asked questions when she did not understand.

At night, while the baby slept, Laura wrote letters. She wrote to everyone she knew from her old life imploring them to consider forgiving her behavior enough to employ her husband's services. When months passed without a response, she wrote again, reminding her dearest friends of their childhood bond. Even that failed to elicit a response.

One cold night in winter, Laura sat again at her writing desk, considering her failures. Somehow she must convince her old friends to employ George. If only he could have a chance, just one, he could prove the value of his service. Then her acquaintance would gladly employ him.

Laura sat up straight in her chair. Why had not this idea presented itself sooner? She put pen to paper and wrote to her dearest friend from school, but this time she wrote not a plea for assistance, but a letter of joy and pure fiction. She wrote of her husband's recent successes, of his necessity to turn away clients for want of time, of their much-improved situation in the world.

She hesitated only briefly before setting her seal to the wax. It was all falsehood, but what had she to lose?

Louisa brought the letter to post and endeavored to think no more on the matter. Weeks later, George came racing into the house. "I have a new client," he said, reaching down to pick up Louisa and kiss her cheek. "I just received a letter from a gentleman in London; he says his wife went to school with you, and he would like to talk to me about what I can do for his country estate."

Laura bit her lip. She knew exactly who the gentleman's wife must be, and she had no wish to acknowledge her role in this connection.

"He is looking to make improvements and knows not whom to hire," George continued. "This could be the opportunity we have awaited. With the income from this project, we might afford a larger home."

Laura crossed the kitchen to her husband. "Not yet," she said. "Louisa is still small. We can manage in the space we have. You must use this opportunity to expand your business contacts. This project might very well lead to others."

George frowned, shifted Louisa to his hip, and grasped Laura's hand with his free one. "I know you are not happy in this tiny home."

Laura hesitated. She had tried so hard to hide her misery, and yet he had known. She felt tears prick at her eyes but hardened herself against them. "It is temporary," she said, moving closer to her husband and child. "But if we save for the next several years, and if your business grows, our children shall have so much better. If we work hard and save now, we can send them to school in London. We will be able to give Louisa a dowry to attract a man of fashion. We might purchase a grand estate and live out our days in comfort."

George smiled. "Our *children?*"

Laura leaned into him, resting a hand on her abdomen. "Yes, *children.*"

He released her hand and put his arm around her shoulders. "I think I should like that." Together, they looked at their daughter. "And you, my dear," George said, bouncing her on his hip. "Whom shall you marry?"

"Fashion," she said in her childish voice. "Fashion man."

Laura smiled, and George laughed. "Indeed?" He turned to his wife. "You start early, do you not?"

"I must." She caught her daughter's hand in her fingers, completing the family circle. "For only then shall I bring the Bingleys from jewelers to gentlemen in a single generation."

"Well, my dear." George chuckled and kissed the top of her head. "I do believe you shall."

Timothy Worthy Teddybear and Spring Cleaning

Will Wright

It wasn't that Timothy Worthy didn't like spring. He loved smelling the air that came alive when the windows were first opened, taking walks in the field with Milly, and holding a buttercup blossom under her chin to see if she liked butter. Then there was the rain. Timothy Worthy would stay awake at night and listen to the soft rain tapping on the roof and window pane. He liked almost everything about spring, except . . . Spring Cleaning!

Spring cleaning meant nearly constant activity throughout the house. Mom kept the children busy every moment cleaning the garage, cleaning the closets, cleaning the basement, cleaning the attic. They never had time for Timothy Worthy.

"Hey Andy, how about letting me ride behind you on your bicycle?"

"Sorry Timothy, I have to paint the shed."

"Terri, wanna play checkers?"

"Sorry Timothy, I have to beat the throw-rugs."

"Milly, would you like to play house?"

"Sorry Timothy, I have to fill my donation bag."

Timothy Worthy shuddered. Every year Mom gave each child a donation bag to fill with old clothes and toys for the needy. One year, Andy put his Sunday suit with the scratchy wool trousers in his bag. Timothy told him that Mom wouldn't allow it, and sure enough, the following Sunday, he was wearing the suit, looking more miserable than usual. To Timothy's dismay, old friends sometimes found their way into one of the bags. Timothy Worthy knew his friends were going to loving homes and that the children would never send *him* away, but the idea of the bag disturbed him.

One year they sent away the bear's favorite cookie jar! They replaced it with a much larger jar shaped like a pig.

"Looking at the pig will help me keep my weight down," said Mom. Timothy Worthy, who couldn't imagine wanting to be less than completely full of cookies all the time, moped for days until Terri pointed out that the new one held a lot more cookies.

One of the most frustrating things about spring cleaning for Timothy Worthy was how hard it was to find a place to snooze. No sooner would he settle into a comfortable spot than that comfortable spot would be invaded by Mom's army of obedient workers. Even the doll house offered no relief. When it came to cleaning, Mary, the porcelain doll, was just as eager as Mom.

Timothy propped himself against the wall in Andy's room to catch his breath. Andy always tried to do the least spring cleaning, so it seemed the safest place. He was just nodding off for a much-delayed nap when he sniffed a strange scent. "Hmm," thought Timothy, "I suppose I'm going to have to open my eyes and see what it is."

The first thing Timothy Worthy saw was Sebastian. There was something different about his friend. He looked strange. It wasn't just that his smile was crooked, or the smell, for it was Sebastian that Timothy Worthy smelled. Much about the hippo had changed. His dark gray hide was now brighter, almost shiny. His teeth shone white instead of a dull yellow. Strangest of all, his right side seemed overstuffed and tight while his left was loose and baggy.

"What happened to you, Sebastian?"

The hippo stomped his left front hoof. Some of the stuffing shifted, and he looked a bit more like himself. "Spring cleaning, Timothy," he said. "Do you remember that spring when Terri was five?"

"Sure, Sebastian, that was the year we moved from Andy's room to Terri's."

"Do you remember what happened to *us* that spring?"

Timothy Worthy Teddybear and Spring Cleaning

Timothy scratched his head. He was good at remembering hugs and cookies and comfortable places, but less important things slipped his mind. Suddenly it came back to him in a flash. "The machines!"

"Yes, the machines," said Sebastian. "Mom threw me in with a lot of towels. I'm still dizzy."

"Do you think Mom will throw me in, too?"

Sebastian sniffed at Timothy Worthy and then wrinkled his nose. "I'm pretty sure she will."

"Oh, I hate spring cleaning."

"Timothy!" said Sebastian, shocked. He'd never heard Timothy use the word "hate" before.

Timothy gave Sebastian a stubborn look. "I won't go through that again. I have to find a place to hide until spring cleaning is over."

"Where are you going to hide during spring cleaning? Every bed and chair is moved. All the closets are turned inside out. Every box and drawer is sorted."

"I could go to the attic."

"I heard Dad's supposed to work there tonight."

"I bet they won't find me if I hide outside."

"Maybe," the hippo agreed, "but there are dogs and cats out there, and what if it rains? I think you're better off getting washed by the machines."

Timothy Worthy rubbed his stomach. "I wish I had a nice big chocolate chip cookie to help me think."

"I don't think that would help," said Sebastian, who was, after all, not a big lover of cookies like Timothy Worthy was.

"I'll hide in the basement."

"The basement's no better than any other place. The whole house gets cleaned."

"I know," said Timothy, "but Andy always cleans the basement, and there's one place I know he never cleans."

"How do you know that?"

"I've watched him. Every year, Mom tells him to be sure he cleans the space between the loud metal box and the big drum, but it's too small to get a broom in there. Andy always leaves it dirty, and I'm just small enough to climb in there and hide."

"I'm not sure this is a good idea, Timothy." The hippo shifted another lump to the left. "The machines weren't as bad as I remembered. I think it just surprised me the first time. You're going to get washed sooner or later. Why not get it over with?"

Timothy jumped to his feet. "Whose side are you on, Sebastian? Are you going to help me or not?"

Sebastian sighed. "I'll help you."

Getting from Andy's room to the basement had never seemed dangerous before. Discovery could come from any hallway or door. Of course, Sebastian wasn't afraid, since he was already clean, so he led the way. Timothy hung back cautiously. The hippo urged him to move faster.

I'm too afraid," said Timothy shivering.

"If you stay here, they'll find you."

"But I'm scared."

Just as Sebastian's patience was nearly at an end, the bear made a run for it, all the way to the basement door.

"Sebastian," Timothy whispered.

"Yes?"

"Will you get me a cookie before I hide? A nice big chocolate chip cookie?"

Sebastian frowned.

"Please," Timothy begged. "It may be a long time before spring cleaning is over."

"Okay."

The hippo grumbled as he waddled into the kitchen. "Why am I doing this? He's going to get caught." Getting to the jar was no problem, as the family was busy outside, but, the first cookie that came up was fudge nut.

"I don't see why it has to be chocolate chip." He fished around in the jar until he found a large chocolate chip cookie. He padded back to the basement door and handed it to Timothy.

"Thank you, Sebastian!"

Timothy Worthy Teddybear and Spring Cleaning

They had to grope their way in the dark once they passed inside the basement door. They could hear movement above. Timothy felt his way to the big drum, ducked under the pipes and squeezed himself into the hiding place. The metal box wasn't being loud at the moment, but the walls that rubbed against him felt furry, soft, and a little wispy— not the way concrete or metal should feel. As his eyes adjusted to the light, he thought he saw spooky threads dancing around him. Was something crawling up his leg?

"I don't know if this was such a good idea," said Timothy.

"I never thought it was," replied the hippo.

Timothy could see the machines on the other side of the big drum. He heard a steady drip echoing from the sink. The basement door opened, and light tumbled down the stairs. Mom and Andy followed.

"This year, young man, I want the whole basement clean. I want no dust, dirt or cobwebs left when you're through."

The light above Timothy came on. He could see that his arms and legs were covered with black soot. Cobwebs formed a shawl about his shoulders and draped the top of his head. "Oh my," he muttered, "how am I going to get all this off?"

"And one more thing, Andrew. This year, I want that space between the furnace and the water heater cleaned out. It's filthy in there."

"But Mom, It's too small to get the broom in."

"That's why I got you this hand broom. Crawl in there and clean it. Do it now."

Timothy Worthy froze. "Of all the places to hide," he muttered. Andy was still putting up a feeble protest, but Timothy knew that wouldn't last much longer. He searched the area for some way to escape. Five feet away was a laundry basket with sheets in it. Timothy crawled under the pipe, dove into the basket, and hid under a sheet. Timothy heard the sound of a stuffed hippo laughing from the basket next to him. A minute later, he heard Andy lie down and scrape out his hiding place with the hand broom. Timothy wasn't quite close enough to hear what the boy was muttering.

"Look at how filthy it was!" Mom sounded very excited. "Look at all that soot, and those cobwebs . . . and what's this? Half a chocolate chip cookie? How did that get in there? We're lucky we don't have mice. No, no, don't stop now, young man. I want you to sweep that spot again until we know it's clean. While you do that, I'll throw this load of sheets in the washer."

At first, Timothy didn't realize what was happening. Suddenly he felt the basket move as Mom lifted it up toward the machines. Now that all was hopeless, he wasn't really afraid of being washed. He just felt silly.

Tip, thud, shake, slam, whirl, and click. Timothy was in the dark. Water poured down from above, slowly soaking him and the sheets. He thought about crying for help, but he didn't. It was useless, and besides, he was too embarrassed. The water felt warm, like the time Terri had brought him into the bathtub with her.

"This isn't so bad," he thought.

The machine gave a loud thud. Suddenly, everything began to move. For the next half hour, Timothy could think of nothing other than trying to keep the sheets from twisting around his arms and legs.

When it finally stopped, Mom threw him, along with the sheets into the other machine. This machine was very hot. It spun so fast Timothy thought he would never see straight again. He had no choice but to press against the wall and feel his stuffing shift.

It was morning. Timothy, with Milly's help, had moved all his stuffing to the right places. His fur looked brighter, and he smelled better, too. Milly was whistling in the bathroom, getting ready for pre-kindergarten. Timothy lay back among the pillows and looked out the window. In the yard, a dogwood tree was budding. Soon, it would explode with blossoms. In the branches, a spider was weaving a web.

Timothy Worthy Teddybear and Spring Cleaning

Timothy remembered the cobwebs from his basement hiding place and shuddered. The webs in the trees were different, though. They seemed cleaner. Morning dew hung from the strands, and the early sun reflected off the drops.

"I guess I could learn to like spring," the bear mused, nestling back against his pillow, "but right now, I think I'd like a cookie."

The River

Ralph Hieb

"I found him." I heard Kim's voice over the roar of the water. "There's no question about it . . ." Her words trailed off. Only moments ago, my spirits had lifted when she called. The words cut deep. "He's dead."

Kim worked rescue and, in this case, recovery. We were part of a search party looking for a rafter who didn't make it to shore.

The previous night a group of revelers left the bar and decided to shoot the rapids. Water ran high, and the class four rapid turned into a class six. We were part of a search party looking for the one who didn't return.

"Why would anyone in their right mind go into the river after dark?" Bud asked as we headed towards Kim's search area.

"I have no idea," I mumbled.

"At least the rest survived," one of the other members of the rescue team said. He moved off to the side as we approached Kim.

Ducking to avoid a branch Bud had pushed out of his way, I walked over to Kim.

"I don't see him," Bud said.

Kim pointed down at the water.

"I still don't see anything," he said.

"Down there." Once again Kim indicated the water.

I saw a bright blue jacket sleeve half hidden under a boulder. The rippling water made a hand appear to be waving gently.

"He got caught under a shelf boulder," the rescue guy said, speaking into his radio. "We'll need a rope and some breathing equipment. Looks like he's jammed under it with the water holding the body in place."

The sun beat down. Although the reflection off the water nearly blinded me, I couldn't take my eyes from the waving hand.

It seemed like hours before the rest of the rescue team showed up. By the time the team set up their gear and had retrieved the body, I was dripping sweat.

"I don't know about you guys," Kim said, "but I need to get out of here." She swatted at a mosquito. "The bugs are eating me alive."

Bud and I nodded and followed the rescue team up the embankment to the road.

The following week, a line of silver water glistened in the early morning sun; high rising walls of earth and stone showed where the river had cut its path through the gorge. The breeze blew crisp and cool; I knew that would change in a few hours as the sun climbed higher.

The New River was known for being unpredictable. Its roiling channel, through rock and clay, provided a tempting adventure. The only way to cross was by passing over the highest bridge east of the Mississippi, the New River Gorge Bridge. A group of us made a living taking thrill-seekers down the rapids while photographers snap pictures from the bridge.

Hearing the crunch of gravel, I looked up towards the parking lot. A bright red kayak cruised along the tops of the shrubbery, its vehicle concealed beneath. Steve, our photographer, had arrived. He'd paddle his kayak ahead of everyone, then set up at points along the river and take souvenir pictures of the adventure.

Turning my attention back to the river, I admired its beauty, even knowing how treacherous it could be.

"Thinking about last week?" A female voice cut into my musings.

"Yeah," I answered as Jessie came walking across the small beach we used as a launching point, a four-cup tray of coffee in one hand and a single cup of tea in the other.

The River

Placing her tea on a boulder that had a reasonably flat top, she used the other hand to steady the tray as she set it next to her cup.

"Here you are." She pulled one of the cups from the tray and handed it to me.

"Thanks." I accepted the cup. "No doughnuts?"

"Be happy you got that," Steve said, walking down the trail, carrying his kayak above his head. "I almost didn't stop. We're running late." He set the kayak down and grabbed two cups for himself.

"How soon until our crews get here?" I asked.

"They're a few minutes behind us. Bud had to find a replacement helmet—his was cracked," Jessie answered.

"'Bout time he got a decent one," I said.

The rumble of the old bus's diesel engine brought our attention to the parking lot.

"Wonder if they're ever gonna fix that mosquito killer," Steve said.

"What are you talking about?" I asked.

"The exhaust from that creature," Steve indicated the bus with one of his coffee cups.

"Time to get to work." Jessie picked up her cup.

Before walking up the hill, I took one final look back to admire the scenery.

The guests piled out of the bus and headed straight for the public restrooms. *Some things never change*, I thought and got in line.

A few minutes later, feeling somewhat lighter, I walked up to the trailer of deflated rafts. Bud and the driver worked to unload the first of them.

"Knew you'd find a way to get out of pulling these things off the trailer," Bud said as he grabbed the edge of a raft. I climbed on the side to give him a hand.

With the two of us on one side, we gave the raft an extra heave, its skin making it easy to grab. As the rafts came off the trailer, we lined them up along the edge of the parking lot.

Using pumps, four of us—Jessie, Steve, the bus driver, and I—filled the rafts with air.

Once Around the Sun

On the other side of the lot, Bud gave the orientation lecture to our novice crews.

"Having everyone paddle at the same time helps keep the raft moving forward in a straight line," he explained to the group who stood in a semi-circle around him. "We'll tell you how many times to paddle and in what direction . . ." He continued until all directions and safety practices were covered. "And very important, make sure that you watch how you swing your paddle. These things can easily knock someone's teeth out." He grinned and pulled the side of his mouth back to show a gap in his teeth. "Not watching what I was doing and the handle played dentist." He laughed.

After orientation, we asked the guests to help carry the rafts to the river. Splitting up the people into three full crews, we ventured down to the launch area.

Because the steps were steep, the park service had installed a waist-high rail. Sliding the raft along it made the trip downhill easier. People stood along the sides, guiding the vessels down. When we reached the bottom of the ramp, the group broke up into their respective teams.

"We'll divide up," I instructed, addressing my team. "Four on the left and four on the right. The ninth person can sit in the back with me."

As I launched my raft, I remembered this group had a zip line adventure scheduled in the afternoon. I was glad this would be a half-day trip instead of the usual full day.

Everyone took a place, and we started paddling out into the center of the water. There were two high school boys on either side in the front; both looked athletic.

"You guys brothers?" I asked.

"Yup," replied the one on the left. "I'm Jeff, and this is my little brother Tom."

"But I'm the better lookin' one," Tom said.

The rest of the people introduced themselves: Julie the boys' mother, Debbie their grandmother; Nancy and John, a couple celebrating their anniversary; Lee and Cindy were on a date; and Katherine, who was working on her bucket list.

The River

In a few minutes, the current had us, and the ride began.

"Paddle three times hard," I yelled. The people in the raft obeyed, and we missed the boulder jutting from the side of the river.

I kept bumping into Nancy, who was sitting beside me. "Having a person sitting next to me is making it difficult to steer," I told her. "So if you don't mind, please move to the princess seat. That's a place of honor, really. All you have to do is sit and enjoy the ride."

Smiling, Nancy took the offered seat between two of the paddlers.

I turned my attention back to the river. "Lean left and paddle hard," I yelled. "Don't stop until I say so."

We swerved to the right, sending the raft sideways into the current. Sitting at the back, I used my paddle as a rudder to steer us into the main channel. The inflatable craft plunged down a four-foot slick boulder into the turbulent pool at its base with everyone laughing and yelling as cold water splashed, soaking them. This was the part I loved: everyone having a good time.

We rounded a bend and the New River Gorge Bridge came into view, still a few miles downstream. Its height was so great the local police constantly had to stop thrill-seekers from base-jumping off the rails. I wondered if there were any thrill-seekers up there now. That would be something to enliven our not-so-leisurely journey.

We approached a pool off to the side of the river, and I aimed the raft into it.

"The water is calm here. Take off your helmets, and if anyone wants to jump in and cool off, we can stay in this area for a few minutes."

I looked over at another raft drifting into this quiet area, with only the guide in it. Its former occupants swam around it like playful dolphins, enjoying the cool water.

I took off my own helmet as well as the baseball cap that I always wore under it. I dipped the cap into the river then turned it over on top of my head. Cool water spilled down my neck and back. When I put the cap back on, it was still wet and cold, more than I could say for the helmet.

As the other raft drifted closer, Kim, its guide, called out, "Do you think these folks would like to go surfing?"

"Sounds good," I hollered back. "I'll check with my group. What do you think, Bud?" I said as Bud steered his raft close to mine.

"Okay by me," he answered. "Make sure everyone is up for it first before we promise anything."

"Will do." I waited until I had all of my crew back before asking.

"What's surfing?" Katherine asked.

"That's when we find a spot in the river where the water flows over a falls and the pool is low enough that it seems you can paddle upriver against the current."

Smiling faces and shouts of "let's go" were my only answers.

We paddled downstream, toward the right side. When we passed a certain prominent boulder, I used my paddle as a rudder to steer us around it and face us upstream. Then I gave the order: "Paddle as hard as you can. Don't stop."

Slowly, we emerged on the upstream side of the boulder. It was a lot of work, but I knew the current was only going to get harder. "Keep paddling hard," I shouted.

The raft entered an area just below a three-foot fall in the river and began bouncing not only up and down, but from side to side as I steadied the course.

Suddenly, it was as if we were riding in the middle of a violent whirlpool. It felt as if the raft would jump out of the water at the same time it dropped so suddenly, people lost their seating.

"Wahoo!" Tom and Jeff yelled in unison.

After a few minutes, I started to paddle and got us out of there. We'd had one hell of a ride.

"How come we had to leave so early?" Tom asked.

"Yeah," Jeff added. "It was really getting great. I could have stayed all day."

One after the other, my crew agreed.

"We have to let the others have a turn," I told them.

The next raft in was Bud. He gave a really good show, sort of like one of those adventure documentaries. After he left, it was Kim's turn. By the time she entered, I had arrived at a calm section, where most of my crew had jumped in the water and were splashing around.

"Does anyone want to try and swim through the rapids?" I asked.

"Yes." Jeff and Tom were the first to answer.

"What you have to do is lay on your back with your feet aimed in the direction you're heading. Don't actually swim. Let the current take you. This area is a class one and not really too bad. Try to keep to the right; the rocks on the left can get nasty. So if you're ready, make sure your helmets are on good, then get in the water. I'll run the raft down the center and pick you up at the bottom."

With that, I lost five of the nine people from the raft.

"You folks don't have to paddle," I told my remaining passengers. "Just enjoy the scenery, and I'll guide us down the river for a bit."

Drifting down, I watched the people in the water as well as the four still in the raft.

"A few weeks ago one of the rafts had a real nice nature experience," I said. "There was a bear at the water's edge, and one of the folks who had a camera was able to get a picture of him before he disappeared into the woods."

"Do you often see wildlife along the banks?" Debbie wanted to know.

"Not too often, but sometimes we get lucky."

We enjoyed drifting along the class one until arriving at the bottom, where I picked up my swimmers.

"Hey look!" Jeff yelled, pointing. At the edge of the wood line, a doe stood munching on the grass, her fawn beside her. "And I didn't bring a camera," he said, disappointed.

I waited for everyone to get a good look at the deer before talking. "We need to start toward one last set of rapids."

Ahead of us, the roar of the rushing water once again drowned out the sounds of the forest.

Once Around the Sun

"Get ready!" I raised my voice above the din of the swift, crashing waters. "Paddle now. Four times hard." The vessel plowed toward a steep drop with the current cascading into a pool that spit the churning water back at us.

We hit hard and the raft flipped sideways, spilling four of my crew into the river. Most remembered the brief training Bud had given them back at the start. They swam toward the raft.

I counted them as they returned. Three. My insides went cold. I looked to the river and there was Katherine, swimming toward the center, directly into the current. "Swim toward us. Hard," I yelled, hoping she could hear me above the noise of the river.

She kept swimming in the wrong direction. The image of a blue-sleeved jacket with a hand gently waving flashed into my mind. He had been white-water rafting for years, but it only took one mistake. I was not going to let her make that one mistake. Even with the cold spray of the river hitting me I broke into a sweat.

"Faster! Paddle faster," I yelled to my crew, keeping the rudder oar aimed at Katherine. I shouted so loudly that Bud, in the raft ahead of us, heard. Seeing what was unfolding, he ordered his people to back-paddle, forcing his raft to slow almost to a stop.

All eyes were on Katherine as she seemed to realize her mistake. Turning, she tried to swim toward me. This whole time she'd held onto her paddle, now, forsaking it, she slogged through the water as if it were wet cement.

The torrent pushed her toward an outcropping of rocks—shelf rocks with their treacherous overhangs.

Jeff and Tom dug deep into the water, their paddles working in perfect rhythm, forcing us to plow through the white foam.

As my raft neared Katherine, I saw we would run over her. I cut my paddle toward the left shore to pull up next to her. Nancy reached forward with both hands and grabbed the shoulder straps of Katherine's lifejacket. Clinging with both hands, Nancy kept her alongside of us. Tom, who was in front, grabbed onto Katherine's jacket, but when he tried to pull, the strap slipped from his grasp. Nancy leaned as far back as possible, keeping Katherine next to the raft, the strain evident in her face. Reaching out a second time, Tom leaned further over the side and latched onto the strap, somehow wrapping his hand in it. At the same time Julie, who sat behind Tom, grabbed the other strap. All three of them pulled hard. With a heavy heave, Katherine was pulled from the water.

She lay there for what seemed like minutes. As I climbed past the people at my end of the raft to see if she were all right, I heard her say, "I'm okay. This is embarrassing."

She lay stretched out across the raft some moments longer, then regained her composure. As she reclaimed her position, other members of my crew exchanged high fives, and I released the breath I'd being holding.

"I'm afraid I lost my paddle," Katherine said.

Looking down the river, I could see the raft ahead of us was still holding position. Bud waved a paddle.

"Let's head toward that other raft," I said, forcing a smile.

Catching up with the lead raft, we retrieved the way-ward paddle. Katherine talked about how she'd become disoriented and thought that a large rock was the raft. Once she'd realized her mistake, getting to the real raft was the only thing on her mind. I just nodded my head, taking in another deep breath of relief. I'd heard this before.

We drifted about one hundred yards farther, and the pick-up point came into sight.

"Everyone needs to give a hand carrying this raft up the bank to the trailer," I announced.

As we carried the raft to the waiting trailer, Steve stood on the edge of the parking lot. "I got the whole ride on film. If anyone is interested, you can purchase a copy at the main building when the bus arrives."

I promised myself I'd buy a copy of Katherine's rescue. But not tonight.

Tomorrow would be a full-day trip.

The Muse

Emily P. W. Murphy

He first visited her in high school. Senior year. Study hall. He sat there, shoulders hunched, head hanging forward, long legs stretched out into the aisle. He drummed the fingers of his right hand on the desk before him.

He had penetrating eyes, probably blue, the kind that made a girl's heart jump before she glanced away. His gaze overwhelmed her. She tried not to look.

Even though she could not see them, she knew those eyes.

Over time she met his hair: tousled, not long, but not too short either. Dirty blond. Eventually, she discerned the outline of his face. She knew he was tall and lean. Still, she never saw him.

He attended every study hall, probably even when she was home sick, though she could not be sure. Over the weeks, she came to know a little more about him. Not the whole story, but some of his details.

She learned his taste in music, though she never heard it. She found he liked to read, though he never suggested a book. She discovered his denim jeans and cotton T-shirt. She admired his casual good looks.

By graduation, she knew about his best friend, and how that friend had changed his life forever.

Over the summer, he left her alone. She was free, for a time. If she thought of him at all, she thought he had released her.

Once Around the Sun

* * *

In college, his visits were sporadic. He waited a semester before he appeared. Then one night, as she brushed her teeth, he came into the women's bathroom. Ignoring the other girls, he looked directly at her. She turned away, returned to her room, and locked the door.

The next time he visited, he brought another. It was late at night as she sat alone. He sat with his mother at their kitchen table. His mother was young and beautiful, with long, straight, brown hair.

The next semester, she heard his voice for the first time. He was talking to his mother. He warned her about his brother's problem. Maybe they were at the kitchen table again. She couldn't see. She combed her hair and listened to his mother finally admit he was right.

Junior year, he joined her in the shower. He was shouting at his alcoholic father. Someone threw a glass. She was not sure who. She only heard it shatter.

Most of his visits were less dramatic. Each time he appeared, she learned more. Sometimes he brought friends. Mostly, he came alone.

He disappeared for a while, but she had other visits: the girl from heaven, the wrinkled old grandfather, that unusual tree. Each had its own story to tell.

They came to her one at a time. Never together. Never staying long.

He returned the night before her biggest final, senior year. The final was early, and she was studying late. She knew she needed sleep. As she closed her textbook, he joined her at her desk.

His eyes, definitely blue, held hers. His sadness washed over her. She could not turn away.

"I need you to tell people about me." The words were as real as if he had spoken.

"What do you mean?" The question flowed through her. "You alone hear my story." He held out his hands. "Write it down, so people will know."

She shook her head, reaching for her textbook. "You're not real. Why should I listen to you?"

He smiled. His teeth were straight and perfect. "What is real? Of course, I'm real. I'm right here. I'm talking to you. You know me. I must be real. But I'm small." She felt him sigh. "If you don't write my story, I'll stay small, but you can make me great. You can make me real for everyone."

"I'm tired," she whimpered, resting her forehead on the desk. "I have to go to bed. My exam is tomorrow morning."

His eyes, those eyes she knew so well, pleaded with her. "If you don't write it down, my story will fade away. Please."

She could feel him reaching out to her. She could not refuse. He was too dear to her now. She pulled out a pad of paper and started to write. She recorded his features, his eyes, his hair, and the smile that she had just discovered. She transcribed his conversation with his mother and his fight with his father. She made notes on each of his friends. Who they were to him, how they belonged in the story. No names. She never learned their names. Not even his.

She wrote about his all-important friend—the one who had changed his life. And she wrote how his story ended.

She tore the page off the pad of paper, opened a drawer, pulled out an empty folder, and placed the page inside.

"Well?" she asked him.

"You didn't write it all." His eyebrows drew together in concern.

"I can't write it all." She yawned. "Not right now."

"But you'll forget." He shook his head.

"I won't forget, and if I do, I have these notes." She flipped through the pages in the folder.

"You'll come back for me?" He looked at the pages in her hands.

"Of course."

He hesitated, his eyes searching for the promise. Exhaling, she closed the cover on his gaze.

* * *

Years have passed. She still has the folder. She cannot throw it away. She knows that inside, he waits. He waits for her to return to him, to sit down, to write. He waits for her to release him into the world.

SUMMER

The Farmer's Daughter

Jerome W. McFadden

I saw my first airplane crash on a late summer afternoon in 1920. I heard the chunking first, then spotted the plane far out over Old Man Emerson's place.

This was also the first airplane I ever saw. I thought they were supposed to stay up in the sky, but the motor on this thing was chuk-chuk-*chuk*-chuk-chuking while the plane weaved and wiggled around up there like it didn't belong. The thing grew from a speck into a fragile bi-plane flying in the general direction of our pasture, but not making a great effort to get there.

The motor went into to a full roar at the wrong time, causing the airplane to streak past the pasture straight into our tomato patch. But even then, it wasn't done. The engine roared again as the plane mowed through our tomatoes, but the vines grabbed the wheels and ripped the undercarriage plumb off. The plane skipped like a flat rock across our yard before plowing straight into the pigsty.

Our hogs bolted out of that broken fence, wailing and howling like it was the end of the world. But once they hit the tomato patch every one of them slammed to a dead stop. Apparently the fear of God doesn't outweigh a sun-ripened tomato. Pa always said that those hogs had less sense than a congressman in Washington.

I put down my hoe and walked over to the plane. The pilot sat stock-still in the cockpit, staring at our barn wall as if he was memorizing the advertisement for *Red Man Tobacco, A Good Chew*, or admiring the painted picture of the Indian chief wearing a full war bonnet.

"You okay?" I asked.

Once Around the Sun

He turned his head and used both hands to lift the goggles off his eyes. He unsnapped his leather helmet and rubbed his face and forehead as if they were really sore. "Where am I?"

"In our pigsty."

"Do you think we could work on a broader perspective?"

"A broader perspective?"

"Is there a name for where we are?"

"You're on the Detweiler farm."

The man gave me a thin smile. "Ah, how percipient. Is there any form of civilization near the Detweiler farm?"

"Oh, sure. Schwartz's Junction. 'Bout a mile up the road. But it ain't much. A feed store and a general merchandise emporium. But I don't think you're going to be able to fly there. They ain't got no airport."

The man unsnapped his seat belt and struggled to climb out, saying, "Let's try for a larger metropolis. One that has a restaurant and maybe a hotel."

"What's a *may . . . trop . . . o . . . lis*?"

"A city."

"Oh. That would be Muscatine. It's about ten miles from here. They do have an airport." I was proud of myself that I remembered that. I had never been to Muscatine nor the airport, but I had heard folks talking about it. But how he was gong to fly out of that pigsty with his wheels back there in the tomato patch was beyond me.

"What state is Muscatine in?"

Now that was a dumb question. Muscatine is in Iowa. Everyone knows that. I told him, but I didn't mention the dumb part.

"Damn. I'm supposed to be in Chicago."

"I think you made a wrong turn up there somewhere."

Then he stepped over the side of the airplane and pulled off his helmet, and I fell in love for the first time. He was tall and lanky with straw-blond hair that matched the pencil thin moustache between his nose and upper lip. His leather jacket went down to the mid-thigh, covering light tan slacks that looked like rich men's riding pants. His gloves were the same soft leather as the jacket. His boots came up over his calves. It was the first time I ever went weak in the knees for anything other than a fresh puppy dog or newborn colt. Boys never done meant much to me up to that point. They were mostly a mix between teasing bullies, moody steers, and ornery critters like my brothers. But that notion just came to a skidding halt for me like them hogs out there in the tomato patch.

"You gonna do something about them hogs?"

I nearly jumped outta my skin—someone was reading my mind. But it was just Pa. I hadn't heard him coming up behind me.

"Uh, Pa. This fella just landed in our pigsty."

"Yeah, I noticed that," Pa said. He turned to the pilot and asked, "Mud and pig shit make a soft landing, son?"

The pilot smiled, and I fell further in love. His face was sunburned and dirty from flying. The goggles had made raccoon rings around his eyes, and his nose looked like it had been broken and pushed out of line and then broken again and pushed back into line. Altogether, it was a gorgeous smile.

"I've had worse landings, sir," he said to Pa.

"Damn, I'd 'ave like to seen some of them."

"If you would help me pull my plane out and loan me some tools, I will fetch my undercarriage and wheels, then see if I can repair my plane and then fly away without disturbing you too much longer."

Pa surveyed the tomato patch, the family of hogs happily picnicking in the tomatoes, the busted fence, and the plowed stretch of earth that lead straight to the barn. "You thinking of paying for the damages done?"

"I wasn't planning to charge you for the damages your farm did to my airplane."

Pa's face flushed redder than the tomatoes. "Say again?"

"If your farm wasn't in the way, I might have been able to make an excellent landing on that grassy field just over there," the pilot said, pointing at the flat pasture on the farm across from us.

I understood his logic. He had been flying low, and our farm blocked his path. It wasn't like it jumped up to grab him, but it did get in front of him, where maybe it shouldn't have been. But I didn't think Pa was going to buy into that.

"Your boy saw it all. Ask him," the pilot said, nodding at me.

It was my turn to flush from the top of my head to the end of my knobby toes. *Boy? Boy?* Just because I was barefoot, wearing bib overalls over a denim work shirt and a straw hat, and aside from the fact that my boobs were smaller than a pregnant cat's, he shoulda been able to see that I was a girl.

I took my sun hat off and shook out my long blond hair and glared at him in anger.

"Oh shit, you're a girl," he said.

That made me madder. That's what Pa says all the time, *ah-shit-you're-just-a-girl.* Three boys and a girl, which put me on the hind tit in this family. Ma and Pa claimed they wanted another girl, and it ain't like they weren't trying, 'cause I could hear them on Saturday nights in their bedroom just above mine. But it wasn't happening yet. In the meantime, I was treated like a sissy boy by everyone but Ma.

"Go get the axe, Jenny," Pa said. "We're gonna chop this airplane into kindling wood. All that lacquered fabric should burn good."

"We could discuss this like gentlemen, sir," the pilot said in a quiet voice.

"You did more damage to my farm than I did to your airplane," Pa pointed out, his voice not so quiet.

"Your farm can still farm. My airplane can no longer fly."

"The axe, Jenny."

The pilot sighed. "I will pay damages, sir. Reasonable damages."

"Reasonable?"

The pilot leaned back against the side of his airplane and folded his arms, nodding at the scene in front of him. "A broken fence, some damaged tomato vines. Those skid marks have little effect on anything."

"Them hogs are eating more tomatoes than they've ever had in this life time," Pa said.

"Your hogs. Your tomatoes. Not my problem."

Pa managed to maintain his control. "Eighty dollars."

"Twenty dollars."

"Sixty dollars."

"Forty, but that includes dinner and a place to sleep tonight."

Pa shook his head. "You done this before."

"One of the joys of flying, sir."

Pa had to fight back a smile. "We'll help you pull your plane out and fetch your wheels, and you can see what you can do about it, and then you can come in to supper." He turned to me to add, "Go fetch your brothers. They're fixing the fence out by the creek. Tell 'em we need some help. As soon as we get that plane out of this here sty, I want you to get them damn hogs back here where they belong and put that damn fence back together."

"Yeah, Pa," I replied, mortified that the pilot was looking curiously at me, like he had never seen a girl before.

The boys traipsed in, all excited to see an airplane. They enthusiastically pulled and pushed the plane out of the sty, the pilot supervising but not doing much work.

"You got two seats in this thing," I said in surprise, standing beside him.

The pilot nodded. "They are called cockpits. I have two cockpits."

The older boys snickered at the word cockpit, and Pa slapped them both on the head, saying, "Mind your manners."

"I give people rides in my airplane," the pilot said. "That is what I do for a living. They ride in the second cockpit."

The boys nudged each other but didn't say anything, trying not to smile at this new word.

Pa snorted. "That must be a real thrill for them if you land like you did this morning. You charge them extra if they don't get shit on their shoes?"

The side of the plane said *The Great Bronson.*

"Who's Bronson?" Pa asked.

Once Around the Sun

"That's me," the pilot replied.

"Damn," Pa said, laughing again.

The pilot walked away in silence to fetch his wheels.

"You don't gotta be that mean, Pa."

Pa looked at me strangely, then said, "Jenny, you get them hogs back into their pen and fix that fence. And I don't want you hanging around making moon eyes at the great Mr. Bronson. When you get done, you get back into the house to help your ma with dinner."

He walked off with the pilot while I swatted the hogs with a long switch, herding them to the barn. They squealed in protest and tried to outflank me, but I was in a really bad mood and wasn't gonna take no nonsense from a bunch of porkers that were going to be part of breakfast one day soon. I swatted my brothers, too, just for the hell of it, and they yelled and threatened revenge but were too distracted by the airplane to follow through.

They got skids under the plane and pulled it over to the tool shed and put it up on blocks. The five of them were now underneath the airplane banging the undercarriage back into place while they fitted on the wheels, all of them yelling at each other as if everyone else under there was an idiot.

That's how we fixed things on the Detweiler farm.

With no one paying attention, I opened the hood (the Great Bronson would later instruct me that, on an airplane, this was called a cowling) to peek at the engine. It was a little fancier than our tractor, but it looked to work the same, so I fiddled with some of the moving parts, then pulled off some of the hoses to look at them.

"What are you doing?" the pilot asked in an annoyed voice, inching out from under the plane.

"Your radiator's cracked and your propeller is split in two, and your fuel line was clogged, and your fan belts are frayed and loose. Other than that, your engine looks okay."

"What the hell do you know about airplanes?"

"Nothing. But I know tractor engines."

"She damn well does," Pa said. "If it's mechanical, Jenny can make it work. Makes the boys madder than hell."

"We can fix most of that. But I think Pa should charge you extra."

There was a long silence from under the airplane. Then, "How long will all that take?"

"Day or two."

"I'm supposed to be in Chicago before that."

"Guess you're gonna have to walk," I replied.

"She is definitely your daughter, sir."

Pa laughed again. "I knew that."

So the pilot stayed for two days while we fussed and hammered and sanded and glued and bent parts back into place, and in the evenings after supper he told us war stories about flying over France. The boys hung on every word. I could see Pa was impressed with the Great Bronson, the war hero who claimed to be an ace that shot down a dozen Germans.

But he behaved himself, polite to Ma at the dinner table and drinking only a little 'shine with Pa on the porch, then going out to the hayloft to go to bed after everyone got tired of talking.

I became restless and moody and irritated, and Pa said I wasn't fit to be around, but he said it kindly as if he knew what was wrong with me.

On the last night on the porch, the Pilot told us that his plane was called Jenny, too.

"You named your plane after a girl named Jenny?" I asked, crestfallen. He was in love with another girl.

"No, silly," the pilot said. "The plane is a Curtiss JN4. But everybody calls it a 'Jenny' for short."

"How about that, Jenny," Pa said, "A plane named for you."

I looked at it again standing next to the tool shed and memorized its long frame and snubby nose and its trim wings and knew it was the most beautiful thing I had ever seen.

The next morning everyone agreed we were done. The Great Bronson walked around the plane, jiggling the wings, thumbing the wires, wiggling the tail section, then came around to the front to admire our handiwork.

Once Around the Sun

"On to Chicago, I guess," he finally said.

"Watch out for them farms over there in Illinois," Pa said. "Don't let them get in your way. They got some pretty big tomato patches over there."

"Anyone want a ride before I leave?" The pilot asked. But he was getting to know Pa. "For free?"

Pa backed away. "No thanks, son. I saw you land one time, and that didn't inspire confidence."

The boys were all over themselves, shoving and pushing like boys do, ready to resort to fisticuffs to establish priority.

"Jenny?" the pilot asked.

I looked at Pa. He smiled at me. "You're a big girl. Do what you want."

The two older boys went first and then little Buck and me. It was cramped, but we wedged ourselves in and managed to buckle the seat belt. I forgot about all that as the plane raced along the ground to lift into the air. I discovered that love was not a lanky blond pilot with a handsome pencil thin moustache. It was scattered puffy clouds in an endless blue sky, with the earth isolated and small below us.

The pilot did barrel rolls, *Immelman* turns, and loops, then swooped low over the farm while me and little Buck waved crazily at Pa and Ma.

The Great Bronson shook Pa's and the boys' hands and kissed Ma and me on the cheek. My knees went weak again, but I managed to keep my feet.

Away he went, the plane lifting off the grass, then climbing high until it turned into a speck going east towards Chicago.

I left the farm, too, a few years later. Ma and Pa decided I should go to that teaching school in Des Moines. It was something that women could do to get off the farm. My two older brothers eventually moved on to their own farms. Little Buck hung on with Ma and Pa. I finally got a job teaching—in Chicago. But I never came across the Great Bronson again.

The Farmer's Daughter

I managed to save enough to take flying lessons. In a Jenny. They were calling it an "old" Jenny then, but that didn't matter to me. It still had its long frame and snubby nose and trim wings and was beautiful. And my love continued to blossom up there, among the scattered clouds in the endless blue with the earth isolated and small below.

Sandal Season

Emily P. W. Murphy

You know, I've had this business for ten . . . no eleven years now, and you'd think I'd get used to them, but no. How can I? They're gross. Disgusting. Warped. I knew I hated mine for a long time, but only when I went to college did I realized how much I hate them all.

What do I hate? Why, toes of course. How could you do anything *but* hate toes? They're stubby mutated fingers that never grew. They have disgusting nails. They have toe jam. And don't even get me started on the smell. I'm telling you, they have nothing to recommend themselves to discerning human beings.

So, you ask, why on Earth did I ever get involved with shoes? Well, I always knew I wanted to help people, but it took me a while to figure out just how. As a child, I flipped through the possibilities, a new idea each week: fireman, policeman, doctor. Army, navy, air force, and peace corps; they all seemed trite—over done. I wanted to *really* help people. Then one day I noticed an opening for a manager at the Shoe-Less store 257 in the Acorn Valley Mall, and I knew in my soul that I had to apply.

Shoes. Those wonderful coverers of toes. I thought of all the barefoot children that I could help if I could just get my foot in the door. I'd sell buzz saws if I thought people'd remove their toes entirely, but I figured selling shoes was the next best thing.

So I applied and got the job because, according to my boss, very few people saw shoe sales as a calling, and she wanted to see how long it lasted.

Once Around the Sun

Well that was ten . . . no eleven did I say? Eleven years ago, and here I am, the proud manager of Shoe-Less store 257. Of course, humanitarian or no, I have my limits. I couldn't just toe the line. I had to implement some changes.

I put my best foot forward with my first managerial decree: changing the footies that ladies use when they try on heels. The store was stocked with those transparent nylon ones, but I gave them away to Goodwill and invested in some heavy opaque ones, thus reducing the time that the ladies' toes were visible.

After the footie success, I kicked up my efforts by increasing the store's stock in slippers and swim shoes. That way people would have their toes covered both late at night *and* when they went to the pool or beach. No more of that nails-on-a-chalkboard feeling of some child's toes brushing up against your leg while you're enjoying a dip in the pool.

Thank God.

I'm stubborn as a mule, so I also increased the store's supply of socks. Socks are great, you know, because they hide your toes even if you insist on taking off your shoes.

Despite my little victories, all these battles served as mere preparation for the great toe war ahead. Within months of my hiring, I realized there was a reason God put me on this Earth, in this country, state, and county. There was a reason that He placed me just a short commute from the Acorn Valley mall. God made me the manager of this very Shoe-Less store to defeat my arch nemesis: sandals.

You see, in Acorn Valley, Shoe-Less store 257 is the primary outlet for toe lovers to purchase their sandals, and, it was clear to me, the reprehensible trade had to be stopped in its tracks.

Now, I knew it would be a mighty task, and none too easy, but I'm no loafer, and, as I saw it, if that was what the Good Lord put me on Earth to do, well then, I'd better do it.

To truly understand the nature of my arch enemy, you must understand that there exist in this world toe junkies who actually think their toes are *attractive*. These sickos refuse to acknowledge how they nauseate the rest of us by lewdly displaying their toes in public. Some even paint them to attract attention *down there.*

Exhibitionists. But for some reason, Shoe-Less wants *their* money, too. Blood money, I say, but then I'm not corporate. No, I am just a lowly foot soldier on the front lines. From my position in the trenches, I realized I couldn't actually eliminate the sandals from the store; I had to come up with a sneaky solution. Somehow I had to save Acorn Valley from the sandal epidemic without cutting them off at their primary source.

I started out by trying to hide the sandals where people wouldn't find them. I'd stuff them behind boxes of high tops and pumps; between cleats and sneakers. I put the kids' sandals up high and the adult sandals down low. I hid sandals in every way I knew how, but my effort was a flop. When people couldn't find their sandals, they just asked me to help.

I tried lying. I said they were sold out; they weren't in season; we didn't carry them anymore. But you know, once people are addicted they have trouble quitting cold turkey. Sure enough, about a week later I got a call from my district manager ordering me to stop hiding the sandals. She said she'd drop by for a surprise visit in a few days, and if the sandals weren't displayed as was outlined in the Shoe-Less Display Regulations packet, I'd get the boot.

This decree caught me flat-footed. I wanted to sock her, but she was the boss, so I had to bring out the sandals.

That day was a nightmare. As soon as I revealed the sandals, the people whirled in on a veritable toe-nado. Scores of junkies plopped down in the sandal section and whipped out their toes. Believe me, I had a tough time keeping my lunch down.

That night I lay awake, desperate for a way to defeat those wretched sandals. I tell you, I fussed so much I lost one of my socks and had my toes uncovered for a good five minutes while I looked for it. I thought about sandals the next morning as I made my bed, brushed my teeth, and shined my shoes for the day ahead.

Once Around the Sun

The great solution first whispered in my ear as I was changing from my slippers to my shower shoes, eyes squished closed. I was just putting my toes into the shower shoe when my right pinky, the most mutated of all toes, caught on the ankle of the shoe before I could shove it in properly. The idea started then, but came to fruition as I was shampooing my hair.

Well it was such a good idea that I nearly forgot to rinse the suds before jumping out of the shower, pulling on clothes, changing my shoes, and dashing to work. I arrived at Shoe-Less only half an hour before opening, and had a lot to accomplish before the toe-obsessed customers came in for their fix. As soon as I arrived, I cut all of the tags off the sandals. I then replaced the tags with those of the sandals a size bigger, so the size eights were now size sevens, the sevens were sixes, and so on.

Now, since there were so many sandals in the store it took me the whole hour just to switch the tags, so, I opened the store with my task just half-finished. But half-done is better than not started, and it was all I could do in a pinch.

I let the toe junkies in, and you know, it worked about as well as you can expect. The people came in looking for their sandals, and they just didn't fit. Too short, too narrow . . . *too bad*. The wilier ones caught on and switched sizes, but a good chunk of the dumb ones left the store disappointed.

That night after closing, I kicked into high gear and went toe to toe with the sandals. One by one I "fixed" them. I used fire, water, and steel, just enough to make them uncomfortable. I melted the plastic sandals so they'd rub those awful toes, I shaved a bit off the cork ones so they'd scrape the heel; I even soaked the leather ones so they'd be stiff and unwieldy.

Now I wouldn't presume to call myself a saint or anything, but if those sandals weren't all altered by morning, I'll show you my toes.

The next day, I was pumped. I waited right in the middle of the sandal section to enjoy my victory. Sure enough the addicts came in and headed straight for the sandals, and

Sandal Season

sure enough some figured out about the mixed up tags, and—sure as I'm standing here in our black loafers—Shoe-Less' most popular men's shoe last month; sure as that, I didn't sell a single sandal that day, or that week. And I haven't sold a single sandal since—except once, and that was an exception because I threw in a free pair of socks. You see, the sandals just don't fit right anymore. But boy does 257 make a killing on slippers and pool shoes. Thank God.

My First Red Sox Game

Carol L. Wright

Until age eight, my only experience with baseball was being dragged along to my big brother's games at Little League—an organization which, at that time, required all participants to have a Y chromosome. As "just a girl," I had to entertain myself during those seemingly endless, six-inning walk-a-thons, so I looked for four-leaf clovers, swatted mosquitoes, and killed time on a nearby swing set.

Then, in 1963, my grandmother moved into an apartment nearby. Suddenly I was spending a lot of my free time at Nana's place. That summer, she and I sipped lemonade in front of her oscillating fan and watched the Boston Red Sox on her black-and-white television. To my amazement, my Nana—a girl—was a baseball fan. She taught me how to keep a box score, making a chart out of notebook paper. Together we recorded each at bat, every hit or error, every score or strike out.

Nana was a kid when Fenway Park opened in 1912. In those days, the Red Sox were good. She even remembered when they last won the World Series in 1918. And she hoped, every year, that the Red Sox would win it all again. Her enthusiasm was infectious. Nana loved baseball, and I loved Nana.

I looked forward to every game at her place and was sad when the season ended. That year, Nana's team finished in seventh place in the American League, twenty-eight games behind those darn Yankees.

"That's okay," Nana said with a twinkle in her eye. "There is always next year."

Once Around the Sun

By the following spring, I was eager for the season to start. I knew most of the stars: Carl Yastrzemski, Frank Malzone, Bob Tillman, and Felix Mantilla, but this year they added a new guy. Tony Conigliaro was a young *phenom*. Soon he was hitting home runs like no other teenager in major league history. And it didn't hurt that he was kind of cute.

Then, one day, Nana asked me if I wanted to go to a game with her—in Boston. I said yes, almost before she finished the question. The date was set for early July—a game against the Minnesota Twins.

It took forever for the day to arrive. I dressed in my school clothes even though it was summer; Nana said we had to dress up to go into the city. She dressed up, too, but still wore her old Red Sox cap.

Nana didn't have a car, so we took the commuter train from West Concord to North Station. Then we got on the green line to ride to the park. The noisy, bone-shaking rumble and the smell of sweat and tobacco in the trolley added to the agitation in my stomach. We got off at Kenmore Square, and Nana helped me cross the street. Such a wide street, and so many cars.

After a short walk, she pointed ahead of us.

"There it is," she said. "Fenway Park." I stared with my mouth open until she pulled at my hand, and we trudged on toward the stadium.

As we approached the gate, I couldn't wait to be inside watching Yastrzemski, Malzone, and of course, Tony C. I held tightly to Nana's elbow as she bought our tickets and navigated our way inside.

When we got into the park, I was amazed at how green everything was: the grass, the seats, and the huge green wall in left field. Having only seen Fenway Park on a black-and-white television, I hadn't expected it to be in color.

"I love this old park," Nana said, a smile on her face. "Babe Ruth played here, you know. He was a pitcher for the Sox in the old days."

I was surprised. I thought Babe Ruth was a Yankee.

My First Red Sox Game

We found our seats on the left field line, and I tried to get oriented. I had never seen the park from that angle before.

"Who's that?" I asked Nana, pointing to a big sign with a drawing of a boy in a wheelchair. The sign said, "I can *dream*, can't I?" Nana explained that the boy was named Jimmy. He was a baseball fan, but he had cancer.

"Some people started the Jimmy Fund to help him get a television in his hospital room so he could watch the games," she said. "Now it pays for research to cure cancer." I thought about Jimmy and wondered if he were watching this game.

Soon my attention shifted to the many vendors hawking cotton candy, tonic, ice cream, and popcorn. Mom had told me that this was an expensive trip, and Nana didn't have much money, so I should not ask her to buy me anything. I didn't ask, but I gave her my best smile as the popcorn man approached our row. She grinned and told me to close my eyes and hold out my hand. I did, and the next thing I knew she placed a quarter in my palm. I looked into her sparkling blue eyes and thanked her.

But a quarter wouldn't cover it. Popcorn was fifty cents. It came in a cardboard funnel, and when the popcorn was gone, you could pull a plug out of the narrow end, turning the funnel into a megaphone. I really wanted a megaphone. I tucked the quarter into my dress pocket, trying to figure out what to do.

The Red Sox took the field, and Nana and I took out our score sheets. Jack Lamabe was on the mound. Tony C. was playing in left. I waved and called, but he couldn't hear me. I needed one of those megaphones.

The first batter for the Twins, Versalles, hit a double. Then Rollins walked, filling first base. Tony Oliva, their star rookie, was next at bat. Lamabe got him swinging. I crossed my fingers for a double play—or at least a strike out. Lamabe pitched, Oliva swung the bat and connected for a three-run homer—with no outs.

Lamabe watched it go and dug his toe into the mound. *Don't let it get to you, Jack.* He picked up the rosin bag and threw it down as the Twins' clean-up batter, Harmon Kille-brew, came to the plate. A quick single and he was on base. Next Allison, their center fielder, got a hit. Now there were two men on. Their first baseman, Mincher, came up and hit a long fly ball. It looked like it was going out, but Yaz caught it in deep center field. By the time he got it back to the infield, two more runs scored—with only one out.

Lamabe was done. Bob Heffner replaced him on the mound and got us out of the inning, but after half an inning we were down 5-0.

That was okay; it was our turn to bat, and our boys did not disappoint us. They faced the Twins pitcher, Jim Kaat, and scored two runs in the bottom of the first, including a hit by Tony C. We were down by three, but we had eight more innings to catch up.

Heffner pitched solidly and shut them out in the second and the third. Unfortunately, Kaat shut us out, too. Then in the top of the fourth, the Twins scored again—only one run this time, but that put us down by four.

No one else scored until the top of the sixth. Heffner lost his stride, and the Twins pounded in six more runs. Fans were making noise, but instead of cheering for the Red Sox, they were yelling at them. I heard people call them the Boston Bums, or the Red Flops. I had to admit, that one was kind of clever.

Another pitching change—we brought in Arnold Earley who got us out of the inning. But we were down 12-2.

Some Fenway fans started leaving as if the game were over, but Nana showed no signs of deserting her team. Two men in front of us stood and threw down their programs. Using a word whose meaning I did not know, they left—abandoning their popcorn funnels.

Careful to keep my skirt down, I climbed over the seats in front of us and grabbed one of the megaphones. I looked up at Nana, half expecting her to tell me to leave it there. Instead, she grinned.

"Can you hand me the other one?" she said. I giggled and passed it to her.

My First Red Sox Game

After I regained my seat, we took out the stoppers, and for the next half inning we yelled our brains out. Fortunately for our vocal chords, it was a short inning. No score.

Earley kept the Twins' bats quiet in the top of the seventh inning. Then, in the middle of the seventh, everyone stood up and the organist played "Take Me Out to the Ball Game." I knew the words and sang along, but I was pretty sure I heard someone get the words wrong. It sounded like they sang, "Root, root, root for the Red Sox. If they don't win it's the same."

After the stretch, their pitcher started to tire. We scored three runs with the help of a pinch hitter for Earley and a home run by Mantilla. *Go Mantilla!*

We were down 12-5 with two innings to go.

Our new pitcher, Dave Gray, was not as good as Earley. The Twins got those three runs back in the top of the eighth.

The stands were nearly empty by the bottom of the eighth. Nana suggested we move down, closer to home plate. From there, we could see the expressions on the hitters' faces as they went up to bat. We brought our megaphones and cheered each one on. At one point, I swear, when Tony C. was on deck, he looked right at me and smiled. But he didn't get to bat. We finished the eighth inning down 15-5.

Gray shut the Twins out in the top of the ninth inning, but we still needed ten runs just to tie it up.

I was beginning to think the Sox were in trouble.

Conigliaro was up first. It was his fifth time at bat, and he already had two hits and a walk. Could he get a rally started?

There he was, at the plate, looking as if he were ready to slam at anything the pitcher threw him. The pitcher set, and threw. Conig hit a screaming grounder right past the short stop and out into center field. He was safe at first.

Next came Yastrzemski.

"This is the guy you want up in a situation like this," Nana said. "He's great in the clutch."

He waved his bat over his head like a weapon, and when the ball reached the plate, he hit it deep into the right field

Once Around the Sun

corner. Conigliaro scored from first, and Yaz had a stand-up triple.

The fans who were still there stood up, cheering. Nana and I screamed through our megaphones. If willpower alone could decide a game, the Sox would win this one for sure.

With the score at 15-6, Dick Stuart was up next. He'd had an off day, and this at bat went south for him fast. Three quick strikes and he headed for the dugout.

Dick Williams came in for Malzone. I stood there, crossing my fingers, my toes, my arms, and my legs. *Pu-leeze let him get a hit.*

The count went to 3 and 2. Williams fouled off one ball after another. *Okay—a walk will do. Just don't get an out.*

He finally saw a pitch he liked and powered it into the net over the left-field wall. *Home run!* Two more runs scored.

"Now we're only down by seven," I shouted to the entire stadium.

Next up was our right fielder, Lee Thomas. He walked, keeping the rally alive. Then came Eddie Bressoud, our short stop. He also walked, moving Thomas into scoring position.

We could win this!

Our catcher, Bob Tillman, came to bat. He'd had a tough day at the plate, but maybe, just maybe. . . . He hit a fly ball directly at the right fielder. Thomas tagged up and raced for third. Bressoud held at first. Two outs, with two men on.

It was time for our pitcher to bat. Did we dare bat Gray? Did we have any pitchers left in the bullpen for the tenth inning if we tied the game? The manager must have thought so because he sent in a pinch hitter named Chuck Schilling.

Ball one . . . strike one, foul . . . ball two . . . ball three. *A walk is as good as a hit—well, almost anyway.* Strike two—looking. Full count.

By now, almost no one in the stands had much of a voice left, but we managed to make noise anyway. I pounded my feet and banged the hollow megaphone on the back of the seat in front of me. *C'mon Schilling.*

The pitcher looked in and nodded. The throw came in low, but Schilling dug it out for a single. Thomas raced home, and Bressoud got to third. We were down by six, with men at the corners, two outs, and the top of our order coming up.

Mantilla strode to the plate and took a few practice swings. The pitcher glared in at him. I hoped he was thinking about that homer in the seventh inning. The pitch came in. Foul ball, strike one. Mantilla was swinging for the fences but didn't hit it squarely. The next pitch was high; Mantilla chased it. Strike two.

C'mon Mantilla. You can do it.

The third pitch came in. Mantilla hit it hard and raced for first. I watched the ball rise toward left . . . and I saw it fall . . . into the fielder's glove.

Game over. Twins won 15-9.

The fans who were screaming only a moment before fell silent. The teams cleared the field. We collected our score sheets and megaphones, and headed for the exit.

"Pitching. It all comes down to pitching," Nana muttered as we left. "A team that scores nine runs ought to win the ball game." She shook her head and looked at me. Then she took off her Red Sox cap and swatted me with it. "But did you have a good time, at least?"

"Are you kidding? It was great. I love this game." My smile felt like it would break my cheeks.

As we filed out of the stadium, we passed people with metal canisters, collecting for the Jimmy Fund. I remembered the quarter in my pocket and considered all the things I could buy with it. Then I thought about how much I loved watching baseball with Nana. I pulled out the quarter and put it in a can. I looked up at Nana, hoping she wouldn't mind that I spent it that way.

"So sick kids can watch baseball, too," I said.

Nana winked and put her arm around me. We might have lost the game, but we were happy because we were together.

The Red Sox finished that year in eighth place in the American League, twenty-seven games behind the Yankees.

Once Around the Sun

But Nana and I remained loyal fans, watching them together for the rest of her life. And forty years later, when they at last won the World Series again, my first thoughts were of her. *They finally did it, Nana.*

I have gone to many games in Fenway Park since that July day. Now tickets are costly, and nearly impossible to get. Young fans know only a world in which the Red Sox are contenders.

Still, for me, baseball will always be the game Nana introduced me to: the team you love whether it wins or loses, the park you love because of—not despite—its age, and the game you love because of who you're sharing it with.

And no matter who I'm with, I still share every game with Nana.

Tomato Blight

Marianne H. Donley

When Detective Eleanor Reed peered through Miss Addie's big basement window Saturday afternoon, she expected to see a lifetime of clutter. Instead, she spotted a man lying on his back in a mess of broken glass and blood.

The guy waved at her.

She took a step back, slipped on the rain-soaked grass, and almost dropped her flashlight. She regained her footing, called for an ambulance, and then ran for the back door. *Good. Not locked.* She fumbled for the lights in the storm-darkened day before clopping down the basement stairs with more speed than grace.

Power went out two-thirds of the way down. She froze mid-stride and heard a scraping. Once. Twice. Behind her, the kitchen door slammed shut. Then she sensed the whiff of gunpowder.

Holy hot cow crap.

She drew her gun, refusing to consider what that rookie mistake might have cost her. After snapping on her flashlight, she finished going down the stairs with more care. She should've believed Miss Addie.

At the bottom of the steps, Eleanor's flashlight lit up broken glass littering the floor, along with lots and lots of blood. The sharp scent of recent death overwhelmed that hint of gunpowder.

In the center of the chaos was the body of a young man. His face dead white. His eyes wide and lifeless. His chest a gory red mess.

Once Around the Sun

She searched the basement for a shooter, a gun, another victim. Nothing lurked in the shadows, just rows and rows of metal shelves stacked with Mason jars full of put-up vegetables.

Eleanor holstered her gun and walked back to the body. He couldn't have waved at her. But his ghost could have. It hovered about a foot off the floor, between two tall shelves to the left of the basement window.

Chills chased down her back. She squared her shoulders. *I should be used to this.* But she wasn't. She never understood why the ghosts of murder victims talked to her. But if it helped put a murderer behind bars, she was willing to ignore her discomfort.

The spirit paid no attention to her, but seemed to be intensely interested in what was on the shelves and in the large cardboard box dumped catawampus on the basement floor. She turned back to the corpse.

In death, he lay on his back with his arms stretched over his head. Next to his right hand was a broken Mason jar with its contents spilled over the floor and mixed with his blood. She didn't see a gun.

Eleanor checked for a pulse, just so she could say she had done so. As she touched the body, the ghost floated closer. He looked at her and around her, appearing surprised, maybe confused. He reached out. She allowed him to touch her. It cost her nothing but a momentary chill.

"Why did she kill me?" he asked.

"Who shot you?" Eleanor kept her voice quiet.

He shook his head as if he couldn't quite understand what she was saying. "I was just trying to help. Why would she do this? Who's going to take care of Raul? Of Angie?"

As she considered what to say, the power hummed back on. As the lights flickered brighter and brighter, the ghost faded to nothing.

At the hospital, Eleanor found Miss Addie sitting on a gurney in the back room of the ER—a nasty goose-egg on her forehead, her white hair spilling out of her usually tidy French twist—regally directing her own care. The room smelled: an odd combination of bleach, sweat, blood, and White Shoulders perfume. Eleanor estimated the air temperature hovered one degree above rock-solid-frozen fish. She was thankful she was wearing her blazer.

"That's still too tight," Miss Addie snapped at a grim-faced nurse trying to wrap a bandage around her arm. From the looks of the tray full of gauze next to the bed, this wasn't the first attempt.

A man from housekeeping swept the floor, and another scrubbed the bathroom. They twitched every time Miss Addie looked their way and then resumed their jobs at a more furious pace.

"Bad time?" Eleanor asked. The nurse glared. The men from housekeeping moved as far from her as the room allowed and looked away.

"Did you get there in time?" Miss Addie asked. "Is Luis going to be all right?"

"No ma'am."

"Damn. Damn." Miss Addie's shoulders hunched, and suddenly she looked every one of her seventy-plus years. She pointed a skinny finger at Eleanor. "You have a lot of explaining to do, missy."

"That's not how this interview is going to work," Eleanor said.

"Oww. Just stop," Miss Addie said to the nurse. She snatched away the bandage then clasped her injured arm. "I'll do it myself. All of you get out."

As the nurse and housekeeping staff fled the room, Eleanor wondered at the ethics of starting a pool to see how many hours it would take for Miss Addie to be released. She turned back to watch Miss Addie wrap her own bandage.

"Don't just stand there glaring at me, missy. Make yourself useful. Put that piece of tape here. No." She moved Eleanor's hand. "Right there."

Eleanor taped the gauze as directed.

"Thank you." Miss Addie shifted her shoulders before regarding Eleanor with a measuring look. "Ever been shot?"

"No, ma'am."

"Hurts like hell."

"Stop stalling. What happened?" She pulled her digital recorder from her pocket and put it on the tray with the bandage debris. Then she fished out her notebook and pen.

"Am I a suspect?"

"Yes, ma'am." She expected Miss Addie to bristle at that, but instead she frowned at Eleanor as if she were dim-witted. So Eleanor asked, "Why did you kill him?"

"Why would I kill Luis Garcia?"

"You tell me." Eleanor wrote down the name.

"I wouldn't."

"What happened?"

When Miss Addie didn't answer, Eleanor let the silence stretch. Finally, the old woman squared her shoulders. "You had better not blame Luis for this. He's a good man."

"Miss Addie."

"Fine. Luis and I were stocking shelves with the canning we did yesterday. I store the overflow from the co-op in my basement. The power kept going off with the thunderstorm, so I went upstairs to get a flashlight. I heard shouts coming from the basement. One of the voices I knew was Luis. The other was Innis Irving. Luis has been having trouble with him. The co-op's been having trouble with him. Hell, *I'm* having trouble with him. If he wanted to be president of the co-op board, he shouldn't have insisted I run. He's such a damn old fool."

"Let's skip Innis for a minute. You heard voices. What happened next?"

"I shouted that I was calling the cops. I ran down the stairs with my cordless phone. I thought I stumbled, but it turns out that idiotic man shot me. I hit my head on the stairwell wall when I went down." She rubbed her forehead. "That hurts, too. Thank you so much for asking. I fainted. When I came to, I got out of there as fast as possible."

"Miss Addie, did you see Innis Irving?"

Her mouth snapped shut. She folded her arms across her chest, the white bandage in sharp contrast to her dark brown pullover. She leaned forward as she spoke. "I. Heard. Innis. Shouting. At. Luis."

"Wait. How did he get into the basement without you seeing him?"

"It's a walkout basement. The door is on the far side, away from the kitchen." Miss Addie got that far away look in her eyes as if she were reliving the memory.

"And you didn't hear him drive up?"

"No, but the storm was loud with the rain, the thunder, the power going on and off. A semi could have driven up my driveway, and I wouldn't have heard it."

"Okay. How would he know he could get into your basement?"

"I leave the door unlocked for the co-op."

"Are you kidding?" Eleanor hadn't meant to shout. "How many people know you leave your house unlocked?"

"I changed your diapers, Eleanor Reed. Don't you use that tone of voice with me. It's perfectly safe."

"Said the woman with the gunshot wound sitting in the hospital ER."

Miss Addie folded her arms across her chest and narrowed her eyes. Eleanor recognized the stubborn look and knew it was time to get the interview back on track. "All right. You heard voices and threatened to call the police. Why didn't you?"

"I have one of those damn wireless contraptions; it went out with the power."

"So you threatened to call the police but couldn't actually make the call?"

"It's called a bluff." Miss Addie looked uncomfortable. "I thought he would leave. Innis was annoying, but I really didn't think he would hurt anyone."

"Why did you go to Uncle Walt's?"

Miss Addie shrugged. "Walter's home is the nearest."

"It's at least three miles."

"Not if you take the short-cut through the corn field. It's less than a mile, and I walk it every day."

"But the storm, I don't understand why you didn't drive."

"Because Luis's car was parked in front of my garage door, and I couldn't get the door open. No. Wait. That wasn't Luis's car. He was driving a cute little car."

"There is a small silver Honda in your driveway now. It's registered to Luis, and I'd consider it a cute little car. Is that the car you mean?"

"No. Wait. I don't know." Miss Addie paused for a few seconds while she rubbed her forehead. "Maybe. But Luis didn't park it in front of the garage. He followed me back from the co-op this morning about eleven-thirty. I parked in the garage. He parked on the side, so I could get out if necessary."

"Did he leave—"

Miss Addie interrupted. "No. Luis parked on the side so I could get out. He didn't leave."

"Did you touch the body?"

Miss Addie hesitated. "Yes. I did. I had to see if he was breathing."

"Was he breathing?"

"No. I hoped I was wrong, but no."

"Okay. This is important. Did you move anything?"

"Do I look befuddled to you? I skedaddled to Walt's and then called the cops—who took their own sweet time coming to my aid." Miss Addie looked down at the thin white hospital blanket covering her legs.

Eleanor noticed the question hadn't been answered, so she put it more directly. "Miss Addie, did Luis have a gun?"

Miss Addie's gaze snapped right back to Eleanor's. "You listen to me, missy, don't you try to blame this on Luis. I don't care what that old fool tells you. Luis wouldn't hurt a fly. We reported the first two break-ins. It was Innis both times. He practically admitted it. Cops did nothing. Now Luis is dead, and I'm in the hospital."

"Wait, someone broke into your house?" Eleanor wrote a quick note to check that out. No one had mentioned a burglary at Miss Addie's.

The old lady snorted. "Not my house. The co-op. You have to ask yourself why someone would break into a co-op and stock it with badly canned tomatoes. Not steal. Stock.

Especially this summer. It has rained so much our whole crop got tomato blight. You couldn't pay me to put up those tomatoes. No one in the co-op would do it either. Innis was trying to make the co-op look bad. Make me look bad."

"Why would he do that?"

"I told you, he was furious he lost the election."

"Miss Addie, people don't shoot each other over a co-op election."

"Innis Irving lost his mind. The cops did nothing about it. Now, leave me alone. I'm old and I'm tired and I'm wounded."

Less than an hour later, Eleanor stood on the back stoop of Luis Garcia's home getting soaked in the pouring rain. The yummy scents of cooking, something with onions and garlic, wafted their way around her. Her stomach growled, but she had no hope for dinner anytime soon.

In life, Luis Garcia had been an unemployed CPA with a wife, Baylee, and a young son, Raul. From all accounts, Luis had been a devoted father, a member of Eleanor's own church (not that she knew him), and well-liked. His ghost had been worried about his son and someone named Angie, but not his wife. Who was Angie, an illegitimate daughter? A mistress? This would not be an easy interview. She knocked on the door.

The woman who answered the door bristled with piercings, and had several tattoos and a heavy hand with the make-up. The baby on her hip, however, looked clean, happy and well cared for. The little guy grinned at Eleanor as she showed the woman her badge. "I'm sorry for your loss, Mrs. Garcia. Can we talk?"

"I'm not Mrs. Garcia." She glared at Eleanor for a second, and then her face crumbled. She blinked fast, but the tears came anyway leaving a trail of black mascara down her cheeks. She wiped them with her free hand making a blotchy mess. "*Ay dios mio.* This is so awful. I'm sorry. My sister-in-law is sleeping right now. Would you like me to get her? She took a sleeping pill, but I can get her up."

"Could I talk to you first?"

The woman nodded. "This little guy is Raul. Right, *mijo*? Can we talk while I feed him? It's late for him, I know. But he has to eat. Poor little guy. Oh, and I'm Angie. *Ay*, I am rambling."

Just a sister or sister-in-law, but why was Luis worried about her and not his wife? But his sister-in-law? Maybe still an affair. Eleanor followed Angie into a large country-style kitchen painted an eye-popping salmon. The far wall sported a built-in bookcase covered with ceramics—bowls, plates, teapots—in a rainbow of colors. The teal-colored teapot, almost identical to the one in Eleanor's kitchen, triggered a memory. "You're Angie Perez. I bought a teapot just like that one last year at the Artist Fair. You are an amazing potter."

Angie flushed bright red before mumbling a quick thanks. She put Raul in a high chair where he laughed and clapped. Angie dropped a whopping key ring, larger even than the one Eleanor's aunt lugged around, on his tray. He grabbed them with glee, banging them while shouting, "Momma. Eees."

Angie gestured to a stool at the kitchen island, well away from Raul. "Have a seat here. I reheated spaghetti for him, and he will make a mess. Are you hungry, detective? I can reheat something for you."

"No, thank you. I am sorry to intrude on your dinner. Can I ask a few questions about Luis?"

Angie nodded, so Eleanor took out her recorder and placed it in front of her; then, she opened a small notebook. "For the record, how are you related to Luis?"

As Angie cut spaghetti in child-sized bits, she answered, "I'm Luis's sister, Anjelita Garcia."

There goes the mistress lead, Eleanor thought as she jotted a note.

"Angie Perez is the name I use for the pottery." Angie continued talking while handing the child his dinner, then fussing a bit with his hair. "I moved back in when Luis got sick. This was our parents' house. They left it to us both. I moved out when Luis and Baylee got married. But it's hard—it *was* hard—for Luis to take care of a baby with a full-time job and his dialysis treatments. So I moved back in. My pottery studio is over the garage anyway. It just made sense for me to move back in. And I'm rambling again. Sorry."

"Understandable." Eleanor hadn't known Luis had been sick. She wrote a note to check on that. Illness would put tension on a young family. "How was their marriage?"

"Um. Well. They had their ups and downs." Angie shifted her shoulders as if uncomfortable with the question.

"Down enough for murder?"

The woman bit her lip, but shook her head. "If you want to investigate someone, try his old boss."

"Let's get back to Luis and Baylee's relationship. How down?"

"They separated for a while. Baylee was having a hard time dealing with Luis' illness. That was when I moved back in. And then he was fired. I was so glad I had moved in because his life just seemed to snowball out of control. But after Luis settled the lawsuit, things worked out for them."

"So once Luis had money, his wife had an easier time dealing?" Eleanor let the implication hang without explaining. Money was always a motive for murder. Angie seemed smart enough to figure that out.

"It wasn't like that. It wasn't." Angie shifted on her seat. "Things were working out. They were."

Eleanor wasn't sure Angie really believed that, so she decided to try a different approach. "Tell me about the lawsuit?"

"Luis was fired for being sick, so he sued. The company settled, forced his ex-boss to retire. The man was furious."

"How furious?"

"Enough to make us change the phone number three times. He'd call constantly. Sometimes he didn't talk. Sometimes he threatened Luis. He egged the house a few times and slashed our tires."

"Luis reported all this?"

Angie nodded.

"Do you have the guy's name?"

"Innis Irving." Angie hopped off the stool then rummaged through one of the drawers by the stove. She picked out a business card, handed it to Eleanor, and then sat back down. "He's on the board at the co-op. Now that I think about it, he fought with Luis about that, too. Something about tomatoes."

Tomatoes, again. What would the DA say if Eleanor brought her a case about blighted tomatoes? Eleanor stifled a sigh and put the business card into her notebook. "Where were you all day?"

"She was here with me and Raul. The whole damn day." The voice came from behind Eleanor. She turned on her stool and saw a small blonde with messy hair and red, tear-stained eyes standing in the doorway.

"Momma," Raul shouted.

"Baylee?" Angie's voice squeaked. "I didn't see you there."

There was such a strange sound to Angie's voice that Eleanor looked back at her. Angie shifted on her seat, biting her lower lip. Her gaze darted to Baylee and then to Eleanor. "You don't have—"

"Don't worry, Angie. I'm okay." Baylee Garcia walked across the kitchen and placed a hand on Angie's shoulder, giving her a little squeeze. She turned to Raul and managed to drop a kiss at the one spot on his head not covered by hand-mushed spaghetti. "Hi baby."

"I'm sorry for your loss, Mrs. Garcia."

Baylee arched one eyebrow and said, "And yet here you are harassing my sister-in-law instead of finding that crazy old man."

"What crazy old man are we talking about?"

"Innis Irving." Baylee lifted her chin.

"How do you know that Innis Irving killed your husband?" Eleanor didn't appreciate the way everyone was wrapping up "that crazy old man" and handing him to her in a nice shiny gold package with a large red bow. Especially since Luis was sure he had been murdered by a woman. But the dead could lie. She had to remember that.

"Because he threatened him," Baylee said. She stood straighter, squaring her shoulders. "Didn't the old lady . . . Miss Addie . . . tell you who shot Luis?"

"I can't discuss what Miss Addie saw," Eleanor said. She thought it interesting Baylee was attempting to direct this interview.

"*Ay dios mio,* Miss Addie. I forgot about Miss Addie. She's going to be okay? Right?" Angie frowned, worrying her fingers together. "I should have asked about her right away."

"Miss Addie's a tough old bird. She'll be fine." Eleanor scribbled another note in her book.

Baylee seemed to lose some of the starch in her spine. She pulled out the stool next to Angie and sat, crossing her arms. "Any other questions, detective?"

Eleanor thought she sounded weary and was sorry for that. But she had more questions. "Did Luis own a gun?"

"No," Angie said. The word was sharp and definite.

Baylee put her hand on Angie's back. "He does. I bought him one for protection a few weeks ago. We were going for safety lessons at the gun club, starting next week."

"You didn't tell me." Angie's voice shook. "You know how I feel about guns."

"I know, but Innis scared me. I thought we needed to be able to defend ourselves."

"Where's the gun?" Eleanor asked.

"In a locked box in Luis's closet." Baylee continued to pat Angie on the back. "I'm sorry Angie. Luis didn't want you to know."

"Can you show me?" Eleanor asked.

"Sure." Baylee slid off the stool and hurried across the kitchen as if she were happy to be doing something active. Eleanor followed her down the hallway and into a small room decorated in sleek black and white, a stark contrast to the rest of the house. Baylee pulled a metal box down from the shelf and placed it on the bed.

It was unlocked and empty.

"Did Luis take it with him this morning?" Eleanor asked Baylee.

"I didn't see him do it." Baylee stared at the empty box. "He must have. I hope he used it. I hope Luis shot that nasty old man."

Eleanor watched Baylee's face for a beat of silence. "What about Miss Addie?"

"What?" Baylee jerked her head up and scowled.

Eleanor couldn't decide if she were surprised or confused. "Would Luis have shot Miss Addie?"

"No, no, of course not." Baylee's eyes filled and she blinked the tears back. "Innis shot both of them. I know he did."

"There's no physical evidence to support that."

"I don't care. Luis defended Miss Addie. He's a hero." Baylee wiped tears from her cheek with a furious and quick jerk of her hand. "I want you to leave now."

By the time Eleanor left the Garcia home the rain had slowed to a gentle mist. She felt unsettled, but at least she had a short to-do list: Find Innis Irving. Find the gun. Talk to Luis' ghost.

As soon as she thought of him, his ghost coalesced in the middle of his driveway. He paced between two cars, a sporty little blue car with a vanity plate QTLTKR and an older SUV. Eleanor walked over to him glancing in the SUV as she went by. Its passenger seats were stacked with the custom boxes in which Angie packaged her phenomenal ceramics.

Luis focused on the other car. He carried a box, like the ones from Miss Addie's basement, around the side of the vehicle and then leaned over as if he were loading it into the back seat.

"Hi, Luis," Eleanor said.

He stopped his task and looked at her. "Why did she shoot me?"

"Who Luis? Angie? Baylee? Or Miss Addie?" Eleanor coaxed. If she had to be haunted by a murder victim the least he could do was tell her who had killed him. But, they rarely did. She had a few theories as to why. Sometimes they didn't know. Sometimes they didn't want to know.

Tomato Blight

Sometimes they refused to believe her they were dead. "Come on, Luis. Who was it?"

Instead of answering, he glanced over her shoulder and smiled. Eleanor turned to see Angie with Raul on her hip rushing out the front doorway of the house. "Detective, wait. I need to tell you something. *Ay.* Two things."

"Okay."

"First. Baylee wasn't with me all day. She thinks she's protecting me. I know how I look, the tats, the piercings, the makeup. It's part of the art, you know. It doesn't mean I'm hard or evil, or I kill people or want to. Sorry. I feel so rattled. Anyway, I know you will check, and it makes no sense to lie. She didn't need to lie. I had an artist show at the Off Topic Gallery. I took Raul with me. Jake Williams has a little girl the same age as Raul, and he hired a sitter for them. He does that a lot. He has a play room . . .*ay* Jake owns the place. Here's his card. Call him. He'll tell you. I *was* there all day."

"Thanks," Eleanor said. She took the card and put it in her pocket.

"The next thing, Luis did not have a gun. He didn't. Luis was shot when he was six. It was an accident. That's why he's sick. He lost a kidney, and now the other one is failing. He would have needed a transplant."

"Who shot him?" Eleanor asked, but she could guess.

"I did. I was four." She flexed her arms around the baby as if making sure he was still safe, and he burrowed his head into her shoulder. "Luis would never have allowed a gun in the house, especially with Raul. He wouldn't." Angie turned and hurried back into the house.

Luis watched his sister go. "I was taking care of everything. I would have taken care of her, too. No matter what." He looked down at the box in his hands. "Tell Miss Addie, not to worry about Innis Irving. I got rid of all the blighted tomatoes."

"Talking to Luis' ghost hadn't helped much, but Eleanor still had other items on her to-do list: find the gun, and find Innes Irving.

Once Around the Sun

The co-op office building was burning.

Eleanor got the call on her way home from Mass the next morning. She did a quick U-turn in front of her house and headed back. She pulled into the parking lot just after the fire truck. She parked well out of the way of the fire-fighters and got out of her car. She identified herself to the incident commander, but he was too busy to do more than nod at her.

The co-op office was housed in a one-story, wood-and-glass building. Despite the amount of rain they'd had this summer, the building burned hot and furious. Even at her distance she felt the heat, smelled the smoke, and had to brush ash from her face.

"Why?" Luis asked, appearing beside her.

"Gee, Luis. It's daylight." Eleanor blew out her breath. A crowd had gathered to watch the fire, but no one paid the least bit of attention to her. Still she didn't want to take a chance that anyone would notice her conversing with thin air. Since there wasn't much she could do until the fire was out and she could talk to the commander, she decided to walk between the raised garden beds to the small patch of grass away from the fire and the throng of looky-loos.

Luis floated along with her, silent. Eleanor could feel sweat dripping down the center of her back. She shifted her shoulders and focused on this case. What was bugging her about this mess?

Besides the ghost floating alongside her.

The car in Miss Addie's driveway for one. Why didn't Miss Addie get Luis' keys and drive away? She took another look around and wondered if Miss Addie really could have walked this far in the rain and the heat, with a gunshot wound in her arm and that goose egg on her forehead. Eleanor was afraid Miss Addie had taken the gun that may or may not have belonged to Luis. Maybe she took it for protection as she walked to Walt's, or maybe she lifted it to frame Innis Irving. Eleanor had to consider Miss Addie as a suspect even if she didn't want to. Dear-God-in-heaven, she didn't want this case to be old people fighting about tomato blight.

Next there was Angie Perez. Her information that she shot Luis when he was a child added a new twist. Could she have killed her brother? Was that why Luis was so confused? Had the sister he loved and to whom he trusted the care of his baby, blown his chest out? Her alibi hadn't been confirmed, yet. But Eleanor expected that Jake Williams would corroborate her story. Still, Luis' concern for Angie *seemed* to suggest someone else had shot him. Or was he protecting Angie?

Why had Baylee lied? To protect her sister-in-law like Angie insisted last night, or to give herself an alibi?

Luis and Baylee had separated. Eleanor only had Angie's assurance that things were better between them. Luis had his lawsuit settlement and an insurance policy. Maybe Baylee decided she didn't want to share. Money always seemed a motive for murder.

And money brought her right back to Innis Irving. But she couldn't find him. He couldn't be ignored, despite Luis' insistence a woman shot him. Dying had to be traumatic. Maybe Luis was genuinely confused about who pulled the trigger. But what would Innis gain by killing Luis? Did Innis think he could get out of paying the settlement if Luis were dead? And why shoot Luis at Miss Addie's house? Did Innis go to her house to kill *her* and Luis just got in the way? Or did he want both of them dead?

"Look," Luis said. He floated around to her other side shaking his head. "Why? Why would someone do that? I threw those tomatoes out. I didn't even save the jars."

She took one step in Luis's direction. Another, larger parking lot lay behind the co-op building. At the far end of the pavement was a stand of pines, and in front of the trees was a large construction dumpster. Cardboard boxes, like the ones in Miss Addie's basement, were jumbled around the trees. Broken jars spilled out of the boxes.

Eleanor walked across the lot. The litter wasn't scattered as she first thought; it marched in a direct line to an old pickup truck parked haphazardly a few feet behind the dumpster.

Eleanor glanced at Luis. He shifted from side to side as if he knew something was very wrong and couldn't decide to stay or fade away.

"Why is Innis Irving's truck here?" Luis asked.

Eleanor got out her cell to call dispatch.

Once she finished her phone call, she walked in a wide arc around the litter, around the dumpster, to where the truck was parked. A man's body was crumbled beside the right front tire. He cradled a gun in his bloody hands.

"Innis Irving?" Luis asked.

Eleanor assumed it was a rhetorical question and didn't answer. She checked for a pulse.

"Holy hot cow crap. He's alive."

She pulled the gun out of his hands as she called for an ambulance. The old man latched on to Eleanor's wrist. She was surprised at the strength of his grasp.

"Miss Addie," he said.

"What?" asked Eleanor. "Where are you hurt?"

"Hands."

"Have you been shot?" Eleanor looked at his hands. They were cut, blistered and bleeding. "Did you start the fire?"

"Miss Addie did."

His expression took on a sly cast, and Eleanor knew he was lying and not just because Miss Addie was still in the hospital. Innis took a shallow breath and blew it out. She smelled the alcohol on his breath and—leaning closer to see if he were bleeding anywhere besides his hands—the gasoline on his clothes. "You're drunk," she said.

"Naw. Just took a little nip. It's Miss Addie's fault."

"Right. Miss Addie's fault. Sure it is." Eleanor heard the snarky tone in her voice but didn't care. "Did she pour rotgut down your throat?"

"She killed Luis. She thought—she thought—she killed me. But she didn't, did she?" He hiccuped and squinted at Eleanor.

"So what happened?" Eleanor asked.

"She missed. She missed. She missed. Then she drove away in a cute little car." Innis lowered his voice to a whisper. "I snuck out of there."

"No, he's lying," Luis said. He patted his pockets as if looking for something. He shoved his hand into the front pocket of his pants and pulled out a small set of keys. "I have the keys to that car."

While watching Luis wave his ghostly keys about, Eleanor considered her aunt who lugged a giant ring around with every key she might ever need. She didn't mind the size; she just threw it in her purse. But her dad had separate rings, one for his car, one for her mom's car, and one for his workshop. He hated the bulk in his pocket.

As Eleanor thought about aunts and dads and keys and cute little cars, she realized who had pulled the trigger.

By the time the ambulance arrived, Innis Irving was singing *Burning Ring of Fire*. He went to the emergency room for his bloody hands and then right to jail where he sobered up and screamed for his lawyer. Eleanor let the arson investigator handle Innis.

She spent the rest of the day and all of the next looking into her suspect for Luis's murder. She found a pile of bills, a desperate need for money, and a flight reservation out of the country.

After a trip to the evidence locker and impound lot, she sat in her car, peering through the steaming twilight at Luis Garcia's home. Luis' ghost paced between the same two cars parked in the driveway: the little sporty blue car and the older SUV.

Eleanor pulled out the key ring Luis had in his pocket when he died. It had three keys on it plus a keyless entry fob for a car. None of the keys or the fob had opened the silver Honda that had been in Miss Addie's driveway. How could Luis have driven to Miss Addie's house without a set of keys? He couldn't. So he must have driven another car that morning.

After killing Luis and shooting at Miss Addie and Innis, the murderer panicked. With the storm raging outside, she ran to her own car, forgetting that Luis had driven it that morning. That huge key ring little Raul played with the night before belonged to the woman who killed his father.

Eleanor got out of her car. The wet heat surrounded her making her feel as if she had leaped, fully dressed, into a hot bath. She crossed the street. In Luis's driveway, she stopped beside that sporty little blue car—the one with a vanity plate QTLTKR.

The front door of the car was slightly ajar; the interior lights glowed yellow, and she noticed a box of Mason jars next to the baby seat in the back. Eleanor bumped the door shut with her hip and was rewarded by a clap of thunder, a flash of lightning, and rain mixed with the nasty sharp sting of tiny hail.

She aimed the keyless entry fob at the car, and it beeped.

"How did you know?" Luis asked.

"The plates—QTLTKR—cute little car." She held up his key ring. "Plus there wasn't a key for the car left in Miss Addie's driveway."

"Why?" Luis asked. "Why did Baylee shoot me?

"She wanted all of your money, Luis."

"But I would have taken care of her," he said.

He faded as Eleanor walked up the sidewalk and knocked on the door.

First Impressions, Second Chances

Diane Sismour

Interesting. For months, 2C's parking space has remained empty, with no noise coming from the apartment below me. But this morning, the sound of a coffee grinder startled me awake, and I walked outside to find a black Viper glistening in the early sun parked beside my dust-coated Prius.

"I hope this neighbor isn't as noisy every morning. The least she could do is offer coffee after waking me so abruptly," I grumble under my breath while pulling the pet-store's trash bags from my car.

The apartment building's entry door slides open behind me. I turn to see a model-thin blonde slink out. The ruched fabric on her simply cut tank dress shimmers, rippling with each step.

Heck, my thigh wouldn't fit into that dress.

The perfect size two heading towards me can't be the new tenant. Not at this hour, dressed in those clothes. The sexy, bed-messed hair completes the bigger picture. No, she is doing the dreaded morning-after walk-of-shame. I return to my task of shoving the pet store's trash into the dumpster.

"So sorry to bother you, but where does the transit stop?"

I jump, caught in the act of illegal dumpster use. She is right behind me. I can't just ignore her hoping she will shrink another size and disappear. Without turning around, I say, "Across the lot at the corner."

The transit? Geesh, it's the bus stop. I glance across the parking area to make sure she is heading in the right

171

direction. A wind gust slams the heavy plastic lid closed on my arm.

"Ouch! That will leave a bruise."

By the time I extract my limb, a taxi has stopped and whisked Blondie away. I can stand on that sidewalk all day and the cabs just fly past me making me wait for the bus. It figures, I'm a size twelve woman living in a size two world.

The sports car and this early departure can only mean one thing: a hottie moved in downstairs. I can't wait to get a glimpse of the guy under me. Not under me, but beneath me; I mean in the apartment below me. Phew, my hormones are running rampant.

The sun shines above the treetops as I approach my grandparents' small brick home on the five-block walk to work. The property is still for sale after a year. But, who would want to buy a house where the previous owners had died from carbon monoxide poisoning? Even after replacing the coal stove with a new furnace, I no longer want to live there.

A newspaper boy flies down the center of the sidewalk flinging papers onto porches. My grandparents had a lifetime subscription. Apparently, the paper doesn't read its own obituaries because every day it's in the hedges. I can't help but think my fate might have ended the same as theirs if David hadn't whisked me to Manhattan that night. Then again, if he didn't, maybe I could have saved them.

I retrieve the newspaper from between the brick wall and the shrubs. The *Forum's* headline announces Hillsborough's new fire chief, Maxim Arsov. What an odd name and no picture either.

A story below the fold reads, "David Bernhart named 'Man of the Hour.'" P-lease, he's more the "Man for a Minute" type. I scan the pages while walking the next few blocks. The rest is the usual local drama: political posturing and stupid criminals.

I reach the shop, turn the skeleton key in the lock, and push open the heavy wooden door, entering Little Darlings–Second Chances. The chime awakens the rescued dogs, cats, and birds. In the calliope of noise, thoughts of the hottie in 2C are history.

Albert squawks. "Hel-lo, Sam. Hel-lo."

"Good Morning, Albert," I say to the large white cockatoo. It took months to break the parrot from spouting profanities at everyone who entered.

After feeding, all is quiet again. I head to the office and leave Albert to guard the shop. Nobody walks through those doors without him noticing. I dread this part of self-employment: paperwork. A stack of unpaid bills sways before me. Rifling through the envelopes, I select one to pay.

It is mind-boggling to think my grandparents survived on the shop's income. Their house had better sell soon. After funeral costs and repairs, the insurance money is depleting fast.

The door opens. Albert whistles. "Sign here. Sign here." By his greeting, I know it's the feed mill delivery and hurry from the office to the storefront.

"How's it going, Pete?" I scramble for a pen beneath the clutter surrounding the antique cash register.

"Sorry, Sam. You have to pay on delivery today."

I cringe and return to the office for another check, taking the recently written insurance payment back to the stack. The due date was ten days ago. I pray, "Please don't cancel me."

The phone rings and goes to voicemail while we are piling the cedar chips and feed into the storage room.

Pete hauls the last bag onto the heap. "I didn't get your response about Linda's surprise party tonight. You should come. I know she'd like to see you there."

This is embarrassing. I didn't want to show up alone and hoped no one would notice my absence. "Sorry, it's been crazy busy here. It's probably buried somewhere on the desk. Wow, I can't believe we're turning thirty."

"That's right; you two have the same birthday. Three decades old," he teases.

"Don't remind me. I'll miss the surprise, but look for me after."

He taps a code into the delivery tablet. "Five o'clock at the pub. Bring a dance partner. Shawn's band is playing. See you later."

Albert squawks, "See you later."

No sooner does the door close, than I start panicking. "Albert, where am I going to find a date?"

He shakes his head feathers.

This is terrible. Now I'm asking the bird for dating advice.

I wouldn't be in this situation if David hadn't given me an ultimatum. He wanted me to choose between him and these forgotten pets. He lost. That was a month ago. Living in his luxurious world did have benefits. Visions of pedicures, shopping trips, and fancy dinners are now nothing but a memory.

When we first met, his love seemed real enough and he always smiled. Then he went into private practice and his legal work consumed him. It's as if he loved money more than me.

Time to get back to work or I'll never make the party.

Two hours later, the church bells ring in the noon hour. It took until lunchtime, but the birdcages are clean and relined—one with David's picture directly beneath a perch—and the kittens are playing in fresh chips. The only cages left are the puppy pens.

I gather the sliced bread and two jars from beneath the counter to prepare the same lunch I eat every day. The peanut butter–and–strawberry jam sandwich oozes around the edges. I lick off the excess, tear the crust off one side, and hand Albert the bread.

"What do you think, Albert . . . did I make a mistake not marrying David?"

"Make a mistake. Make a mistake."

I should know better than to ask for his opinion. "I didn't make a mistake. David's a jerk. What did he ever see in me anyway? There is nothing extraordinary about me. I'm certainly not trophy wife material. My hair is brown and frizzy, my clothes' size is in the double digits, and he never thought me worldly enough because I enjoy simple pleasures. I can't even remember the last time he smiled at me."

Thinking about David has me so worked up that I'm pacing around the center displays, taking large bites from my PBJ. I sit behind the small counter and sigh. Where can I find a date?

The door opens abruptly, and the animals greet our visitor. The watch-bird moves side-to-side. His yellow plume fluffs in agitation. "Samantha. Samantha."

Great, it's the Man for a Minute.

David walks to the counter. "Hello, Samantha. I see you haven't changed your mind . . . yet."

"David's a jerk. David's a jerk."

For once, the bird's statement has perfect timing. "Albert, hush."

"Sorry." He hides his head beneath a wing.

I give Albert a big eye roll before facing David. "And give up all this for you? No."

"You're looking as lovely as ever, Samantha."

I can only imagine how bad my appearance is after cleaning all morning, and force myself from throwing him an eye roll, too.

The phone rings again, and I let it go to voicemail. The lawyer's voice sounds urgent as he insists I contact him immediately.

"That's the second time he's called today. What does he want to speak with me about?" I say to myself and reach for the receiver to take the call.

David steps forward and stops only a breath away. He places his hand on mine to let the caller finish speaking.

When the message ends he says, "You can still come back to me and have it all. I can arrange a quick ceremony."

Marrying him would make life so much easier. I look down to avoid him seeing any truth to his statement. His black wingtip shoes gleam beneath his creased slacks. The gold fraternity ring he polishes daily glints in the lighting as his hand lifts my chin to meet his green eyes. His black hair is perfect, parted to one side and groomed.

Once Around the Sun

I could never live up to his expectations: constantly faking a smile, always dieting, and knowing I'll never be perfect enough.

David looks from me to the cockatoo. "You're wasting your time on these rejects."

I shake my head free from his grasp. "Leave, David. We're not getting married. It's not happening. Not now, not ever."

"You have until midnight to choose."

Squawk. "Not now, not ever."

He glances at Albert. "We'll see about that." He taps his Rolex. "Time is running out, Samantha."

I turn away and hear his footsteps stomp across the store. The door slams as he leaves. The scent from his over-applied cologne lingers. Its sweetness cloys the air.

Whistle. "Time is running out."

What's with the deadline? Seriously. My thoughts are sarcastic, but my hands are rubbing the goose bumps covering my arms. I could use some sunshine after David sucked all the warmth from the room, but it's time to get back to work on the dog pens.

I carry the last of the puppies to the small kennel behind the building. "Here you go little guys." The puppies romp, pouncing upon and chasing each other. There are only six more large cages for me to finish scrubbing before I can call it quits.

The great thing about simple work is it gives me time to think. So far, I've gone through a list of every available single man in town, and I'm still coming up empty handed. Not that there was ever a line out the door to ask me out, but there has to be someone out there for me. The early morning blonde comes to mind. Now she could find a date in a snap.

The animal pens are all clean, but I'm a mess. Puppy puke stains my shirtfront, my ponytail is falling out, and I smell much worse now than when David visited. I carry Albert to the clean perch and re-tether his leg.

First Impressions, Second Chances

The door chime rings and the animals greet the arrival. Normally, the parrot squawks at everyone. Instead, he tilts his head sideways to get a better look.

Cool, a new customer. Well, it's too late to clean up now. I turn towards the door and *yowza . . . he is definitely not a local.* With clear blue eyes, dark brown hair and day old stubble on his jaw, this man couldn't hide under any woman's radar.

"Please tell me you're a stray looking for a home." My hand slaps over my mouth. *Did I just say that?* Heat is racing up my neck and over my cheeks, and I force myself to look at him again. "I call a do-over. I meant, are you looking for a stray to bring home?"

"A do-over?" Amusement creases the lines around his eyes. His smile catches the hook on my heart and tugs me closer. His nose wrinkles up, and he takes a step backward.

I can only imagine the stench surrounding me, and feel the heat rise further to my hairline.

I extend my hand out extra far before introducing myself. "Hi, I'm Sam Darling, chief caretaker and owner of Little Darlings–Second Chances."

He reaches his hand just as far to shake mine. "Max Arsov."

A puppy yelps. "Would you excuse me for one moment?" I say and slide my fingers from his. "It sounds as though the little guys have had enough play time for today."

Instead of staying in the store, he follows me to the pen and past the bathroom stocked with a clean shirt, comb, and soap. Darn, I hoped to at least make a quick change and wash my face before returning. He foiled my excuse to get a second chance to redeem my first impression.

The younger puppies are sprawled out sleeping in the sunshine while others are sitting in a line. Their noses touch the fence as they watch the children walk home from school.

"Hey guys, let's go." All their heads pivot towards us, followed by their big paws.

"Where did I see your name? Now I remember . . . the *Forum.* You're the new Fire Chief. Welcome to Hillsborough,"

Once Around the Sun

I say and drape two small puppies in each of my arms. "So what brings you to Second Chances today?"

"The Fire Department needs a mascot." He glances into the kennel. "I was hoping to find a Dalmatian."

"We're fresh out of spotted pups today, but I'll keep my eyes open for one."

He walks into the pen, catching the two larger dogs.

They squirm against him, and I find myself fantasizing at doing the same thing. We head into the building to deliver round one to the pens.

Max releases them into their cages. "Word travels fast around here. I just hit town yesterday."

"Yesterday? Oh my gosh, you're the hottie in 2C." Groan. I did not just say that out loud.

"And how do you know my apartment?"

"Lucky guess?"

He's not buying it and leans against the counter, crossing his booted feet.

"Someone moved into the apartment under mine. I noticed a new car in the lot this morning. A Viper. Your girlfriend asked where the cabs stopped."

He stands there all dimples.

"That's my car, but she's not my girlfriend."

"A friend with benefits?" Wishing to vanish, I cover my face with both hands. "Gosh, what is wrong with me today? Sorry, your sex life is your business."

"Darla is my sister. She ended up in a bad situation last night, and big brother came to the rescue."

I audibly exhale. "So you're single?"

He nods, and the smile turns into a grin. His dimples deepen.

I'm doing everything possible to keep my distance, but—but nothing. This man is way out of my league. However, I have put my foot in my mouth so many times concerning him, and he's still standing here. What is there to lose? "Do you have plans for tonight? There is a surprise birthday and a band . . . do you dance?" gushes from me before I chicken out.

Max walks back to collect more puppies, and again he captures the two larger dogs. With a couple more trips, we manage to wrangle all of them into their pens.

Other than asking where the pooches go, he still hasn't answered me yet. I place the last one into its cage and scratch the cocker spaniel behind the ear. "What do you think, Harvey? Will he say yes?" I glance over my shoulder at Max. He's shaking his head, but he hasn't run yet.

"What time is the party?" he asks.

"At five, but I'll never make the surprise. I have to feed these guys and take a much-needed shower. I can meet you at six in our parking lot."

Max uncrosses his feet. "What are you wearing?"

"Jeans, nothing fancy. What you have on is perfect."

"Okay, I'll see you at six." He throws me one more gleaming smile before walking out the door.

I lift Harvey into the air and spin around. "He said yes! Oh my goodness, he said yes. What am I going to wear?"

Thank goodness for forethought. I had filled the water dishes after cleaning each cage so feeding will not take as long. The five blocks home is also done in record time, half jogging, half gasping, leaving me forty minutes to go from ghastly to gorgeous.

I hurry past the hot rollers and flick on the switch, crank the shower spigot to hot and run to the closet to flip through the hangers. "No, no, maybe, okay, yes. The soft neckline on the draped tank makes even me look sexy. My favorite jeans and a pair of cowboy boots that match Max's complete the ensemble. An outfit David would never approve of, but I get the feeling Max will love it.

There are only thirty minutes to go before D-time. I double condition and stand in the shower spray, relieving my aching shoulders from all the work done today.

Twenty minutes. One hand is plucking eyebrows, and the other is drying hair. I finish setting the rollers, with seven minutes left to dress and apply minimal makeup. At 5:59 the doorbell rings, I'm dressed, made-up, and yanking rollers as I open the door.

Once Around the Sun

Goodness, will this man ever see me looking better than bad. "Max, I thought we were meeting downstairs."

"We were, but you mentioned living above me. I had to see if this apartment is different from mine. It's the same. More girlie, but the same layout. You missed a few. Spin around, I'll get them."

I turn and speak without thinking. "Please tell me you're not gay?" At least he can't see my face cringing from another blunder.

In response, I hear him snort. "I have a diva sister, remember."

"Ah, that explains it. Give me two minutes." I dump the curlers into the bathroom sink, spray perfume on my hot points and stand before the mirror loosening the curls with my fingers. "You look good. Have fun tonight. You deserve this."

I bounce into the living room. "Ready to go."

He's standing by the window enjoying the landscape overlooking the park. "You have a better view."

Don't I know it? I'm noticing the view—of him in my apartment. He stands there unaware of my thoughts, and the actions I'm considering. "Let's go before I do something totally inappropriate."

I hear him laughing from behind me and grab my Prius key fob from the side table. "I'm driving." He's seen me at my worst already. My butt looking like a big harvest moon as I'm leveraging out of his sport car's low seat is not an image I want him to see tonight.

The party is in full swing when we arrive. The band is warming up and food covers four tables. Half the town is here, including David. Wonderful. He sees me with Max and walks in my direction. I head towards Linda, and Max turns towards the refreshments.

"Happy birthday, you old lady." The woman doesn't look a day over twenty-five. Unfortunately, I can't say the same.

"Look who's calling who old." She hugs me and whispers, "So the salon gossip is that you and David are done."

"You always tell me, where there's smoke, there's fire."

She just smiles. My stylist, and friend since forever, knows every word is true. "So, who's the hottie?"

I look for Max. He's surrounded by women, available and otherwise. "Max is the new fire chief. We just met today."

"Sam, you better put a leash on him soon or someone else will."

Not having any claim on Max, I can only smile and dream.

David comes within earshot.

"Linda, Max is such a gentleman, too," I say just loud enough for David to overhear. "Earlier today, he helped bring in the puppies, and he always carried the larger ones."

"Really. Good looking, manners, and he doesn't mind getting his hands dirty either," she says just as loudly, playing along.

Pete stands beside Linda. "Glad to see you could make it, Sam. And you found a dance partner, too."

I glance towards Max and we make eye contact. I feel heat flushing my cheeks. When I return to the conversation, Linda and Pete are now talking with another couple, and standing directly in front of me is David.

He grabs my wrist. With a clenched jaw and eyes narrowed, he digs his fingers into my flesh. "Did you think you can replace me so easily?" he snarls. His grip tightens.

In an instant, Max is beside me and says, "Release her."

"This is between Sam and me," says David, but he loosens his hold.

"I have nothing to say to you, David. Let go of me."

"We need to talk," he says and drags me after him towards the exit door.

"Buddy, I said to release the lady's arm," Max says in an even tone.

David pushes me away into Max's arms. "Fine. You can have her. She's not worth my time anymore."

Everyone turns to watch David leave. He slams his hands against the door's bar handle to exit. It bounces against the entrance wall and closes hard. Now everyone is staring at us. The room becomes awkwardly quiet.

Linda walks over and stands beside me. "Are you okay?"

"Yes," I say and rub at the red finger marks.

The wait-staff places plates of sliced cake on the table. "Thank goodness. I need cake," I say. Without another word, Max walks to the dessert table.

"David seems really jealous. Be careful," says Linda.

"He's harmless," I say. But all I can think about is how quickly Max came to my rescue and what could have happened if he hadn't.

The band's amp screeches, breaking the silence. The crowd is cringing. The focus is off me and now on them.

Max returns from the food table. He lifts two pieces, "Vanilla, or chocolate? Silly question," he says, handing me the chocolate cake with chocolate butter crème icing.

"What planet did you come from, and are there any more men like you?"

"Nope, I'm one of a kind." He scoops a forkful into his mouth. "Good cake. What's going on with that guy?"

"He's my ex-fiancé."

"Ex, huh. He doesn't think so."

"Trust me. David is history." I take a last finger swipe of icing off the plate before he disposes of the trash.

The band breaks into a slow song, and Max leads me to the dance floor. His arm wraps around my waist, and we sway together. His spicy cologne intoxicates my senses. It is the only reason I can think of as to why my brain has turned to mush. All my thoughts are of how to get him this close, but horizontally.

"I'm curious, why did you say yes? I mean, I'm happy you did, but . . ."

He looks into my eyes, halting my babble, and says, "Because you make me laugh."

"For real?" I'm ready to give him a big eye roll.

He pulls me closer, and my body feels the vibration rumbling his answer. "Yes, for real."

My head is nestled into his chest. I can sense that he is teasing me, but I don't want to think past this moment.

First Impressions, Second Chances

My body softens into his, and we're both relaxing. One song leads into another, and I'm dreaming of the next date.

Suddenly, there's a chirp from a dozen radio transmitters in the room including Max's phone. "Fire alarm at two fifty-seven Main, origin lower level. Repeat, fire alarm at two fifty-seven Main, origin lower level."

I bolt upright. "Holy crap, that's my store." Max and I and all the volunteers run for the doors. Electronic car lock blips surround us as we dash to our vehicles. My hand is shaking so badly I can't push the button to unlock the car.

He guards the fob against my next attempt. "I'm driving."

I'm not in a position to argue and hurry around to the passenger's side.

The parking lot is pandemonium as everyone races to the scene. Giving him directions is impossible because I'm gulping for breath. He follows the others to the fire while I panic.

Glancing behind the seat, he finds a fast food bag and dumps the contents. "You're going to pass out. Breathe into this."

The paper bag sucks in as I inhale. The smell of stale fries makes me nauseous. I open the window. My hands are shaking, and I can't stop a torrent of tears from falling. Not much air is refilling the bag.

We turn the corner to find smoke billowing from the pet shop. The tenants from the two upper floors are standing across the street. Some are crying, and all of them appear in shock as their memories burn. Fire hoses aim at the upper windows in an attempt to keep the blaze from spreading along the other Main Street buildings. The firefighters already axed the pet shop door open, and they are hurrying out with armloads of puppies and kittens.

"I know you want to go in there, but stay here. Please." He pulls the bag away and kisses me.

The kiss is a quick smooch and unexpected, but an effective way to halt all my brain activity. His lips are soft, and five seconds pass before I realize he is no longer beside me. I focus on the shop and wring my hands to keep from opening the door.

The smoke billows thicken, and I hear, "Help! Help!" through the din.

"Albert." I have to save him. Racing across the street, I follow a yellow suited firefighter into the doorway.

"Sam, don't go in there." Max's caution reaches me too late.

Water is raining on me through the ceiling. Large clumps of plaster are falling. The smoke is thick, and fire is licking up the walls from the back rooms. Flickers enthrall me to watch the fire dance, like a cobra entrances its victim. I shake my head to break the flame's hold over me and rush to open cages, praying the lovebirds escape before the smoke kills them. Some fly out, others are lying dead already.

Albert's yellow plume puffs making him appear menacing, but I know he is just scared.

"Help. *Squawk.* Help!"

I remove the leg tether. He leaps into the air before I can grab him and flies around the room, disappearing into the smoke.

"Albert. No!" I run back to find him. The air is hot, thicker, and more acidic. It's impossible to see through my tears. "Albert," I shout above the fire's roar.

"Help." His cry is weak.

I drop low and sweep my hand across my path to feel ahead of me in search of the stupid parrot. Pulling the shirt over my mouth, I struggle towards the office. Albert is on the floor lying limp. I tuck him into my neckline, and I try finding my way back to the door, but the smoke is getting worse. The heat is too intense, and there is no way to escape. We end up trapped in the office beneath the metal desk.

From out of the blackness, yellow clad legs appear. Hands reach in and lift me—no easy feat for any man. His shoulder smashes into the rear door to safety, but while backing out through the doorway, he stumbles over the puppies' cast iron watering trough. My rescuer is flat under me. The stubble on his chin looks familiar.

My head flops onto his, clunking foreheads, and I hear Max call for the medics. Dark spots dance in my peripheral vision and funnel to a small point. The last thought before blacking out—this is not how I pictured the hottie in 2C beneath me.

Someone is taking my blood pressure as I awaken with an oxygen mask over my mouth. Sirens are screaming, and red and blue flashing lights are bouncing off the white doors. Max is looking in to oversee my treatment. His eyes flutter closed.

I call to him, muffled by the mask, but he hears me. Relief reflects on his face before he smiles and his eyes light up. A feature I'm getting all too comfortable seeing. One day I'll look good enough to deserve that smile.

Abruptly, the assisting attendant closes the ambulance's rear doors. The medics are asking me questions, attempting to keep me focused, but instead of rushing to the hospital, I want to help my animals.

"Please, I want to stay and help." I'm thrashing my arms, and they strap them to the stretcher. The attendant nods to the driver, and the vehicle lurches forward, bouncing over every pothole to the north end of Hillsborough.

The rear doors open, the gurney clatters open, and the medics roll me into the emergency room. "She's stable, smoke inhalation, first degree burns, minor contusions." A clipboard with the vitals is set on my stomach, and the curtain whips shut. A radio squeals, and the EMTs' footsteps clap against the tile floor as they race out to assist another call.

Although I arrived by ambulance, the hospital is busy with other accident victims. Patients with worse injuries are bumped ahead of me. My arms are still immobile. I'm reading the clipboard's information upside down.

The curtain flips open, and a man hurries to my bedside. "Samantha, I'm here."

Once Around the Sun

He is the last person I expect to see. "David? What are you doing here?" My voice drips sarcasm.

Undeterred, he stands beside me. "I came as soon as I heard the news. Tragic that your shop burned."

"Yes, tragic," I say cautiously. There is no reason David should have come to the hospital for me. It hasn't been long since the fire call went out. How does he even know I'm here?

"I see your fireman couldn't save your store. What will you do now?"

"My fireman? David, he's not my anything. We just met today. Again, why are you here?"

"You should have taken me up on my offer, Samantha. Now you have nothing. No family, no pet store, no one."

This leap to the present situation sinks into my mind. A knot grows in the pit of my stomach. Bile is rising from the acids churning. My arms are still strapped to the gurney or I would slap him for bringing my reality so sharply into focus.

I goad him. "I know you weren't the biggest fan of me owning the shop, so what aren't you telling me?"

David leans over me. His eyes are manic. He pushes my shoulders into the padding; his face is inches from mine, stifling the air within the curtained area. A sneer crosses his face. "You didn't think I would let anyone or anything stand between us, did you?"

My tears stream unchecked as I realize David deliberately set the fire. How could I have loved him? A person so vile, he wouldn't think twice about killing innocent animals.

My eyes widen as I fully comprehend David's implication. "You said anyone. Oh my God, did you kill my grandparents?" I inhale sharply and gag on his overpowering cologne. I'm drowning in mucus.

He grins triumphantly, then realizes his mistake too late. His face turns hard, malicious, transforming into someone I never knew. His fingernails are digging into my flesh. I manage to fumble my fingers along the hospital cord wrapped around the side support and manipulate the wire close enough to press the emergency aid button, praying a nurse can help me to evade this monster. The curtain whips open, and David is snapped away. Max's hands are around his neck. I can only imagine that the slimmest shred of humanity is all that's keeping Max from strangling him.

David doesn't fight back, he stands glacial, but his eyes burn with hatred. He glares at me. "No one is safe, Samantha." He stares up at Max. "No one."

My chest is pounding. I'm struggling to breathe. I'm either hyperventilating again or drowning in my own snot.

"Sam, are you okay? Sam?" Max's voice booms above the emergency room noise, "Code orange. Emergency violator, code orange."

My eyes are swelling closed from crying and smoke damage, making it impossible to see anything that is going on around me. Someone is using a cold stethoscope to probe my chest, and another person is taking my pulse; then I hear bone smashing into flesh. A needle pricking my arm is the last thing I feel before the chaos dims.

Soft shoes squeaking on a hard floor wake me from a light, dreamless sleep, but I continue to lie still, not ready to wake. Curtain rings slide on metal, and someone forces one eye open. Brightness blinds me. Seconds later a blood pressure band is squeezing my arm, and a hand is sliding along my wrist to find the pulse point.

"Good morning, sleepy head."

I jolt to the present, and a nurse is staring down at me. A bright light behind the pink-clad woman is haloing her short, curly, brown hair.

"What happened to me?"

She reviews the chart. "Looks like you had a panic attack. Dr. Givens gave you a mild sedative. He said to wake you and check your vitals. If they checked out, you could leave. You're good to go now. I'll process your discharge papers."

My clothes stink from adrenalin, sweat, and smoke. The blood pressure monitor is wrapped around my forearm, filling every twenty minutes. The band is clean against the black smudges, and red welts cover my arms.

Max walks through the partially-opened curtain. His left eye is black and blue.

"What happened?" I ask.

"He sucker punched me and ran when I called for assistance."

A man in blue scrubs rushes through the curtains. He lifts the chart off the side counter. "Miss Darling, how are we feeling?"

"Groggy. My throat is sore, and my eyes hurt."

"The grogginess will dissipate shortly. The heat and smoke from the fire over-dried your eyes and throat. He digs around in his hip pocket and removes a prescription pad. "Use these drops as needed, and gargle with a salt water solution four times a day for a week to help your throat heal. Do you have any questions?"

"Doc, about the panic attack. Is that something to be concerned about?"

"Only if you continue to have them. It's something we'll have to monitor," he says and scribbles another prescription. He hands Max the notes to fill at the hospital pharmacy, before exiting through the curtains just as quickly as he arrived.

Max stashes the papers into the inside pocket of his jacket before removing a small clear plastic bag from the outside pocket. A gold ring slides to the corner. "Is this yours? It was found in the store."

David's fraternity ring. He did set the fire. Tears slide onto the pillow as the words lodge in my throat.

He moves to my side and caresses my cheek. "Sam, what's wrong?"

I shake my head, not wanting to believe what David told me. None of it made sense. "It's David's ring. He set the fire. I think he killed my grandparents too."

"Are you positive?"

"He didn't say so exactly, but I've never seen him so angry. If you hadn't come in when you did . . ." I'm hiccuping breath, unable to speak.

First Impressions, Second Chances

Max grabs a tissue from a box on the counter and dabs under my eyes. The tissue comes away black. He places the box beside me and plucks them one by one, wiping soot my face. Dirty tissues cover my gurney. "Come on, let's go home."

What did I do to deserve this man? I try to move. The straps that kept me from defending myself are still holding me down, reminding me that nothing will stand in David's way. He'll hurt Max just to get back at me. What happens if David is watching outside? I can't leave with Max and put him at risk.

I look away. "Linda is on her way to get me. She's my contact person."

He knows it is a lie. Max discards the tissues and removes the straps. He smooths the hair away from my face and tenderly kisses my chapped lips. He's smiling, but it doesn't reach his eyes. "If you need me, you know where to find me," he says and removes the notes from his coat, placing them on the counter before walking out.

Inside I'm screaming, "Don't go," but the words don't spill from my lips. Instead, I drape an arm across my eyes to shield myself from my own fear. Max is the man I want to smile at me forever, and I have to let him go. David is still in control.

When the nurse returns, I ask, "Can you please call a cab for me?"

She scribbles more information onto the chart and returns with a wheelchair to transport me to the exit.

The cabbie glances in the mirror at me after the nurse relayed my address, but remains quiet until we reach the apartments. "Six dollars and forty cents."

My purse is still in the Prius. "Can you come upstairs? My purse is at the fire scene."

Once inside the elevator, he asks, "What floor?"

It snaps me from a daze. I'm not sure how long we stood there, but the doors had already closed. I press the third floor button.

Once Around the Sun

I enter the keyless code, and the apartment door unlocks. Fishing through the kitchen junk drawer for money, I find enough cash to cover the fare.

"Are you going to be okay?" he asks.

"I hope so." A chill runs through me as soon as he leaves, and I bolt the door and slide the chain.

On the way into the bathroom, I glimpse the reflection in the hallway mirror and stop in abhorrent shock. My clothes are ruined, my skin is black with soot and inflamed welts, and my hair is uneven, seared off by the intense heat. I can't cry anymore. There are no more tears.

I throw everything I'm wearing into the trash, and I double knot the bag to contain the odor before stepping into the shower. It takes three scrubbings to remove the grime embedded into my pores. Hair clogs the drain and forces me to stop and remove the fist-sized clumps as the shampoo loosens the dirt matting it together. I step from the shower, pink skinned and scraggly headed, and go to bed wet, collapsing from exhaustion.

The next morning, I wake to someone knocking on the door. "Go away," I say into the pillow.

"Rise and shine, Sam. It's Linda. Let me in."

I put on a sweatshirt and pants, and go to let her in. She's holding a carrier with two coffees and a bag from the corner bakery. When she sees me, Linda almost drops everything.

"Oh Sam, your hair . . . " She walks into the kitchen, setting the treats on the counter, and digs through her purse until finding her shears. "Sit. I'll trim the worst off now, but you need to come see me at the salon for a good cut later."

I peek into the bakery bag to see what she brought to sugarcoat my dark mood. "Are these chocolate-coated doughnuts with raspberry filling?"

"Of course. I know they're your favorite." She sits across the counter from me. "Let's eat first. Did you hear anything about your animals yet?"

I lick the confection off my fingers and wash it down with coffee. "I kept waking, hearing the messages coming in on the recorder. The Uptown Pet Rescue took most of the dogs and kittens. The other one had room for the rest, but neither had received a cockatoo." I feel a hollowness fill my chest. "It can mean only one thing. Albert didn't survive."

A second donut follows, and in quick succession a third, to fill the void. The sugar buzz will hurt later, but I grieve better with chocolate. I'm already considering buying a small marker for Albert to place beside my grandparents' stones. I'll find the money somehow.

Linda makes quick work of repairing the worst damage by cutting the hair to just below my chin. I run my fingers through to the ends. It will take time to adjust to the new length—to everything.

She pulls the broom from the pantry and sweeps the mess covering the kitchen floor into a manageable pile. "Go get dressed, and we'll go to your shop."

I walk into the bathroom to look at the results and can still smell the soot emanating from the knotted trash bag. My long curly locks are gone. My hair will never be the same. Another wave of depression hits.

Digging through the closet I find old jeans, a T-shirt, and sneakers that I won't mind tossing in the trash later. There's no time for makeup. Heck, there is nobody to bother impressing anyway. David was right . . . I have no one.

I return to the kitchen and sit across from Linda. She sips her coffee and pushes her last gooey donut towards me. I savor every calorie, before leaving to see the charred remains of Little Darlings–Second Chances.

Max's car is missing from the lot as we leave the apartment. Linda parks across the street from the fire scene. Yellow caution tape surrounds the building. The tenants are gone, and the charred windows from the two upper apartments stare back at me.

"Linda, I appreciate your help, but this is something I have to do alone."

"I understand. Call me if you need me."

Waiting until she drives away, I duck under the tape into what is left of my store. Water is still dripping through the ceiling. I think about the tenants above. They must have lost everything, too.

The cages are empty and deformed from the intense heat; the wood shavings added fuel to the fire, incinerating any small animal remains that didn't survive. Only the metal base remains to Albert's wooden perch. Cautiously, I move farther into the store, stepping over debris.

The office didn't completely burn. The small fireproof wall safe is exposed, but still locked. I turn the tumbler, pausing at each number, and the latch opens with a soft click. Inside is the insurance policy, a thousand dollars in emergency cash, and a photograph of Grams and Pappy.

"I'm sorry for losing everything," I say and sit on the floor staring at the picture.

Grams had warned me against dating David. She said, "It doesn't make sense. Him coming from the uppity side of town." I should have listened. They would still be alive if I had paid heed to her advice.

"Hello. Who's in there?" a man shouts from the entrance.

I wake from a trance, huddled beneath the desk, still holding the snapshot. I shove the cash and papers under the denim's waistband, dry my tears with the back of my hand, and carry the photo out of the building.

Milton Cooper, who owns the hardware store across the street, is waiting just outside the door, holding a long handled flashlight like a club. He reminds me of an English bulldog, big and brawny, but a real softy inside. He lets out the breath he held. "It's you, Sam. I wasn't sure if somebody was looting the place." He looks inside the doorway. "Not much to take though. It's not safe to go in there. This old building went up fast."

I hear him, but I'm not really listening. At least until I realize he was here when the fire started. "Did you see who torched my store?"

"Nope. Didn't see anyone suspicious. I called 9-1-1 though," he says, standing proud.

I walk away and, out of habit, follow my usual route towards the apartment. Stopping to fish today's *Forum* from between the bricks and shrubs, I read the headline: *Arson*

First Impressions, Second Chances

Suspected in Downtown Fire. I drop the open newspaper on the porch and continue home. The photo is crinkling in my hand.

Once again, I strip out of my soot blackened clothes and scrub until my skin is pink. No matter how many times I shower, the smell from the fire lingers in my sinuses, a constant memory of everything lost. Again, I stuff the clothing into a plastic bag and double knot it.

After redressing, I trudge the two sacks of smelly clothes to the dumpster. Max's car is still missing, and so is mine. The Prius remains across the street from the pet shop.

Next is to call the insurance agency. A recorded message tells me that the office is closed and to call again between nine a.m. and five p.m. on weekdays. "Great, so accidents can only happen during working hours," I say sarcastically.

I go back to bed. Sleep takes me into nightmares where David is chasing me with a torch. I wake up only to fall back into the same horrific pattern. There are knocks on the door, but I ignore them. The food is running low, and I just stop eating.

I'm not certain how many days pass, but I lose all ambition to leave my bedroom until I hear a faint knock and then a familiar voice, "Hello. Sam, hello."

"Albert?"

"Hello. Sam, hello."

This is another nightmare, but I have to check the door. I look through the peephole and see nothing.

Again, I hear. "Hello. Sam, hello."

After fumbling with the safety chain, I whip open the door ready to scream at whoever is playing this cruel joke on me. Max is holding a box of mail in one arm, and the cockatoo is perched on the other.

Tears spill down my cheeks, and I rush out to take Albert. Max pulls me tightly against him with his free arm. I realize not everything is lost. The human contact unhinges my emotions. One moment I'm sobbing, and then the next, laughing.

Albert squawks, "I love her. I love her."

Once Around the Sun

"Hey, that was our secret." Max holds me tighter. "Are we going to stand in the hall or are you letting us in?"

I back into the room, not quite able to release him so soon after reconnecting, and still dumbfounded at seeing Albert alive.

"Go take a shower, and I'll make breakfast." He looks in the cabinets and opens the refrigerator. "There's nothing to eat."

I stand in the living room, and my stomach growls so loudly he hears it in the kitchen.

"Don't worry, we came prepared. I'll be back in a minute. Please don't lock me out." He hands the parrot to me. "Albert, keep her out of trouble."

The cockatoo is dancing side-to-side, happy to see me. His head is butting against my shoulder, "Hello, Sam." Squawk.

I smooth his head feathers. "Albert, I missed you, too." Some of the emptiness surrounding me lifts at having my companion returned.

Max carries in a bag of groceries. "After we eat, I have good news to share, but first, go shower."

I realize that, once again, he just saw me at my worst, but he is still happy to see me. "Albert, stay with Max," I say and place the parrot upon a stool.

On the way through the bedroom, I grab jeans, a T-shirt, and the essential underwear before washing off the stench of depression. When the water hits my body, the smell is overwhelming, and I add an extra squirt of body wash to the face cloth.

I'm finished showering, and the scent of bacon wafts into the bedroom, drawing me back to the kitchen and life. On the counter, two plates heap with food: bacon, scrambled eggs, and toast. He even has coffee brewing. We sit across from each other at the small dinette table. Max reaches over and combs his fingers through the shorter hair, toying with the ends.

"So tell me the good news," I say while forking food into my mouth as fast as I can chew.

First Impressions, Second Chances

"David was arrested at the airport. He was trying to leave the country."

"So the mighty has fallen." There is a smug satisfaction in knowing he will hate prison. I slurp the coffee, glad to revisit my addiction.

"Also, the police have reopened the investigation into the deaths of your grandparents. I called a friend, the best detective I know, to help with the case."

I choke. The liquid sputters, and I block the spray from hitting Max with my hand. He stands to hunt for a towel, but I wave him down, dabbing the mess with a napkin.

He continues, "David's behind bars with no chance of bail. He'll be there until your grandparents' deaths are investigated. David still has to face arson charges and won't be going anywhere for a very long time."

Shocked at the news, I stare at Max with my jaw gaping.

"I thought you'd be happy to hear your ex-fiancé is out of your life for good."

"I'm just overwhelmed. Here, I felt abandoned like one of my animals, and all this time you were helping me." My knees wobble as I stand. One meal is not going to fix the nutritional meltdown. Walking around the table to his seat, I place one hand on each of his shoulders for balance. "Thank you," I say in a whisper as my mouth meets his.

Max steadies me before lifting me onto his lap. "You're turning into a feather-weight." He moves closer; his lips are inches from mine. "I like my woman to have some heft. Makes for better loving."

I smile against his kiss and realize he said that I was his woman.

He places a box on the table beside me. There are dozens of letters to sort through; most are bills for Little Darlings and junk mail. Two letters take precedence. The insurance company sent a cancellation notice. I knew this was coming. The other letter is from my grandparents' lawyer. I never did return his calls.

Once Around the Sun

To: Samantha Darling

It is imperative that we meet as soon as possible. I have left multiple messages for you without reply. Please contact me at the phone number listed in the letterhead.

Regards,

Reginald Bailey, Esq.

I dial the phone number and the call answers immediately.

"Reginald Bailey."

Wow, a direct number. I explain the reason for calling.

"How soon can you meet with me?" he asks.

"Whenever is convenient for you." I say offhandedly, "I could leave now and arrive in twenty minutes."

"Wonderful, I'll cancel the next hour of appointments. There is personal information for you to consider. I suggest you come alone," he says and disconnects.

The last appointment I made took six weeks to see him for a fifteen-minute meeting. The lawyer was never this nice to me. What personal information does he have . . . and come alone? He is totally freaking me out.

I leave Albert with Max and hurry along the sidewalk to uptown. This practice is from old money and sustained by old money. I have no money and no clue why I'm here.

When I enter the office, the receptionist whisks me into the inner sanctum where Reginald Bailey awaits.

"No interruption, no calls, Stephanie," he tells her.

Reginald Bailey turns towards me. A trickle of sweat is beading from his hairline. "Miss Darling, please sit. Can I offer you coffee, tea perhaps?"

I decline, wondering why he is nervous speaking to me.

"Before your grandparents died, they left strict instruction not to contact you until your thirtieth birthday." He hands me a wax-sealed and embossed envelope and stands across the desk from me. "Please open the letter and then we will speak further."

First Impressions, Second Chances

The wax snaps easily, and I remove the paper. Gram's precise handwriting scrolls on the lawyer's ivory letterhead. The bottom is notarized and stamped on my birth date two years ago.

Our dear Samantha,

If this letter finds you, then we have moved on and are watching over you from another place. Although we raised you simply, we loved you as our own and want you to be happy through life.

We set this trust fund in place for you with stocks we bought many years ago. We hope they provide all you need so you can continue Little Darlings–Second Chances, as we had, without hardship.

There are twenty-eight original IBM stock certificates at this time. We know you will use them wisely.

We love you,

Grams and Pappy

I'm stunned. This explains how they managed to survive on the shop's meager income. "How much are these worth?"

"The stock has split multiple times and with the dividends reinvested . . . millions."

I watch a second rivulet of sweat trickle along his forehead. "What aren't you telling me?"

"In light of recent events, I have to confess a breach of ethics. An outside party saw this document. That person came into the office while this letter was open on my desk."

The document's date and my social life started within days of each other. "Let me guess . . . David Bernhart."

"You have to understand, he is no longer working for this firm. I'm so sorry, and I do hope you can forgive me for what happened to your store because of David. But with your inheritance, you can rebuild."

I am shocked, almost speechless, at the indifference he has towards my misfortune. "Do you know that he threatened my life and killed my grandparents, too?"

His face blanches as he sits with a thud onto his leather chair.

I stand abruptly to leave. "Now I know what he was after . . . not me, just the money. Millions of dollars worth. Mr. Bailey, you'll hear from my lawyer."

I walk to my apartment elated at having my financial worries solved, but still dumbfounded at discovering how David had manipulated me. This past week has been an emotional rollercoaster.

Months pass, permits are approved, and the building is almost finished. Milton identifies David as the person who entered the store just prior to the fire, but hadn't considered him suspicious because of his standing in the community. He is charged with arson and destruction of private property.

Mr. Bailey testifies against David in exchange for no jail time. His practice is closed. The evidence against David's murder case is building as he sits in jail. I can't wait to stand before him during sentencing and watch the contempt drain from his arrogant eyes when he realizes that he will never see freedom again.

It took time to find a lawyer and a financial advisor. I debated about telling Max about the inheritance. They both advised me not to disclose my financial freedom to anyone.

Six months later, Max moves into 3C with Albert and me. It's getting harder to come up with ways to hide the undisclosed income. I have to explain the inheritance to him or risk our relationship crumbling from telling lies.

We're clearing dishes from the table after dinner, and I pull a bottle of champagne from hiding out of the cabinet.

"What are we celebrating?" he asks.

First Impressions, Second Chances

"My financial freedom. Remember when I went to Attorney Bailey's office?"

He continues drying plates and placing them in the cupboards.

"I mentioned there was an inheritance, but never told you how much it was worth."

He reaches for the bottle and begins unfurling the wire cage. "That's because it doesn't matter to me. I did guess there was something, though. It's not as if the tooth fairy was leaving bundles of cash under your pillow."

"Pappy had bought IBM stocks years ago. Now they're worth millions."

This caught him by surprise. The cork hits the ceiling, and champagne fizzes over the top before I have the glasses ready.

"With this money, I can rebuild the store and design an apartment to live above it. Maybe even donate some to the families who lost everything in the fire."

"That's a great idea. You do know I fell in love with a woman who has a big heart . . . not a big bank account. I'm not like David."

In answer, I wrap my arms around his neck and kiss him long enough to forget all about the champagne. For the first time, I'm happy with someone who loves me for just me. His dimpled smiles still melt my heart.

I'm walking to the newly opened Little Darlings–Second Chances. Corn stalks lean against the lampposts for Halloween, and some block my path, but not much can divert my new attitude. The hardships have only made me a stronger person. There really are second chances in life.

Redheads by the Cement Pond

Jeff Baird

I've been around pools all my life. I guess you could call me a Pool Guy. Okay. No one ever *has* called me a Pool Guy, but someone *could*, right? Right. Now, I know I said I'd been around pools all my life, but I should point out, those pools came in a box. You know, the inflatable kind that you fill with a hose? Don't laugh, they count. Coupling my Pool Guy status with my membership in the elite league of Redheads, I bring an interesting mix of skills and talents to the "Pool" Table.

One of the things that drew me to my current home was the fact that it came with an in-ground pool. While the more rational corners of my brain were shouting "Oh good, more work for me," my Redheaded genes were dreaming about the killer tan and beach bod I'd undoubtedly gain with ready access to a pool. Besides, my wife and kids were thrilled at the prospect, and seeing as I love my family to a stupendous degree, no sacrifice on my part seemed too great if it would benefit my loved ones.

So there I was, the Redheaded Pool Guy, embarking on the maintenance of his first non-pool-in-a-box. Like all real men, real Redheads don't read manuals or ask for help— we're *way* too manly for these trivial matters. Besides, I already knew all the jargon from my pool-owning friends: filter, skimmer, backwash, chlorine, vacuum, water.

In fact, the breadth of my knowledge was virtually limitless, which explains the ease with which I picked up on this in-ground pool stuff. No, really, I could skim and chlorinate and backwash with the best of them. In my Redheaded mind, I was a pool-owning god. There was only one thing that I wasn't quite up to speed on, and that was diatomaceous earth or DE. For you non-redheads deficient in pool jargon, DE is made of ground-up sea shells and acts as a filtering agent, picking up the minute particles suspended in the water that are too small to be caught by the filter baskets. Pretty cool, huh?

When we moved in, the previous owners (also Redheads) left us—meaning me—the rundown on the intricate directions concerning the house and pool as well as a one-minute dissertation of the joys of pool maintenance. After hearing the abbreviated version, I started to daydream about jumping in the cool, refreshing pool water.

I didn't actually return to work on the pool for the next couple of weeks because I was somewhat preoccupied with other minor details, like hooking up the TV in my new man cave so I could watch my beloved Philadelphia Eagles and Florida State University Seminoles. I was much too busy to bother with minor issues, like maintaining the PH balance of the pool, or to vacuum or backwash.

Hmmm, you might be wondering what the term backwashing refers to. Let me assure you, it has nothing to do with sharing a drink. You see, sometimes a pool filter has sucked up all of the minute particles in the water and can't suck or filter any more. When this happens, the pool owner needs to perform a backwash to clear out the filter.

You can tell when a backwash is necessary if one of a couple things occurs: first, you can read the pressure dial on the filter and do the mathematical calculations necessary to determine the DE capacity. The second way you can tell that backwashing is necessary is when the water flow grows so weak in proportion to the force of water blowing out of the water-return from the filter, that frogs will use the water-return as a whirlpool Jacuzzi. As I am slightly deficient in the mathematical area, I opted for the Frog Early Warning System. Frogs vacationed in my filter as if it were the French Rivera.

Searching my photographic memory for clues about DE and backwash, I thought back to the one-minute pool-owning dissertation. I could remember with perfect clarity my plans for a tan and six-pack, but the details of back-washing were a bit fuzzier. Still, a fuzzy photograph is worth at least five hundred words.

I made my way down to the filter at the bottom of the incline in the back of my yard. I turned off the filter, and I then made sure to eat my spinach so that I could "bump" the filter handle up and down to clear any clumps of DE that had gathered inside. I bumped it five times and then thought to myself, *if five is good, seventeen times will be even better and also allow me to get my cardio workout all in the same operation.*

However, there comes a time in pool maintenance when you have reached the break-even point, and bumping will no longer free up space in your filter. When you reach that spot, the only way to keep your filter from Frog Friendly levels, is to drain it of all of the gunk, and replace the dirty DE.

I survived several weeks as a pool owner before I reached that break-even point, but when bumping ceased to do the trick, I proceeded to both backwash and drain the filter and replace the old, overworked DE with the fresh DE that the former homeowners were so kind as to leave in the shed for just such an occasion.

No sweat; it worked like a charm. In no time, I was off to enjoy my aquatic recreational activities, although I did notice that the water flow back into the pool, while much improved, was not super-duper. I figured the filter hadn't totally circulated the DE and the pressure would pick up gradually.

When I returned the next morning, the pool was some-what cleaner. However, I noticed some smallish white gran-ules forming into clumps in the water. While swishing the water around didn't dissolve them, the skimmer seemed to be picking these pellets up, so I didn't give them a second thought.

Still, I continued to watch the backwash for water flow intensity to determine whether the frogs were still using my skimmer as a summer resort. I didn't see any frogs, but the nodules continued to appear, and the flow still wasn't as strong as I liked.

I determined that I hadn't added the DE correctly, so I decided to backwash and drain and replace the DE a second time. This time I made sure to add the DE powder into the pool slowly so it would totally dissolve. I painstakingly added the DE at a rate of one teaspoon per hour into the skimmer. Three weeks later I finished up, only to be dismayed by the reappearance of the nodules shortly thereafter.

I must admit that I was baffled and went back and forth on whether or not to stay the course or reach out for assistance. I compromised by turning to cyberspace. I googled the terms "DE," "water flow," and "frogs" to see if anyone had come across this problem before.

I came up empty on the frog angle, but my other searches brought me to the conclusion that I should have trusted my initial instincts. According to the Internet, I was doing everything correctly. I felt vindicated that the World Wide Web had confirmed my previous efforts. However, it was a hollow victory as I still had to deal with lack of water flow and the return of the nodules. I began to harbor a deep resentment towards the frogs as the main culprits and to plot a way to wreak havoc on these amphibian freeloaders.

Before going out to buy a new filter, I decided to try once more to figure out what the problem was. I tore apart the filter to see if I had clogged the tubes by putting in too much DE or, though it was unlikely, putting it in too quickly. When I pried off the cover of the filter, I saw what can only be described as dozens of the tendrils, like the tentacles of the aliens in Will Smith's blockbuster, *Independence Day,* clogging up its inner workings.

Overcoming my revulsion I tried poking them with a knife. They were solid. Upon further inspection, I realized these alien tendrils were caked up with a white dirty paste, undoubtedly due to the fact that the previous owners had not changed or cleaned the filter in a long time.

As I scraped them away with my knife, my Redheaded side cursed the previous owners for passing this chore on to the newbies moving into their home. My more rational side whispered that perhaps my waiting to get around to cleaning had allowed an excess of gunk to build up, but I ignored it. I cleaned it out as best I could; then, figuring that I had solved the problem, patted myself on the back for my hard work and perseverance.

Going into my shed to fetch the remaining DE to clean the pool, I thought, *yessiree, I am one Redheaded manly man, master of my domain.*

That's when I accidentally knocked a box off a shelf, and some of the contents spilled out onto the floor. Thinking that I had found a small spare box of DE, I placed the box back on the shelf, I glanced at the label but didn't think anything of it. I picked up the bucket of DE and started to walk towards the pool, when just like in the movies a moment of clarity made me stop in my tracks.

If someone made a cartoon version of my life, this would be the moment a light bulb, or a dunce cap, appeared over my head. *Slowly I turned. Step by step, inch by inch.* I returned to the scene of the crime. Haltingly, hesitantly, I stared at the box that was to be the undoing of our Redheaded Hero.

Possibly germane to this story is the fact that, due to repressed memories of living in a wood-shingled house and having to paint said house several times during my formative years, I vowed never to buy a house that required painting. My first home was a red-brick ranch home. This one, the second, was off-white—I believe the term is "weeping mortar stucco." Yep, that's right; I lived in a stucco home, and the previous owners had kept a certain amount of the white powder to use for basic repairs. Apparently they had x-ray vision and did not need to label containers, instead knowing by the sense of touch and smell what the different buckets contained.

Did you know that stucco powder looks surprisingly similar to DE powder used in pool filters? Let me tell you, it does.

So, let's recap; those white pellets or nodules were the result of pool water and other pool chemicals mixing with small amounts of stucco cement. Yep; all the time I thought I was cleaning my pool; I was actually well on my way to building my very own "Cement Pond."

I have two questions. First, does anyone know if homeowners' insurance covers damage to swimming pools due to inadvertent cement additions? Secondly, does anyone know if Hallmark makes an apology card for frogs?

Keeping Promises

Sally W. Paradysz

Last night, watching the moon
turn its color with you beside me,
I concealed our love because of prior sorrow.
I left, but not with any desire to go,
and brought you home in my heart for safe keeping.
One day there will be greater freedom,
turning separation into a field in harvest.

With the scent of slaughter fresh in the air, Kimi faced the heavens and wept.

When the shock of her grief eased, she opened her eyes and took in the scene. A young doe. Shot dead. Her body had oozed blood onto the ferns that surrounded the sanctuary of the feeding stations. Dropping to her knees, she stroked the fur around the doe's ears and face. Her tears cascaded to the ground, each drop settling into the dirt.

She heard footsteps behind her and knew it was Adele.

"Oh no. God, so sorry." Adele sat next to Kimi and pulled her into an embrace. "How many deer have you lost this year?"

Kimi rested her head on Adele's shoulder and sniffed. "Eight. Two bucks last September. A fawn was shot in early spring shortly after it was born, then three does in June, one in July, and now this," she said gesturing to the body before her. "That one makes eight."

She shuddered at the horror. This land, once so safe and sheltered for her deer, had recently seen far too many murders. She loved these acres, felt protected by them, and worked hours each day maintaining them. She had never dreamed of living anywhere else.

Now, her land dishonored, Kimi felt violated.

After a few moments, she touched Adele's cheek with the back of her fingers then pushed away to stand. With a hand resting on each knee, she looked down at the doe once again. She held a finger to her lips to listen for sounds while she checked the ground surrounding the doe for anything out of place. She smelled the air, searching for clues that might lead her to the doe's assassin. She found nothing.

She wiped tears from her cheeks. "I don't know who I've angered, but someone is out to get me. Why else trespass onto this land to shoot my deer at the feeder? It's not for meat or antlers. It must be a message."

"That makes no sense," Adele said. "Who could be upset with you? You keep to yourself, take care of your land, and leave the rest of the world alone. I don't get it."

Kimi took a deep breath. "Me either. Do you see anything out of order, Adele? Something I might have missed, like footprints, or shell casings? I've never once found a damn thing. Just the carcass. Why would someone go to such trouble to kill my deer?"

Adele studied the ground before answering. "I don't see anything. You're right. Whoever did this was careful." She looked toward the lake. "I guess I'll go to the fire-pit and make sure there's enough wood."

"Be there as soon as I can. I need to walk back to the barn," Kimi said, watching Adele saunter away.

Kimi returned with the tractor, a box of matches, and a tattered old sheet. Gently, she rolled the carcass into the front-end loader, covered it and drove to the edge of the fire pit. Her great-grandfather, a Mahican, had built this ceremonial space many years before. It had seen rituals for generations, and now would again.

The two women built a pyre from deadwood, then lifted the sheet-wrapped body from the tractor and placed the doe on top. With the tractor safely to the side, Kimi gave the matches to Adele. It had always been difficult for her to set flame to a deer's remains; she loved their stunning physical bodies.

Flames licked the air at first, but then settled into a glowing fire that dried the cattails nearby. The woods stayed silent.

Kimi's sadness helped her stay in her heart rather than in her anger. She squinted at Adele through the smoke. "Grandfather said the fire guides the animal's soul back to the Greater Spirit."

Adele removed her Red Sox cap, pulled her thick hair into a ponytail, threading it through the cap as she returned it to her head. "I like the ceremony," she said. "It gives you time to grieve. She looked at Kimi's tear-stained face and added, "Don't worry. We're going to find who's doing this."

Kimi looked into the blaze. "At least it's not my albino deer," she mumbled.

Adele's head snapped around, her eyes bright and large. "Albino? Just now I thought I saw a white deer through the smoke."

"You probably did. I thought they had died out. Hadn't seen any for three years, but this spring I saw a set of twins, and one was an albino." Kimi scanned the woods. "I love the little doe so much that even whispering about her makes me afraid that she'll disappear. I keep hoping to catch a glimpse of her. Native Americans believe that all-white animals are magical."

Adele shifted her weight, a slight smile on her face. "One day when I was about fourteen I came into the woods to hide from . . . well life, I guess. Your grandfather found me, and we sat for hours talking about the animals on your land. He told me about an albino strain of deer in the area. I've kept my eyes peeled ever since, but I've never seen one."

"Now I think you have." Kimi took Adele's hand. "Grandfather always had a soft spot in his heart for you."

Adele squeezed back. "I know. It was an honor to spend time with him. He was a perfect father figure for me." Whether it was smoke or emotion that got into Adele's eyes, she wiped the tears away and said. "I wish he were here with us now. He'd find the bastard responsible for the killings."

Kimi nodded. "Well, we'll just have to do it ourselves."

They sat by the fire until it burned to embers. Her prayers offered, Kimi rose and brushed off the seat of her pants.

Adele checked her watch. "I have to run if I'm going to make it to the office on time. Can I hitch a ride on the tractor back to my car?"

"Sure," Kimi said, rubbing her hands together. "I have an appointment with Arthur around three o'clock, so I'll see you there."

"Okay, I won't say anything to him. No reason to let him prepare for your meeting." She gritted her teeth. "He's such a jerk."

Kimi tightened her fists. "Thanks. I'm going to give him a piece of my mind."

At the car, Kimi gave Adele a hug. "I don't know what I'd do without you," she said closing the driver door after Adele got in.

She watched the car drive off before going into her cabin. It was one room, with a wood stove and an upper loft. It held a rough-hewn table and bench she had made herself. On the walls hung the few works of art and objects important to her: a snapping turtle shell, snowshoes, and a birch-bark basket ornamented with feathers. On the floor lay a mat of woven cedar bark, a gift from her grandfather.

As she showered, Kimi rehearsed what she'd say to Arthur Green, the County Game Warden. He had originally run for the position ten years before, winning because of voters' sympathy after he was maimed in an accident only a week before the election. Once in office, he'd used his considerable powers of intimidation against anyone who dared run against him. Kimi knew. She'd tried. His not–so-veiled threats had pressured her out of the running.

Standing at the antique mirror, Kimi gathered her silver hair in a knot at the base of her neck and stared for a few seconds at her image—tall and fit for a woman of sixty, with no bend to her solid body. *I am confident of who I am,* she thought. *I can handle this meeting.*

Outside, she drew in a deep breath of pine-scented air and followed the sun-dappled deer path to the road. At the forest edge, she hesitated before she took the last step into the bright daylight, hating to leave the comfort of her land.

Her aged pickup truck sat at the fork in the road, next to the triple-white birches marking the trailhead opening. There were times when she liked walking to her cabin from there, rather than driving in to the barn.

She was delighted as the engine turned over on the first try. *The gods are with me,* she thought heading for town.

Kimi shuddered remembering her last meeting with Arthur. She'd gone to see him when the two bucks were killed. Not only did he refuse her any help, he slid his boning knife out of its scabbard and let it rest on his knee. When she didn't take the hint, he took the knife in his three-fingered hand and waved it in front of her face.

Voters who had elected Arthur out of sympathy probably didn't realize he'd lost those fingers in a trapping accident. The man, who was supposed to catch poachers, was one. She never felt sorry for someone who trapped for the thrill of the kill.

Kimi didn't feel ready to approach Arthur. Nothing had changed, so why did she think he would help now? But as she drove into town, she noticed the chief of police's car in front of the police station and had an idea.

Dakotah Whitewood, the new chief, was the only woman the town fathers had allowed into a position of authority. She'd arrived eight months before from the mid-west, but Kimi was so rarely in town she'd never met her. According to Adele, Dakotah's resume said she'd had twenty years experience in police work. She'd wanted to come east to care for a dying friend.

Kimi entered the office and waited. A tall, broad-shouldered woman in a tailored suit walked around her desk and greeted her. "Kimi," she said extending her hand. "It's a pleasure to meet you, finally. I'm Chief Whitewood. But, please call me Dakotah."

Once Around the Sun

Kimi would have felt threatened that Dakotah knew her name, but her firm grip and open expression set Kimi at ease.

"Thank you," she said, accepting the chair Dakotah offered. "How did you know who I was?"

"Your cheekbones," Dakotah said. "And your eyes. I noticed your name on the town rolls. 'Kimi' is Native American, isn't it? Iroquois?"

Kimi shook her head, impressed with Dakotah's observation. "Algonquin for 'secret.' Grandfather said he gave it to me because he knew I harbored something deep inside."

The sheriff nodded. "Dakotah is Sioux, and means 'friend or ally.' Looks like we have something in common."

"It does."

"Townsfolk say you're a seasoned freelance photographer and writer. I envy you. I'd love to be able to work from home."

"I'm seasoned all right," said Kimi, laughing. "Nothing like town gossip to precede you."

"What can I do for you today?"

"I've come by to introduce myself, but I also want to talk about some deaths occurring on my land."

Dakotah straightened her shoulders and pushed away from the front of the desk.

"I've found deer in my woods. Shot. It's been happening since last fall. I tried talking to the game warden about it, but he's done nothing to stop the killings. In fact, I was just on my way to complain to him again."

Dakotah sat at her desk and scribbled notes on the pad in front of her. "Have you seen tracks at the killing site, or markings of any kind?"

Kimi shook her head. "Nothing. In July, I found a gash at the edge of the lake where someone beached a canoe on my property."

"Did you see the canoe?" Dakotah didn't look up as she spoke.

"No, just the groove on the beach."

The chief put down her pen. "I'll look into it and stop by your land. Okay with you?"

"Anytime," Kimi said, standing up. "We'll walk my land and talk about our ancestry. She turned toward the door and paused, looking back. "Actually, I have a question you may be able to help me with. When my grandfather was dying he told me about people with two spirits. Those who walk in two worlds within reverence and respect. I'm not sure what it meant. Have you heard of that?"

Dakotah met her eyes. "My mother also told me about people with two-spirits. She said the legend came from Great Plains Indians."

"Did they mean the physical world and the spirit world, because sometimes I sense my grandfather's presence."

"No." Dakotah said. "I think it means some people can walk with two spirits in the physical world." She tilted her head and looked into Kimi's eyes. Kimi looked away. "Maybe that's the secret your grandfather knew you held onto so tightly."

Feeling fortified by her new "ally," Kimi drove to the other side of town.

An available parking slot opened two spaces down from the county office building, and Kimi deftly backed into it.

She pulled the outer door of the office open, crossed the vestibule, then turned the knob on the door to the Game Warden's office and entered without hesitation. "Hey," she said, walking to the only desk in the small but well-lit room.

"Hey," Adele said staring at Kimi. On first glance, Adele's eyes appeared gentle, vulnerable even, but Kimi knew if she looked closer she'd see the strong woman behind them. Focused, stubborn, with a low tolerance for bullshit—at least most of the time. "He's here, but on the phone. Coffee?"

"Please."

Adele grabbed a cup from the wide sill and poured from the ancient machine. "Be careful. I tried talking to him when I came in, and he growled." Adele handed the cup to Kimi. "He's in a mood."

"So am I. This could get ugly."

Adele flicked a squinty-eyed look toward Kimi. "I'm fine with ugly. But I'm not going to take it much longer. I don't even know why I'm still here." Adele lowered her voice to a whisper. "I walk on eggshells every day; just as I did when Arthur and I were married. I don't put up with garbage from anyone else. What's wrong with me?"

Kimi glanced toward Arthur's door and whispered. "Nothing's wrong with you. It's an old pattern from your past. Just do your best to be safe. You told me a month ago that you were going to quit. Do it, Adele."

"I will. I'll leave before he explodes and hurts me or someone else."

Too late for that, Kimi lamented. Arthur had been an abusive husband. Kimi was so proud of Adele when she found the strength to leave him, but then she'd taken the job as his assistant when he was elected to the Game Commission. She had a number of excuses: county jobs are stable and pay well, no one else would know how to handle Arthur as well as she did, she could leave any time if he got to be too much for her. Kimi had often wondered if the last of these were true.

Kimi snapped out of her reverie and glanced at the clock. She was about to complain when the door to the inner office opened. Arthur, six-foot tall and bald, swaggered forward with hat in hand. He leered at her with intimidating arrogance.

"Oh no you don't, Arthur," Kimi said, positioning herself between him and the door. "You're not going anywhere 'til we talk." He moved to push her out of the way, and she felt a wave of panic. "I've talked with the police chief." Her voice was piercing but insistent. "I've got rights and concerns, and I can force you to take them seriously." It wasn't exactly true, but she hoped her face didn't betray her. "I told her the entire story before I came here."

Arthur rolled his eyes but didn't touch her. "Calm down, Kimi." He spoke as if she were an irrational child. "Let's go into my office." He held the door open for her, and Kimi walked through.

She glanced back, meeting Adele's eyes over Arthur's shoulders. "Go get 'em." Adele mouthed, giving Kimi a thumbs-up. The door closed between them, but it didn't latch. Kimi knew Adele would hear everything.

Arthur's office was as unpleasant as he was. Piles of disheveled paper covered the desk, and books were stacked carelessly. Open soft drink cans littered every available space. She waited for Arthur to sit before she settled in the wooden chair that was in front of his desk. She placed her elbows on its well-worn arms and tented her fingers.

"I think you know why I'm here. Someone is killing my deer. I think it's suspicious that you're not doing anything to stop it."

Arthur held up his three-fingered hand. "You know, you're a real pain in my ass. How do I know you're not killing the deer yourself?"

"What?" Kimi had expected unpleasantness, but not an outrageous accusation. "I . . ."

"You're just like your grandfather with that short temper. It's not attractive on a woman."

Kimi was startled from her indignation. "If I'm like my grandfather, I'm honored." She sat up a little straighter. "You've always hated him, and now you're taking it out on me. He protected that land, and I'll follow in his footsteps until the day I die. I've waited far too long for you to do your job. Now I'm going to have to take matters into my own hands. Someone is killing deer for no perceptible reason. Neither meat nor antlers were taken. It's murder, plain and simple."

With the bony fingers he had left, Arthur tapped out a bit of rhythm on his large beer belly. "I can't help you. Won't help you, and neither will Dakotah. She's useless, and she knows it. If you don't like what's going on, I suggest you sell out."

Kimi felt her chin drop open for the second time that day. "Sell? Weren't you paying attention? That's the last thing I'd ever do!"

Arthur sat up and shot his jaw at her. "Sell, Kimi. Sell. Maintaining all those acres is too much work for one woman. Sell it to me. I'll give you a fair price."

Once Around the Sun

"Never. You make me sick. And I'll never sell. Never!" Kimi stood, her chair crashing to the floor. She turned, yanked open the office door, and stormed out not even acknowledging Adele as she passed.

Trees blurred as Kimi drove home. Her pulse raced with determination. No longer would she rely on others to help protect her land; she would do it herself. For the first time in months, Kimi felt in command of her true self. She did what was in her heart. Her grandfather had always said self-esteem could not be faked, but now she realized it could be remembered. And she had just remembered hers.

At home, Kimi changed into her well-worn jeans and flannel shirt. She made herself blackberry tea while considering her next move. Her thoughts kept skipping back to her meeting in the game warden's office. *Something is radically wrong with that man. I think there's more going on than he's letting anyone know.* Taking her tea to the porch, Kimi looked to the sky and noticed the gathering clouds. A cold front was moving in.

It was late afternoon and shadows were lengthening. Realizing she was wasting daylight, Kimi went to the small barn and grabbed a shovel. On her tractor, she headed to the feeding stations to dig out the blood and damaged foliage. The deer wouldn't feel safe to return until she finished.

Ahead in the meadow, she could see the flat rocks, held two feet off the ground by two-by-sixes pounded into the earth. Her tractor had lifted those rocks into place once the foundations were built. They worked fine for her purpose.

For the next two hours, Kimi dug up the blood-stained plants and threw them into the front-end loader. In another hour, she had replaced the ferns, split from the thick clumps close by. Smiling with satisfaction, Kimi spread corn on the level stones. The deer would come back as they had before, but they'd be more cautious for a while.

She walked toward the lake hoping to catch the last of the sunset, but paused when she was only a few steps away from the feeding stations. Something was wrong. She studied the ground. No question, the vegetation had been disturbed up ahead. Walking closer she bent and looked down onto some moss. "Is that a cross?" she said to the birds, bats, and peepers. It hadn't been there earlier, of that she was certain.

The next morning dawned, gray and drizzly. She gazed through the window from her loft and felt the weight of the promise she'd made to her grandfather. She needed to save something that was slipping away.

Tossing her quilt aside, Kimi sat on the edge of her bed. She took her time pulling on wool socks and a heavy sweatshirt. The aged ladder creaked under her as she descended the loft.

The phone rang, and Kimi started. "Damn it," she exclaimed. "I hate that thing!" She grabbed the cell from her backpack on the peg by the door and flipped it open.

"What?" She listened for a moment. It sounded like Arthur's voice. All she heard was slurred words, and then nothing. What the hell? She snapped it shut and hurled it across the room.

After toast and coffee, Kimi hiked out to her truck. Adele was coming to her cabin for dinner, but she didn't want to wait that long to talk to her. She needed to know what Arthur had done after she left his office.

Kimi could see Adele's familiar silhouette through a curtained window as she pulled into her lane. It was as if Adele were waiting for her to come by. Stepping from her truck, Kimi noticed the air smelled fragrant. Balsam. Oh, how she loved that aroma.

The door opened before she could walk in. "Hi, Kimi," said Adele, pulling her into a hug. "I had a feeling you might stop by. Have you heard anything more from Arthur?"

"I think he called this morning, but I'm not sure. He was hard to understand, so I hung up." Kimi took a seat in the small cozy room. "What happened after I left?"

"I quit." A grin spread across Adele's face. "I should have left years ago."

Once Around the Sun

"Good for you. He must have been shocked." Kimi jumped up and gave Adele another squeeze. "What's your plan now?"

Adele shrugged. "Not sure. I have enough money put away to get by for a while, and I don't have a mortgage, so I'll be fine. But—" she giggled with a lightness Kimi hadn't seen in months "—I feel unleashed for the first time in years. He was outraged, but he said he knows I'll be back. Fat chance of that."

"Well, good for you sweetie, I'm proud of you. Adele, did you know Arthur wanted to buy my land?"

"I recall hearing him talk about it once when we were still married," Adele said, running her fingers through the kinks in her wild hair.

"He's wanted it that long?"

Adele nodded. "Your property butts up against his, and for decades he's wanted to purchase a portion of it so he'd have access to the lake."

"How did this happen without my knowing?"

"Your grandfather told him no. I guess he didn't feel he needed to mention it to you at the time since he knew you'd never sell either."

"So what's changed? Why mention it now? Why neglect his job in the hope that I'll sell?"

Adele looked concerned. "After you left yesterday, I heard him talking to someone about establishing a hunting camp on his land. He'd need access to the lake. He plans to lure sportsmen in from Boston and Hartford."

"Oh God. No wonder he needs me to sell. Arthur wants to shoot my albino and have it on the front of his brochure." An idea popped into Kimi's mind. "Do you think it's possible he's behind the killings? Is it probable he *is* the poacher?"

Adele's eyes widened. "I'd never put it past him, not for a minute. Arthur is a dangerous man."

"If it is Arthur, he'd love to destroy the piebald and albino strain. He knows that would break my heart." Pushing off of the sofa arm, Kimi stood up. "I'm not going to let this happen. I'll spend every night in the woods if I have to, but I'm going to protect those deer."

Keeping Promises

* * *

Kimi drove back to her land with Adele's side of the story tumbling through her mind. *Good for her to quit*, she thought. *Arthur's an ass and a dangerous one at that. But sell my land? Not in this lifetime.*

She pulled her pickup into the turnaround, noticing fresh tire tread marks. "Someone's been here."

The wind rose, bringing a scent of the lake through the woods. Kimi made her way along the path, watchful for any indication of an unwanted visitor. She walked in the front door, wishing she'd bothered to lock it when she left. Nothing seemed out of place.

Resolved not to let a little paranoia ruin her day, Kimi reached for her largest pot to make stew for dinner. While chopping the veggies, she kept an eye to the woods beyond the window. "This is my bit of heaven, but trouble is brewing; my bones feel its heat," she muttered.

Setting the stew to simmer, Kimi went outside to check the deer feeders. She walked through the trees hearing the steady whine of a motor on the lake. She thought nothing of it as the sound came closer. The lake was large, and recreational boaters often launched from the public beach several miles down shore. When the noise indicated the boat was near, it stopped. Nothing. Silence. Kimi froze for a moment, then sprinted down the path. She bypassed the feeding stations and continued on to the lake. Concealing herself behind the tall reeds, Kimi carefully separated the stalks to see. There on the lake was the dot of a dark, flat-back canoe with a small outboard motor. A lone figure sat in the boat, but the distance was so great that Kimi couldn't make out whether it was a man or a woman. She cursed herself for not grabbing her binoculars. As she watched, the boat's engine coughed twice, then caught and sped away.

Perhaps the engine had just faltered near her land, but whoever that was, Kimi felt deep in her gut they would return. She walked back to the feeding stations, spread the corn, and then went home to the cabin. Adele was standing on the wide porch.

Once Around the Sun

"Hey, you!" exclaimed Adele. "Good thing I came; the stew needed stirring."

"Damn, Adele, I'm sorry," said Kimi, rubbing her lower back. "I heard a boat's engine stop in the middle of the lake. It made me suspicious, so I went for a look."

"Could you tell who it was?" Adele asked.

"Nope, just that it was a dark-colored canoe."

"Green, like a game warden's boat?" asked Adele.

"Exactly like that."

Kimi ladled the stew into two large bowls and brought them to the table. "We need to come up with a plan to protect the deer," she said once they were seated. "I don't want to kill anyone, only slow them down enough so I can tell who they are. Then we can report them to Dakotah."

"Good idea," said Adele. "You and I can be one tough pair when we put our minds to it." They talked for the next hour until they felt confident in their arrangement. It was an old snare trick, but one that had worked forever.

"Listen, I need to go home and get dark clothing and boots," Adele said, taking her empty bowl to the sink. "I'll meet you back here at midnight."

"I'll be here waiting. Stay safe, my friend."

Kimi wanted to wait until Adele arrived to go into the woods, but it occurred to her that she might get a glimpse of the albino if she ventured out on her own. She dressed in black clothing before leaving a note for Adele. Throwing a coil of rope over her shoulder, Kimi left the cabin. She walked in silence—listening.

The hike was longer in the dark, but Kimi would know her way even if there wasn't a slice of moonlight. She walked to where the moss had been crushed into a cross and paused to see if she could tell what made the impression. Nothing.

Reaching the feeding stations, Kimi placed a rope loop under the dead leaves on the path from the lake. Their trap was set. Holding the end of the line firmly in her gloved hands, Kimi moved behind a large grouping of laurel.

Keeping Promises

The dense night air smelled fragrant, almost sweet, and a lone mockingbird went through its playlist near the water's edge. All of this calmed her racing heart as she sat motionless on a dead log. The sliver of the moon rose higher, turning the setting into a ghostly blue-white scene.

A rustle in the leaves to the left snapped her to attention. She looked up to see Adele moving slowly toward her. Kimi waved, but Adele didn't notice. Kimi turned and saw the albino deer stepping cautiously toward the feeder. It moved slowly, then froze at a sound Kimi couldn't hear. Throwing its head up it sniffed the wind, looked toward the lake and then bolted away.

"Oh," Kimi said quietly, disappointed. She saw Adele turn in her direction and open her mouth.

"No!"

The blow to Kimi's head was sudden and agonizing.

Kimi drifted in and out of consciousness. Once, she realized she was no longer holding on to the rope. Another time she sensed the coppery taste of blood. Another she saw someone hovering over her.

She roused again at the distinct report of a rifle followed by a low-pitched guttural scream. Birds screeching. Women's voices. If only she could remember more. She struggled to sit up, but acute pain brought the darkness back.

Dakotah stood over Kimi with a backboard from her police car. "Let's roll her to the side and slide the board underneath," she said to Adele. In a couple of minutes, they had Kimi strapped on and were making their way down the path. Once they made it to Adel's SUV they opened the back hatch, slid Kimi inside and covered her with blankets.

"You take her to the hospital, but drive carefully." Dakotah said. "I need to stay here and call for backup. Hopefully this mess will all be handled by the time you get back."

"Right. I'm so glad you were there." Adele jumped into the driver's seat.

"I'm so glad you called me," Dakotah said as Adele started the car.

Once Around the Sun

* * *

Kimi smelled wood smoke before she opened her eyes. When she did, she squinted from the sunlight filtering through the window and saw her working fireplace. She lay there breathing in the familiar scent of her sheets. She remembered the hospital visit in town, the effort of steady and capable hands guiding her from truck to cabin, and the sound of a mattress being thrown from loft to floor. The God-awful pain. The blackness. She shuddered.

"The sun's up, and you're safe now," Adele whispered into Kimi's ear from their pillow.

"Tell me what happened, and please don't leave anything out."

"The poacher was in the woods. He hit you over the head. Luckily Dakotah was there to stop him. I called her on my way home after dinner. She said she'd come and keep watch with us. What a good friend she is turning out to be, Kimi. I knew we could trust her."

Kimi frowned; she didn't remember Dakotah being in the woods. "The fire pit?" she asked, unable to form a more coherent question.

"I took care of it. It wasn't the albino; focus on that. You can clean up the blood and foliage when you're up and about. It's going to take a while. Dr. Stevens from the ER said your concussion is borderline severe, but I could bring you home as long as you stayed quiet."

Kimi nodded, not wanting to know which of her precious deer had died. A recollection floated to her consciousness. "I had a dream last night. I saw the albino through the moonlight. She stopped in the middle of the place where the moss was beaten into a cross. But I realized it wasn't a cross, it was an intersection, where two paths had crossed over each other. I think Grandfather put them there to show me his path and mine . . . both of us together as one on this land."

"That's beautiful." Adele sighed.

"It's the truth." Kimi yawned and touched her mat of woven cedar bark. "Thank you, Grandfather."

"I want us to live together, Kimi, openly, to show the world who we are." Adele said. "Ours is not the only town that's been unfriendly toward women being partners, helping each other, loving each other. But times are changing. People are more open to women like us. We will have the opportunity to be an example. Perhaps you can write about it one day. But from now on I want us to share a home filled with love."

Kimi thought a moment. "I feel it's time," she answered, grabbing Adele's hand and bringing it to her chest. "We've been patient, but now we can share a meaningful life. I think it was meant to be, and Grandfather would have embraced us. Now our *two-spirit* hearts will join and be free, walking together like a living prayer."

Adele started to giggle. "I think we sound like two Native American women from long ago, gathered around a fire ring."

"You're right." Kimi closed her eyes to sleep, but she had one more question. "The poacher. Was it Arthur?"

"Yes. Dakotah shot him. He's alive to stand trial," Adele answered, covering them with the quilt. "Shhhhhh, rest now. You've honored your land . . . and your grandfather."

La Quebrada

Paul Weidknecht

As his mother wailed and moaned, Jorge realized she had passed into an emotional place that was beyond reason. Nothing he could say—short of telling her he wasn't going to work this day—would calm her. She was the one who always shushed the family whenever the clamor of some argument became too loud, concerned that the neighbors would hear their business through the wall they shared. Sound travels easily through cinder block, she said. But now, crying as she was, she seemed to have forgotten both where they lived and that she'd ever cared what the neighbors heard, or even what they would say afterward. Jorge knew children could talk their mothers from tears, but not from worry; that was impossible, and probably improper. Worry was a mother's right.

She held onto his hand with both of hers, pulling him back with her full weight, only his grip on the doorframe keeping him from being taken back into the shadows of their little house. It was a tug-of-war Jorge knew his mother would not win. With a turn of his wrist, he freed himself and crossed the grassless yard, the family's chickens flapping in panic, a yellow-gray dust rising from under their wings. The walk to the cliff was short, and the town would soon be behind him, his ocean in front of him. The last thing he saw was *Madre* crying in the doorway, a bunched handful of her apron in each fist, with his little sister, Rosa, at her side, confused and frightened by the things that cause adults to fight. Normally, he would have felt it necessary to turn back, make amends, but after what his mother had told him that morning, he continued on, guiltless.

Once Around the Sun

The driver of the Volkswagen Beetle taxi had the windows open, but Rob's shirt was pasted to his back; August in Mexico. Sitting in the back, he bumped shoulders with Lisa at every turn in the road. The highway followed the contour of the coast, and whenever they hit a straight stretch, Rob stared over the ocean. Farther out, the Pacific was flat and blue, but toward the shore, it became something different, slamming into the cliffs in an explosion of white foam, its spray darkening the lower half of the rocks, remnants of the wave trickling back into the ocean through countless cracks and fissures.

He glanced at Lisa. She was reading a tourism brochure. To Rob, the ocean seemed more interesting. Capture something well enough, and a photograph wasn't necessary. A truly good experience is always glorified by reminiscence.

The taxi driver seemed to be in his mid-fifties. His face was desiccated by the Mexican sun, but appeared open and friendly, and when he smiled up into the rear-view mirror, Rob saw he was missing a front tooth. Rob knew the man was doing his best to get them there on time. The driver explained there was only one daytime show, at one-thirty, so he raced.

Last night Rob and Lisa had stayed out late; easy to do in Acapulco. The club they'd gone to sat on a hillside, the dance floor portion perched on stilts. Floor-to-ceiling glass walls revealed a glittering panorama across the bay, as the lights of the city stretched around the shoreline, reaching up into the valleys until finally dotting to blackness farther into the mountains. Three-thirty brought the house fireworks display, the white embers dropping from the edge of the roof outside like rain during a heavy storm, cascading beads of light enclosing the dance floor in a curtain of brilliance. After this, Rob and Lisa called it a night.

The travel agent had told them Acapulco was a place to experience the real Mexico, although neither of them knew exactly what that meant. Maybe this wasn't the jet-set Acapulco of the '50s anymore, but they had gotten a great deal on the trip, and the city had done fine: in the past seven days, Rob had thought of work only three times.

"It says the divers jump from heights of over one hundred and fifteen feet, hitting the water at up to sixty miles an hour," Lisa said into the brochure. "And that they have to time the dive to coincide with the incoming surge of water, or it will be too shallow. Wow. Ten, twelve feet of water. That's all they're diving into."

"*Sí, señora,*" the driver said, looking up into the mirror. "Very much danger."

Lisa continued. "It says *La Quebrada* means 'The Gorge' or 'The Ravine,' but that the verb, *quebrar,* means 'to break.' Not a good name for a place if you dive from cliffs."

"These *clavadistas,*" the driver said, "they train with fathers, uncles, brothers. For many years."

Eddie, from Rob's office, had told him about having visited Acapulco in the early eighties and seeing young men in wheelchairs near the cliffs asking tourists for tips during show times. The image of a diver hitting the base of the cliff and sliding into the water came into Rob's mind. He shook it off, concentrating on the ocean, the calm part, out to sea.

Jorge walked down the road, thinking of the conversation he'd had with his mother earlier, before her hysteria. Because she had asked him to sit with her at the kitchen table, and this right after his father had left for work, he thought it was something important. He was mistaken.

"You were about to dive, and I was standing next to you on the cliff," his mother had said.

"Were you wearing your bathing suit or your dress?" Jorge asked.

"This is not funny. This is my dream, Jorge, one that was given to me to tell you. It could be a symbol or a warning, maybe from God, and you will listen. So, we are next to each other, and I look down into the ravine. Then something moved to my right, out toward the ocean, and I looked. Men were building a dam at the mouth of the inlet."

"Did you tell them they were taking my job from me?"

Once Around the Sun

"Stop it, now! There were workers and trucks moving across the top of this dam. It was concrete, huge. I turned back to the ravine, and the water was gone. The bed of the inlet was dry and cracked as if the water had never been there. I saw you push off from your perch, your head down, arms out. I tried to grab you, but missed. You were in air."

Her dream was ridiculous and, like nearly every dream, it made no sense except as a muddled collection of fragments with something understandable only here and there. She probably had that same dream other nights and had simply forgotten it by morning. She may have even had a remembrance of one of these forgotten dreams—that recollection that happens during the day—and decided to say nothing.

In any case, she was convinced it was a premonition. Jorge remembered studying her face as she recalled the dream, her pausing now and then, mouth half-open, scouring her memory for something sudden, any scrap of information that would enlighten, or more importantly, caution.

He got her to agree that the images were strange, but she refused to say they were ridiculous. She didn't want him to go to the cliffs today. Diving another day was all right, but not today.

But Jorge had been a *clavadista* for the past five years now. His uncle—her own brother—had trained him. The family enjoyed the benefit of his money just as much as they did *Padre's*. When he got to the cliffs he would pray for his two minutes then dive. That was it. He would do what others were too afraid to do, do what others fantasized about doing, but could not. Standing on the ground looking up is not the same view as standing on the rocks looking down. He would not be like the rest of them, pedaling his bicycle downtown to work in some restaurant or hotel, refilling someone's glass with water or lingering for a *propina* after carrying a suitcase. He was glad for his friends that they had jobs, but such work was not for him. He loved what he did, and how many people could say that?

Jorge heard something behind him. Quick footsteps, hurried. He turned to see Rosa running up in her pink polyester shorts and a white T-shirt with a faded iron-on of a puppy on it. A corner of the iron-on was starting to peel off in a rubbery flap. He waited until she caught up.

"What are you doing here?"

"She sent me," Rosa said, out of breath.

Jorge made a face. "You're nine."

"She is worried. And crying."

"She worries for no reason, over some stupid dream." He pointed to the ground. "This road is more dangerous. I could get killed by some *borracho*."

"You don't know if it's stupid or not."

Jorge put up his hand. "I will tell you something. There is always construction going on in this city. Someone is always building something. She saw that, and she knows I dive. She put the two together in her mind, and that was her dream. Now go back home."

Rosa stared at him, frowning.

"*Vé a casa. Ahora!*" he said. He was already walking away and pointing back in the direction of their house.

Rosa scowled and snapped around, stomping back up the road. She glanced back once and kept going.

Jorge stopped and turned back at Rosa. She was fifty meters off, her small body moving away in sharp steps.

"Rosa!"

She continued. He rolled his eyes. He knew she could hear him.

"Rosa!"

She spun around, her head canted. "What?

"Walk more away from the road."

"I know, we always feel the same way at the end of a trip," Lisa said. "The last day of vacation is like a day of work. Preparing to leave, getting everything together."

Rob stared out the window then turned to his wife. "I guess I'm looking at it differently this time. We always say we're going to leave our jobs, do something new, be our own bosses. Truth is, it never happens. We get back into the rut, get used to our paychecks—half thankful they didn't replace us while we were away—needing the money to pay off our trip. And, of course, we'll continue working so we can pay for *another* week of vacation to forget a whole *new* set of problems at work."

"Vacation is fantasy, not real life, Rob. Other people work while we sit around and do nothing for a week then we switch. Maybe that's the way it's supposed to be," Lisa said, shrugging. "Everybody takes a turn."

"I'd like a little longer turn."

"We still have some way to go," the driver said. He wiped the sweat from his forehead with the back of his hand then dried it on the leg of his pants. "It will be close for you to see them."

The car rounded a curve, sending Rob into Lisa and Lisa into the side of the car.

The driver looked up into his mirror at them. "You are in Acapulco. You must see the *clavadistas*."

Jorge looked down from the top of the cliff. If there was a symbol to be found, that cliff was it, he thought. *That* had meaning, not some dream.

Slope and angle did not permit diving from the entire face, but jutting from the bleached gray wall as if cemented into place was an outcrop of yellow rock perfectly positioned over the water.

God had given him a gift, a talent. Jorge honored that gift and could not waste it. Certainly he'd never fear it.

Jorge would dive from the highest platform after everyone else had taken their dives from the lower points. Felix and Enrique had already gone. The tourists on the walled observation terrace clapped and held video cameras on them as they clawed hand over hand through the roiling water toward the rocks below. Reaching the rocks, the two divers looked up at Juan, who stood on a pedestal of stone only large enough for his calloused feet to fit with his ankles touching. Except for his rounded shoulders, he looked like a statue. Then he went. Seconds after knifing into the water, his head of black hair appeared in the boil and an arm swung out to the crowd.

La Quebrada

After seeing his friends dive, Jorge turned and walked several steps back to the shrine of pastel-blue stone and white masonry. Kneeling on the steps before the shrine, he prayed. His mother always told him to pray before diving, but he never needed the reminder—at the place of the broken, you always pray. Two minutes later he opened his eyes and stood.

At the precipice, whether at the lower platforms or here at the highest, he thought only of the dive and those things that affected it: his form, the surge into the cove, the wind. Everything else was distraction.

The bright sun caused his shadow to fall dark and defined on the platform. Under his feet, the cliff was warm. He looked to his right, out to sea, the place where his mother had dreamed of people, construction, and a dam.

He saw people. Of course, there were people; pleasure boats always sat at the mouth of the cove to watch the divers perform. It was no different now. Boats bobbed in the chop, chrome horns and railings flashing silver. How many were there? Six, seven boats today? On the platform, he never looked at the boat people, or anyone else, but now he did, and he wondered why. He looked elsewhere.

To the left, on the plaza far below, a taxi pulled up, just above the steps leading down to the terrace. The passenger door popped open. First a woman, then a man, squeezed past the folded-down front seat. The woman ran for several steps, a swishing jog, before stopping and bringing a camera to her face. The man paid the driver and wandered toward the woman, his head tilted back, a hand shading his eyes. *Welcome to La Quebrada*, he thought.

Past his feet, Jorge watched the sea rush into the cove, pale green near the sides, darker in the middle. At that moment, it occurred to him that he had never asked her how the dream ended, or what happened to her on the cliff when she reached out, and he felt a tinge of guilt ripple through him.

He was in air.

Fall

Only a Game

Jerome W. McFadden

Being the high school football coach of East Jesus, Texas (*Team motto: Don't Cross Us*) was not a great job. We had exactly twelve kids on the team, and one of those was a girl.

Because of the great distances involved, and the lack of a school bus, we had only three games scheduled. Two of those were on the same day. But that was just a scheduling screw up that no one noticed or thought much about until I was hired.

I brought up the fact that the locker rooms' hot water tank wasn't going to produce enough hot water on the same day for two sets of boy showers, plus two extra ones for Margaret, our female player. And nobody wanted to drive home sixty miles or more with a really smelly, tired, cranky kid—who probably had chores to do the moment he (or she) got back to the farm.

The coach at the other high school, General George Custer (*Team motto: Bring It On!*), understood and agreed to reschedule.

The next crisis was the field. We didn't have one. Neither did our opponents. Our first choice was the school parking lot, but that was going to be confusing with all of the permanent white lines for the parking slots already painted on it. But an argument was made that the blue lines for the handicapped slots made a natural end zone. However, if we played in the parking lot, where would we park all of the cars?

So we moved to the adjacent field, old Mr. Detweiler's cow pasture. Old Mr. Detweiler said he didn't mind, but he had nowhere else to put the cows, so we were just gonna have to shoo them off to the side of the field whenever we wanted to practice or play. Of course, that also meant that we were gonna have to shovel and clean the cow patties from the area we wanted to play on. Old Mr. Detweiler said that wasn't his problem.

The kids were more enthusiastic about clearing that field than I thought they might be. But I shoulda known they were gonna turn it into a manure throw. A few got to seeing how far they could hurl a cow patty. The older, dried-up patties worked best—if you used the discus technique. But, of course, a couple of other kids went for accuracy (wet patties work better here) and that degenerated into an all-out brawl. I didn't stop it though as I thought it brought the team closer together, which is important in any sport.

Equipment also turned out to be a bit of a problem, too. We didn't have any. The helmet part was easy: All of the kids scrounged their bicycle helmets or their older brothers' motorcycle helmets, and we painted them all purple (*our school mascot—the Purple Sage Brushes*) and added big white numbers on the side. Any number they wanted from one to ninety-nine. Our art/social/history/English teacher used that as an art project, encouraging the kids to paint on skulls and crossbones, lightning bolts, or some other menacing symbols. Margaret painted pink hearts and kisses on hers, which scared the hell out of everyone else on the team.

Team jerseys (we didn't have any of those either) were easily resolved. The mothers, aunts, and grandmothers knitted them. However, I forgot to tell them to coordinate the number on the jersey with the numbers on their kid's helmet, so that caused a bit of confusion when we finally got on the field. But the worst problem was that if an opponent missed his (or her) tackle but got his (or her) fingers caught in a knitting loop, which was easy to do, the jersey would unravel all of the way to the end zone. We compensated for this by having the women knit several backups for each game.

Shoulder pads turned out to be the real challenge. The only sporting store we had in a hundred fifty mile radius was Cabela's, and they mostly stocked fishing and hunting clothes, outdoor gear, camouflage tents, and hiking boots.

Robbie Shelmbacher's father hobbled a set of pads together from some short wood slats leftover from some fencing he had done around the farm house, but it came out kind of mean, like putting brass knuckles inside your boxing gloves. But at least he had taken the nails out.

Little Tommie Sooner came up with the best solution. His Aunt Beaula's brassieres were big enough to stretch across the back of his small neck, one generous cup covering each shoulder. Fill them full of old rags and cast off T-shirts, and you were ready to go.

That, too, became a team project. However, not all of the mothers or other women had Aunt Beula's proportions, so the boys started going into the East Jesus Dollar Store (used to be a five-and-ten) to pick up the bigger sizes. But they were too shy to buy them, so they started to shop lift the super sizes.

The manager, Mr. Clarendon, caught on pretty quick, but he was a team supporter, so he just sent me the bill. I tried to turn the bill in as an expense but got a nasty note back from the school business administrator in which she said: *You are an ugly pervert, and if you don't stop this I will inform the school board.*

But what worried me even more was to hear the boys talking about Nylon versus Elastane versus Rayon versus cotton, and padded cups versus lift-up cups, and under-wires. A couple of them even suggested we drive all the way into Amarillo to visit Victoria's Secret, but I told them if we were gonna drive all the way to Amarillo, we might just as well buy regular shoulder pads. All they said to that was "Oh," kinda disappointed.

We didn't practice much, considering we only had twelve kids. We could practice either offense, or defense, but not both at the same time. So we brought over a few of Old Mr. Detweiler's cows. They just stood there staring at us blankly not quite understanding what they were supposed to do, but they gave us something to run around, like blocking dummies. Occasionally one of them skittered, knocking down a kid or two, which is as close we got to full contact.

The first game against Moses, Texas, (*Team motto: Watch Our People Go*) came a little sooner that I would have liked. But I was relieved to see they weren't any better equipped that we were. We managed to line out the field and chase the cows away that thought they were gonna get to play and set up a portable blackboard as the scoreboard and whistled for the game to begin.

The Moses halfback almost ran the opening kickoff all the way back on us, but Margaret stopped him cold on the forty yard line. He jumped up and ran off the field and wouldn't come back, yelling that the kid who just tackled him was wearing lipstick.

I called a quick time out and told Margaret that, to paraphrase the old Tom Hanks movie, "There's no lipstick in football." She wiped it off but glared across the field and yelled at their halfback, "I'll still kick your ass!" He refused to play.

On the next play, their other halfback almost ran around our end but slipped on a fresh cow patty that we had overlooked and slid out through the sidelines, taking out a row of folding chairs the Moses supporters were sitting in. The referee wanted to run the play again, but our principal argued that that was our well-known "Defecation Defense," and the play should stand. Their coach was so angry that he couldn't even respond, so the play stood.

They were so discouraged by now that they wasted the next two plays, and we took over the ball. Margaret knocked their guard on his butt, and little Tommie Sooner scooted through the opening and ran ten yards before anyone could catch him.

He was the only one who noticed that one of the cows had come back on the field, and darted around it just like at practice. All three of their defensive backs didn't see it and ran smack into the cow's side, knocking it over and sprawling across it. Old Mr. Detweiler happened to be watching the game and came out bellowing about him not agreeing to any "cow tipping" and that everyone "should just get the hell off my field."

The game was over. But the referee ruled that little Tommie Sooner had scored before the game was called, so it was East Jesus 6, Moses 0. Our first win.

The other coach was still angry but rational. He suggested we go inside and play basketball, even though it was a bit early in the season. They had driven all this way, and it was a shame to waste the day. As I was also going to be our basketball coach, I thought it was a reasonable suggestion. But I took Margaret aside before the game, as she was going to be our starting center, to tell her there was no lipstick in boy's basketball either. She made a face and asked, "When we gonna get to a sport that has lipstick in it?"

I patted her gently on the shoulder and said, "I think you're gonna get there real soon, but I ain't gonna be coaching it."

We canceled the rest of the football season as we no longer had a field to play on—neither did they. But the basketball season went well. We kept the cows out of the gym and won more than half our games. Margaret even got a basketball scholarship, but she was sorely disappointed that it was *just* for the girls' team.

I gave her a tube of lipstick as a going away present.

Prisons and the Digital Age

In my most innocent and well-mannered voice, I apologized. "I will stop now and not do it again, cross my Redheaded heart," I said, adding a solemn promise that now I would be on my merry way.

"Nope, ain't happening. You need to wait here until my boss comes to check into this matter."

"Corporal Klinger" (the names have been changed to protect the innocent, in other words, me) showed up and again asked me what I was doing.

This was my first chance to explain myself, so I proceeded to tell him the long tale of sightseeing and digital photographing and trail riding.

Things were starting to look up until "Sergeant Schultz" appeared, and I had to repeat the story again. Once more I told my tale. This time I made the mistake of trying to explain the digital camera side of this. I showed him the pictures that I had taken of the prison, of which there was the grand total of—yes, you guessed it—*one*!

I don't believe these three gentlemen understood anything about a digital camera versus an older-style, traditional-film, thirty-five millimeter camera because the threats started at this point, ranging from taking the film, to taking the camera, to taking me.

Thankfully, they stopped short of threatening to take my mother. However, my seventy-five year old mother's maternal instinct must have kicked in at this point as she waded into the fray.

My mother rose to her full five-foot height and began to explain that she had grown up in this area. Somehow the phrase Graterford Prison came into the conversation, go figure, and my sweet, saintly Redheaded mother started vehemently arguing with the prison guards about, and I kid you not, the pronunciation of the town's name: Graterford.

Using a salty tone that reminded me of the times when she'd begin scolding me with a crisply enunciated, "William Jeffrey Baird," she proceeded to correct the numerous *armed* prison guards as to how to correctly pronounce the name of Graterford Prison.

Once Around the Sun

This, of course, eased tensions considerably, as she brought all of her motherly skills to bear on the disagreement. Apparently she'd never learned Pig Latin or was choosing to ignore my whispered pleas to "ixnay on the arguway" with the armed guards.

During all of this time, I continued trying to plead my case about the mistake with the digital camera and explain how I easily could erase the one picture, but they weren't being very "Twenty-First Century."

It wasn't until "Lieutenant Dreben" showed up that I had someone who understood anything about digital cameras. I knew I'd be okay because of his close-cropped red hair, and the fact that he flashed the Redheaded Brotherhood Gang sign. I finally felt I could communicate with someone on my own level.

I showed the lieutenant the camera, displaying the "before and no after" picture. He was about to let me delete the picture when they got word that their captain was on his way to the scene of the crime, and to wait for him before making any kind of decision. So close yet so far!

When "Captain Kirk" showed up, I was immediately in fear for my life. As I watched him put on his hat, I gazed upon his blond hair. Blonds and Redheads, Yankees and Red Sox, need I say more? So there you have it folks; once "Captain Kirk" arrived I had a total of five, I repeat, five *armed* prison guards surrounding little old me and my saintly mother.

While we waited, a heated debate took place about what to do with us. We caught bits and pieces of the conversation, words and phrases such as "confiscate," "Redhead," and "make an example."

We continued to wait while they ran a check on my license plate. At this point, they whiled the time away by asking me questions about where I was from; I believe to determine if indeed I were a true Redhead. I must have passed the test because it was then that they graciously permitted me to delete the picture and let us go, thus giving a happy ending to our adventure.

Prisons and the Digital Age

As we drove off into the sunset, what do you think we saw on our way out to civilization? That's right—the sign to the prison informing passersby that this area was off-limits. It was right next to the sign warning about the dangers of picking up hitchhikers and that photographs are strictly prohibited.

So in closing, if anyone has any questions about joining the twenty-first century and the benefits of using a digital camera, let me offer my own bit of sage advice. Go digital. It could keep you out of prison.

Gramma, How Could You?

Carol A. Hanzl Birkas

"I found it! I *knew* they would still have it," exclaimed my nine-year-old granddaughter.

She plucked a book from the shelf in the children's section of the bookstore and hugged it to her chest. "I wanted this book for a long time, but my mom said it was too expensive."

"Twenty-three dollars *is* a lot of money, Tabitha," I said after scanning the back cover for the retail price.

"But look, Gramma, it's about wizards and magic, and it comes with a magic wand and *everything*. It'll be just perfect for Halloween." The pleading look in her big brown eyes begged for my approval.

"I told you I would buy it for you, sweetheart. As long as it's age-appropriate, it's yours. May I see it?" I asked, reaching for the book.

The Wandmaker's Guidebook was more than just a book. It sported an attractive, leather-like hard cover embedded with sparkling, colored jewels. Inside were twenty-four faux-parchment pages, a pull-out drawer containing a wooden wand with a removable handle, bright-colored feathers, and little pots of glittery multi-colored sand and stones. I could easily see why my granddaughter would be so impressed with it.

"Here, Tab," I said, handing it back to her. "Let's go buy your book."

Tabitha was spending the weekend with her grandfather and me. With Halloween just a few days away, Tabby was caught up in the spirit of the holiday. We had mapped out our plans for the weekend over the telephone. They included:

1. A taco dinner that she and I would make together
2. Going to the bookstore to get her special Halloween book
3. Watching *Wizards of Waverly Place: The Movie* on the Disney Channel.

Tabby had already seen the movie and was very anxious to watch it again with me.

The taco dinner went well; I'm not sure which part she enjoyed most, making the tacos or eating them. The bookstore also proved to be a huge success. Tabitha was thrilled with her book.

She sat Indian-style in the middle of my bed with the book's contents spread out all around her. Short, dark hair framed her pixie face, now scrunched up in concentration as she studied the instructions.

"It says I can create my own powers. All I have to do is choose what I want to put into the wand." Her eyes wide with anticipation, she twisted off the handle and filled the wand with the treasures she liked best. She carefully replaced the handle, then flicked the wand, sprinkling the air and everything around her with glittery fairy dust.

"Abracadabra," she shrieked excitedly, waving it again as she danced around the room with childhood abandon.

I sat there watching my youngest grandchild, amazed at just how enchanted she was, caught up in her whimsical world of make-believe. A sudden thought came to me, and I laughed out loud.

Tabitha was named after the little witch girl in the old television show, *Bewitched*. How perfectly that name fit her at this moment; if my daughter could only see her own little witch girl now.

When it was time for the movie, she placed the wand back inside the book and set it down on the bed between us.

Wizards of Waverly Place: The Movie was about wizards waving wands, casting spells, and making magic. No wonder Tabby wanted that book so badly. She loved the movie

Gramma, How Could You?

and was totally engrossed in it. But the long day was catching up with me, after a while I found myself becoming very sleepy. I could hardly keep my eyes open. I asked Tabby to turn the volume down a little.

"No, Gramma," she pleaded. "I don't want you to fall asleep. I want you to watch this with me."

How could I say no? She'd been looking forward to this for a week. I just had to find a way to keep myself awake. Unbeknownst to my granddaughter, I had an extra remote on the bedside table next to me. I picked it up, unobserved, and lowered the volume just a bit. Tabitha sat straight up.

"Gramma, the TV just turned itself down." I didn't say a word. She turned it back up. After a short time, I lowered the volume again. It didn't work. She turned it back up. We were struggling for power—strange that I should use that phrase—only Tabby had no idea what was really going on.

Wanting to see what she would do, I impishly changed the channel then quickly changed it back again. She bolted up, grabbed her book, and ran out to the living room where her grandfather was watching television. Amused, I heard her say, "Pop, can we leave this book out here with you? We're having a problem with it."

At this point, I was finding it so hard not to laugh out loud that I had to bite my lip to maintain my composure. She padded back to my room, climbed up on the bed, and said, "Let's see what happens now." And she turned the volume up again. I waited for her to settle.

God knows I should have left well enough alone. But curiosity got the best of me. I flipped the channel and then changed it back. I immediately regretted it. Tabby's face went white; her big eyes widened with fear. I hated myself at that moment. Without meaning to, I had scared the living daylights out of my little granddaughter.

I quickly showed her that I had an extra remote, and told her that *I* was making the TV act strangely, that it was *not* doing it by itself. I assured her that there was *absolutely no magic involved.* I apologized profusely. I explained that I was not trying to scare her; that I had no idea how what I was doing was affecting her.

Oh, she got it all right.

She glared at me. "Gramma, how could you?"

Then she stomped out of the room, retrieved her book, and brought it back into the bedroom. She wouldn't even look at me. Had she the power of her namesake, I'm sure she would have rubbed the side of her little nose and made me disappear.

She was very upset with me, and rightfully so. She trusted me with all her heart, and in her mind, I had really let her down. I was *so* sorry. But she was having none of it.

"You tricked me," she said furiously. She stared at me icily with "I hate you eyes," then she stormed out to tell her Pop what her Gramma had done to her.

In an effort to soothe her, I made her a cup of hot chocolate. She drank it, but she still was not happy with me. I promised her that I would never do anything again that would make her mistrust me.

She must have gotten over it a little because I was able to persuade her to come back to the bedroom and go to sleep—*with a very bright nightlight on.*

I did make it up to her the next day. I took her to her favorite restaurant, one we only visited on birthdays and special days, and treated her to a virgin strawberry daiquiri and a scrumptious crab-leg dinner. It was a meal fit for the princess that she was, and she thoroughly enjoyed it. When nothing remained but an empty glass and a basket of crab shells, she looked at me from across the table with a foxy little grin on her face.

"What's so funny, Tab?" I asked.

"I was just thinking that Halloween started a few days early this year," she said. "Last night I got the *trick*, and today I got the *treat*." Then she came around the table, and, giving me a big hug, she said, "Do you think next year we could just skip the trick part?"

As I smiled at her, I said a silent prayer of thanks. I also thanked God for working His own special brand of magic;

creating this adorable child and making her a part of my life.

A grandmother-grandchild relationship is truly magical. And from now on, I will leave well enough alone. The next time I am fortunate enough to have my granddaughter want me to watch a movie with her, no matter how tired I may be, I *will* watch the movie.

The Little Ghost Who Couldn't Say Boo

Courtney Annicchiarico

Once upon a time, high up on a mountain where the sun was scared to shine, was a school for ghosts. They took classes like boo-ology, ecto-nomics, and public shrieking. But the most important skill every ghost student had to master was how to deliver an ultra-scary boo.

Every day, the halls were filled with the echoes of boos. Some were loud and fast like thunder and lightning, some were low and stretched out like taffy. Some upper-level ghosts knew how to knock stuff over or shake chains with their boos. Others used their pets—black cats and bats mostly—to amp up the spookiness of their boos.

But there was one little ghost who couldn't say boo.

Every time Gossamer tried, his boo came out as baaah, just like a lamb. He tried and tried to be like everyone else. He wanted to be scary, but mostly, he didn't want all the other ghosts to laugh at him anymore.

One night, Gossamer and his only friend, Twilight, wandered down the mountain. Twilight wasn't very scary either. She was Gossamer's gray cat, and she preferred to purr rather than hiss. They explored caves and played hide and seek. They chased fireflies and raced along a stream.

"Do you hear something?" Twilight asked, shaking herself off after an unexpected tumble into the water. Her ears stood straight up. "I think . . . it's crying."

Gossamer stopped short. "People who are already frightened are easy to scare more. I don't have to say baaah. I can just fly around. Come on, Twilight."

Once Around the Sun

Gossamer floated through trees and soared toward the source of the crying. He soon discovered a little boy, his cheeks red and streaked with tears, whimpering in the dark.

"Gossamer," Twilight panted as she caught up to her friend. "I think he's lost. He's all alone. Don't scare him more."

Gossamer looked at the boy. He was very young, and it would be so easy. But Gossamer knew how it felt to be alone.

"Go run ahead, Twilight. See if you can find his family." While his little cat was away, Gossamer watched the little boy and scared away any spiders or bats that got too close. After a long while, Twilight reappeared.

"There are people in the woods. A woman is crying. They're all running in circles, though. They'll never find him, Gossamer," Twilight said, worry making her voice squeaky. "What are we going to do?"

Gossamer swooped down to get a closer look, careful not to be seen. The little boy's ripped overalls had a dog on the front. The shirt underneath had blue paw prints all over it. *I've got it*, Gossamer thought. He returned to where his cat waited. "Lead the way, Twilight. I'll get him to follow us."

Gossamer flew up high, so the little boy wouldn't see him, and slowly started flying ahead. "Baa-ah," he called softly. The boy's head lifted, and he looked around. "Baa-ah," Gossamer repeated. The little boy stopped crying and stood up. "Baa-ah."

The boy took a step forward, and then another. *It's working.* Very slowly, Gossamer led the boy to the side of his crying mother.

And with the family's shouts of joy fading behind them, Gossamer and Twilight went back up the mountain. Gossamer smiled as he got to the school. He knew that he would never be scary, and he would never be like everyone else. *But*, Gossamer thought, *that could be a very good thing.*

Mortified

Will Wright

I remember, it started the Halloween my frat brothers hauled a keg out to Woodland Cemetery. While I'm as brave as the next guy—or at least some of the next guys, I spent the night in front of the tube. Why go to a graveyard on the one night of the year when the dead are supposed to rise?

The next morning I felt like a coward. Why was I shy about graveyards? What was I worried about: ghosts, zombies, vampires? I wasn't a child anymore. I was a grad student. It was time to do something stupid.

Anyway, it was All Saints Day. Wasn't that supposed to be an undead-free holiday?

That night, Woodland didn't look very spooky, though it wasn't exactly tidy. Toilet paper hung limply from a marble Jesus, as it did from a massive oak tree. Beer cans leaned against William A. Mayberry's (1870-1921) stone. That had to be high school kids. Even the dead won't drink Coors Light.

Meeting Godfrey gave me a start. Suddenly he was just there, standing straight but not stiff. His clothes were perfect without looking metrosexual. Even the wind didn't bother his natural-looking, perfect hair.

Of course, I hated him immediately. He extended a manicured hand and flashed a cold smile.

"Godfrey Hamilton."

"Stan Plotz," I said, shaking his cold hand and feeling inferior. It reminded me of shaking the priest's hand after Mass. "You're very nicely dressed for graveyard walking," I said.

Once Around the Sun

I was just saying something to make noise. What did I know about graveyard-walking attire? Was there a uniform, maybe from a business fashion magazine? What would that be, *Graveyard Quarterly*?

"First impressions are important, Stanley," Godfrey answered. "People judge you by your outward appearance. They'll never take the time to appreciate your finer points if your presentation shows a lack of self-respect." Pausing, he took in my flannel shirt, grass-stained blue jeans, Demon Deacon jacket, and three-year-old Nikes.

So much for my "presentation."

"You're a grad student?" he asked.

"Yes."

"That would be MBA or law school?"

I'd been turned down for both, so I lied. "No, I decided not to go the money route. I'm getting my MSW at Wake."

"Master of Social Work." Godfrey frowned. "Yes, I suppose it's important to have qualified people in every field."

I felt vindicated. Why, I didn't know.

"As long as you're striving," said Godfrey, "to be the best you can be each and every day."

One never knows what to say when encountering a Dale Carnegie cultie. I hated him more, but I sucked in my gut and straightened my jacket. Then, rebelliously, I unstraightened, earning another frown from Godfrey. I'll be damned if I'll change my appearance to earn the approval of some upper-crust Ken doll.

"So, Mr. Hamilton," I said in what I hoped was a superior tone, "why is it so important to give a good first impression to perfect strangers one meets in a graveyard?"

Godfrey showed no sign of irritation. "Well, Mr. Plotz, in some cases, hardly important at all." He gave me a glance that made it clear I fell in that category. "However, once in a while you'll run across a more formidable type. It's important to keep them off balance so you can do this—"

I was flooded with a mix of sensations and emotions. Incredibly powerful hands grabbed me by my head and shoulder. I felt a sharp, two-pointed stab in my neck. Racing through my head was fear, anger, embarrassment, and the feeling that this all would be a lot better for my self-esteem if Godfrey had been a hot woman.

Everything went black.

It took a few moments to realize that I was no longer unconscious. It was that dark. The air was stuffy, and I had a disgusting flat taste in my mouth. I shifted to ease a lump in my back and bumped into walls to my right and left.

That's when I heard an odd muffled sound, like someone else's phone conversation bleeding through the line. It seemed to be a human voice or a number of human voices. It sounded far away and close at the same time. There was a musical quality to it like singing or, more accurately, chanting. I strained my ears to hear the words, but the harder I strained, the less distinct they became. Whatever I was hearing, it wasn't with my ears.

Did I have a new sensory organ? I touched my face expecting to feel a lump or mutant zit. There wasn't anything there, but the chanting got louder. What do you do with a new sense? I had no recollection of using my eyes or ears for the first time. Maybe that's why babies sometimes look so thoughtful.

Reaching up, I felt cushioned fabric. I was in a pretty tight space. Normally I'd be trembling with claustrophobia. I was never good with closets, elevators, or even small cars, but I felt fine, even comfortable. I pushed against the ceiling. I heard wood cracking and metal complaining as I pushed the roof several inches. Did I just do that? I'd never been particularly strong, as every bully in my middle school could tell you. Maybe the wood was rotten? Freshly turned soil and sand poured down on my face.

The voices were clearer now, and much louder. Working my way through dirt and debris, I got to my knees, then to a crouch. I reached up 'til I felt a breeze on my fingertips. The earth parted above me like water, but when my hands gripped the topsoil, the ground held.

I stretched to loosen tight muscles. It was a delicious sensation. I felt both light and strong. With one heave, I not only cleared the surface, but sailed several feet into the air, landing majestically on a stone.

A grave stone.

My grave stone.

So this meant what, I was a vampire?

Some might have been horrified, but I felt great. I was a lord of the night. No more fear of brawny troglodytes like those who had, a decade past, beaten me with my own violin case. I was now a creature to be feared. Gathered around me was my new brotherhood, fellow members of a mighty pack. I was secure in our mutual admiration. Why else would they be gathered to sing me out of my grave, imbue me with their mighty spirit, and . . . laugh?

Around me, the dread fraternity of vampires rolled about, cackling like so many Shriners at a whoopee cushion trade show.

"Plotz," Godfrey said, "you haven't any pants on."

It was true. I was in my best shirt, tie, and suit coat, but with nothing but boxers below. I suppose I should have been grateful for the boxers, but I didn't feel gratitude at that moment.

"Who did this!" I sputtered.

The vampires laughed even louder. Godfrey, however, only snickered. "Plotz," he said, "you might want to check with your undertaker."

"How do I do that?"

"The cemetery office. You're newly buried; there'll be a file."

I disliked Godfrey Hamilton, even in my newly glorified state. I was also afraid of him, but I took his advice.

The file identified my undertaker as Mr. Feeley Nuzbetch, who ran his establishment in the West End. I knew the place—up the hill from Burke Street Pizza.

There was a light burning downstairs at the Feeley Nuzbetch Funeral Parlor. I didn't have a watch on, maybe Feeley took that, too, but it felt really late or, more likely, really early morning.

I went to the door and silently broke the deadbolt. I planned to sneak in and spring on Nuzbetch. That's what vampires do, right? I opened the door, but I couldn't cross the threshold. I'd heard something about thresholds and vampires. Breaking into the cemetery office hadn't been a problem, but no one lived there. Maybe this was Nuzbetch's home.

That was sort of creepy. I tried to imagine living in a house with a continuous flow of dead bodies. Of course, I was dead now, so I guess I had no reason to be judgmental.

I circled the building. Through a window, I saw a pudgy man in his fifties or sixties. He was working on a body using a machine with tubes attached. The process fascinated me. It also made me hungry. Then I realized–the man was wearing my pants.

And my pants fit the guy. I couldn't be as fat as he was. Maybe he had them tailored.

Something nagged at me. A clock inside read five-fifteen. What time did the sun come up?

I wondered if the government kept records of vampires' mortality or re-mortality on their first dawn.

Maybe you got a mulligan if the sun toasted you on your first night out.

Maybe not.

If dawn meant certain death, or whatever it's called when dead people expire, how much longer could I afford to stand by this window in my boxer shorts watching this pants-altering mortician? If I didn't do something soon, Nuzbetch would find himself a matching jacket. But where could I go? I looked around me. There were plenty of homes I couldn't get into. There were also shops and restaurants, but even if I could enter those, they might not appreciate a corpse resting the business day away. Even worse, they might move my body, and once outside—

So where to go? Saint Paul's Episcopal?

Too chancy.

Inside, Feeley shut down the machine and pulled a large plastic bucket from beneath the bench. He headed toward the back of the building. Silently, I moved with him.

Once Around the Sun

Should I cross my fingers? Crossing anything was probably not a good idea for a vampire.

Before the door opened, I smelled blood in the bucket Nuzbetch had been carrying. I could also smell the mortician's blood. His was more appetizing, like prime rib holding a bucket of chipped beef. I waited for Feeley to clear the door, then I slammed it behind him. He spun around, sloshing blood from the bucket onto his pants—no—my pants.

"Who are yo. . . ?" He never finished the question, maybe because he recognized me. I could smell his fear, but he was also laughing.

I wanted to kill him; I wanted to drain the blood from his body, but most of all I wanted to scare the hell out of him. I knew I couldn't do that partially dressed.

"First of all, give me back my pants." I tried to sound scary and mysterious, and I guess I succeeded because he wasted no time stripping down to his green and orange boxers.

Instead of getting fancy, I put my pants on one leg at a time. With my new undead abilities I could probably jump ten feet up in the air, have my shoes off, pants on, shirt tucked in, and shoes back on and tied before I hit the ground, but I didn't want to give Nuzbetch a chance to escape. I sure didn't want to botch it and have him laughing at me again.

I zipped up; the pants fit. It had to be a vampire thing. No way was I as fat as Nuzbetch.

The mortician shot glances at the door and at me. I made a point of pulling the belt in an extra notch as I casually stepped between him and the door. The move might have appeared more ominous if I hadn't burned my hands on the silver belt buckle. Wasn't it supposed to be were-wolves that hated silver?

"You know, it'll be dawn soon." Feeley sputtered. "You can't enter my house, so you'll be nothing but a pile of dust unless I help you."

The man knew his vampire lore—certainly better than I did—probably came with mortician training. Still, how

Mortified

certain could he be about everything? "It's very simple, Feeley," I told him. "After I kill you, your home will be as open to me as any other abandoned building."

I leaned in and smelled rising terror in his blood. The scent was intoxicating. No wonder vampires didn't just bonk people over the head and drag them off to feed.

I was glad I retrieved my pants before I scared him. A stream of yellow ran down Feeley's leg, forming a puddle by his right foot.

The smell of urine, while unpleasant, did nothing to stem my appetite. The urge to kill and feed was strong, but there was another force inside me.

I never liked my great aunt Agnes. When I was a child, she used to hector me about proper behavior and table etiquette. As much as I wanted to ignore her, I always buckled to her irresistible will. I was the only kid in summer camp who ate his hot dog with a fork.

Here she was again, nothing but a dead woman's voice ensconced in my supposedly demonic, undead brain. "Don't slay your food," she said. What did that even mean? Ridiculous, how could I survive if I didn't slay?

From Nuzbetch's perspective, my inner battle must have looked ominous. The man was on the ground, his bare bony knees in mud and urine, shaking and blubbering for mercy.

"Don't kill me!" he cried. "I can help you. I'll do anything. Please, don't kill me!"

He was a pathetic mess. He stole my pants. But I needed his help.

I waited, feigning uncertainty. The sky was going pink in the east. As much as I enjoyed the groveling, I needed to get under cover. I grabbed the mortician by the chin and forced him to look me in the eye.

"Invite me inside, Nuzbetch."

I suppose things could be worse. Nuzbetch's basement is dry and blocks the sunlight during the day. He set me up in a lovely coffin and asked if I wanted it lined with Transylvanian dirt. I declined; it seemed more messy than exotic.

Once Around the Sun

The funeral business keeps me well supplied with blood. Dead blood makes an uninteresting dietary staple, but it keeps Great Aunt Agnes quiet.

I went back to school, taking only night classes. People were pretty surprised to see me, but it raised less fuss than you'd think. My frat brothers thought it added prestige to the house. They try not to eat too much garlic when I'm around.

I make money for tuition and death's little extras as a night watchman. The black uniform suits me. Feeley packs me a thermos each night.

I do get tired of dead blood all the time.

Maybe someone will show up and make trouble.

Great Aunt Agnes would never defend a troublemaker.

The Banshee

Bernadette De Courcey

Siobhan was twelve years old when she had her first run-in with the banshee. She had heard all the stories grandma told, trying to send her and her brothers to their beds early on dark nights. The banshee, a small, frail old lady with long silver hair, came around people's houses when someone was about to pass to the next world, warning of the inevitable grieving to come. She would wail a soulless cry and comb her hair with a toothless comb— a deep sadness for the person about to depart from this world.

Siobhan imagined how she would look, this banshee, dressed in a dirty white shawl and skirt. Big black boots on her feet. Every old person in Ireland had a pair of big black boots. Her hair tangled and greasy, so long it dragged on the ground. Her face, an open mouth, where ear-hurting wails came forth.

Walking home in the evening, Siobhan was always on the lookout for the banshee. No one she knew, apart from her grandma, had ever seen one. Everyone would want to hear about it at school if she happened to come across her hiding in the bushes, wailing and moaning, combing her grey locks. This was all well and good in theory, but she worried that she may actually faint with fright if it came true.

Barnacrusha was a small fishing village on the Atlantic ocean. A population of less than seven hundred people. In the summer, it was flooded with so many tourists that you wondered how it was possible to fit them all into one tiny town. The summer was great though, lots of fun festivals and regatta's, pony shows, and sail boats. Siobhan dreaded the winters, they were so long and dreary. Rain falling softly or misting into fog in the early hours of the morning as she and her brother Eric got the bus to school.

To make it even more depressing, every November, the month of All Souls, there were at least three funerals in the small village church. The mournful procession driving slowly, respectfully down to the beachside graveyard to inter the deceased into an eternal sandy resting place with an ocean view. Her family always attended these services. They were her neighbors, very old neighbors that she didn't know, but neighbors just the same. The stories would spread at each service.

"Tommy Joe heard a knock on his door at two a.m., that was the same time the doctor's announced his ma's time of death."

"There was a loud banging outside just as he slipped from this world to the next, and when I went out to see what caused it, there was nothing there."

"The mirror fell from the wall. It should have been covered with a towel; it smashed into a thousand pieces. Oh God rest her soul."

Everyone blessing themselves with the holy rosary in their hands.

Siobhan and Eric would jostle for position nearest to the best story tellers at the wake. The strong smell of whiskey emanating from their mouths mixed with the scent of burning candles and the recently perfumed departed.

"When I was a young lad there was a ghost path across our farm. You daren't go near it after dark. The hairs would stand up on the back of me neck as I crossed it during broad daylight, and once across it, I never looked back. No, no, child you never look back at a ghost path. We used to build a stack of turf along the stone wall, and Mamo would warn us not to build it past where the wall ended. One night me and Michael built the turf stack past the part where we shouldn't, just to see what would happen.

"Well, we went off to bed and slept soundly as any other night. The next morning we made sure we were up first, before everyone else, and we ran down to check the turf stack before rounding up the cows for milking." Tommy Joe paused to refill his whiskey glass. All the children leaned in, holding their breath, eyes fixed.

"Where was I?"

"You and your brother were checking the turf stack early in the morning," Siobhan reminded him.

"Oh, yes. Well the turf stack was fine, still standing, or so we thought. But as we got closer, we could see that the four feet of turf we had stacked past the end of the wall was knocked down and spread about the place. We couldn't believe our eyes. We had been the last to bed, no cow was in the field, and no small fox, or dog, could have knocked it so precisely; not without the turf being dislodged next to it.

"No children, it wasn't the work of any living creature, that's for sure. Well, boys being boys, we decided to build it up and see if it would happen again. Four days in a row we built it up, and four days in a row, it was knocked down. That day, the fourth day, as we were crossing the ghost path just after dark, Michael suddenly fell down, and his ankle was twisted bad. My hair was standing up all over my arms and neck. Michael was shouting. *Someone grabbed me by the leg, someone grabbed me by the leg.* He lifted his glass to his lips and threw down the shot.

"That was the last time we meddled with the ghost path."

That was the end of story telling for the time being, so Siobhan and Eric followed the other children outside to play kick-the-can. Now that they were good and scared, they began their hide-in-the-dark game. Siobhan wasn't afraid of the dark; her dad had always told her: it's not the dead that will hurt you, but the living. Winning kick-the-can was her thing. She was never the one looking for the hiders.

There were obvious places you could hide; between the parked cars, behind the hen house, in the bushes, up the cherry tree even, but tonight she chose to go as far from the light of the windows as she could.

Orla had volunteered to be on, and she was a scaredy-cat who wouldn't dare look for Siobhan in a spot too far from the safety of the house. With the hood of her black coat up over her head, Siobhan slipped off behind the shed. Orla counted to fifty out loud with her head turned to the tree, the can on the ground beside her. All the children skittered off looking for hiding places. Once the counting was done, Orla had to try and find each of the children before they could get to the can and kick it. If they kicked the can they were safe.

As Siobhan went farther into the fields, Orla's voice was harder to hear. *She must be done counting by now*, she thought. *Here, I will hide behind this wall.* As she climbed over she could hear squeals coming from the other kids as Orla caught them. *She won't catch me out here, and once she goes to the other side of the house I will run back and kick the can.*

Siobhan smiled to herself. She looked up at the cloudy sky, some of the stars visible between. The moon was covered, and she could barely see the stone wall she was hiding behind. Pulling her coat closer around her to ward off the cold, she began to think about the story of the ghost path. *Not a good idea to start getting all scared while hiding out alone in a dark field*, she thought, so she tried to think about school instead.

Time passed slowly, and it seemed Orla was still trying to catch everyone. Siobhan decided it was time to start sneaking back to kick the can. As she was climbing the wall, a loud shrill noise made her freeze still, one leg up on the wall and one down on the ground. The noise grew louder. *It couldn't be, could it? Not the banshee.*

She hoisted herself up and over the wall, not daring to look around to see where the noise was coming from. She ran as fast as she could back to the group and shouted.

"The banshee, the banshee, she's back there behind the wall. Oh God it was so awful. Did you hear her?"

The children looked at her and said "No . . . no, we didn't hear her."

"She's there. I saw her. She was combing her hair and howling. She tried to grab me." The words came tumbling out before she could edit them. Her imagination was running wild. Her arms flailing between blessing herself and corralling them all into a huddle for safety. The smallest ones started crying and had to be brought inside.

Soon the adults were all fussing over the children, shushing them and then directing them to the car, when they were unable to get them to stop crying and hiccupping. Siobhan's mother and father told her to calm down and not scare the other children like that.

"But Dad, I heard her, she's out there, why don't you believe me?"

He put on his coat and said he would go out and take a look. Siobhan and Eric watched from the window. Once he went behind the shed they lost sight of him in the darkness, only seeing a small glow from the flashlight he had borrowed. Their mom made apologies for them and talked quietly in the kitchen with the neighbors.

After about ten minutes, he came back in the door and called Siobhan over to him. He bent down and put his arm around her. "You may be right Siobhan, you may well have heard the banshee." He pulled her hand forward and in it he put a toothless comb. "I think she left this for you".

The next few weeks in school there was a buzz of excitement. Siobhan had seen a banshee, and she had her comb to prove it.

Autumn Pursuit

David Chesney

Winner of the 2012 Bethlehem Writers Roundtable Short Story Award

When walking too close to a stranger, you have fifteen steps before you must slow down or hurry ahead. People have a very touchy sense of personal space. They'll allow it to be breached only for a moment, and if you make no effort to allow them their space, you'll be labeled as a creep. I have fifteen steps to think of something to say. Something witty that will make her smile.

Two paces in front of me she hurries from class, quickly trying to escape the dreary weather. The wind whips her scarf back just in front of my face. She slows down to step around a puddle. I'm now walking even with her. This is my only opportunity. I can't pass her by and then finally muster the courage to talk to her. This is the only window I have. I can't turn around and casually start a conversation because that would seem too awkward, and I certainly can't let her pass me by again and still stand a chance. Either way would be an obvious attempt at picking her up. Maybe make a joke about her scarf hitting me. No, she'll think I don't like the way she dresses.

She seems like the type of girl that doesn't realize quite how beautiful she is. Her walk lacks any sway in the hips, and her eyes are focused on the ground in front of her. The way she carries herself reveals a bit of shyness. Her coffee-house glasses suggest that she wants to appear fashionably intelligent. I can't believe I even know the term "coffee-house" glasses, nor do I even know if that is the correct term. The glasses are dark, thick-rimmed, and square. Girls from teenage sitcoms used to wear them as geek apparel, but apparently they are fashionable now.

Once Around the Sun

Fourteen steps left. Quit thinking about how much you like the girl and talk to her. Say anything. Puff your shoulders up and ask her in a deep voice if she knows where the nearest weight room is. Sure that didn't work for Chris Farley in *Tommy Boy*, but you've got charisma. When is the last time you even flirted with a girl? A month ago, and you were successful. She liked you. And before that? In the summer when you went with your roommate to a party, the volleyball player with strawberry-blonde hair loved you, if only for the one night. Girls like you when you work up the courage to talk to them. So quit wasting your time and put your foot in the door.

Maybe she will trip any second. I hope so. I could be the knight in shining armor that helps her up. I'd be set if she just fell right now. Maybe she wants me to talk to her. If she does, she should just trip on purpose. Any sensible guy would help her up, and she could initiate the conversation. This should be a universal rule for women: if you are interested in a stranger, and you are walking near him, trip in his view. No room is left for an awkward beginning to the conversation. Sure you may gain a few battle scrapes and scars, or even a hole in your favorite jeans, but you will gain the companionship of a new man.

Thirteen. You don't have time to brainstorm on how women can get the men they want. You are trying to get the woman you want. So stop with your philosophies and start a conversation.

She pulls out her phone from her coat. Twelve. I hope she's not calling someone. I'd lose all chance of talking to her if she stays on the phone. Nope, she's just reading a text message. She laughs. Her focus is on the message, so I'm not sure I'll be able to gain her attention easily.

Eleven. No, you're a mysterious stranger to her. You're more interesting to her than some guy in her statistics class that keeps sending her messages hoping to score this weekend. She doesn't want that guy. She's just friendly, so every guy in her class wants her, but she wants none of them.

Maybe I shouldn't make so many assumptions about this girl I don't know. Who's to say she isn't texting her boyfriend or some other love interest. I usually have the uncanny ability to read people, even when I've never met them. Maybe I should just trust my instincts. What do I know about her? She's in Professor Barrett's course. I saw her walking out of his classroom on Monday and decided I had to meet her. I went through this whole situation then, but I reached my fifteen steps and backed down in defeat. She has a key-chain on her backpack that says Class of '17, so she's a freshman. She's a freshman in Barrett's class. That's all I have to work with.

Ten. Work with it then. Now!

Nine. The sun peaks through the clouds on the evening horizon, forcing me to glance away from the woman momentarily.

Eight. You're wasting your time. You are never going to talk to her. Let's just face that reality. You never take a risk. Quit. Just go home.

Seven. Oh so now you've succumbed to using reverse psychology on yourself. Is your courage really so severely lacking?

Six. All right, I'll do it, but I still don't have anything to say.

Five. Be confident. Be a man. Be a confident man. Stand up straight, throw your shoulders slightly back, and put a cocky little grin on your face. Do this and what you say doesn't even matter. She'll just melt in your hands.

Four. Still though, I need something to say. Anything. I adjust the collar of my favorite maroon shirt as I always seem to do when I'm nervous. I'm not superstitious, but I consider this my lucky shirt. Sure, a couple little bleach stains decorate the lining, and the color isn't so bright anymore, but the shirt has so much history. I make my final adjustment of the collar and turn towards the girl.

Three. "You're . . ." my lips freeze. Any attempt at confidence flees my body as anxiety floods my vocal cords. I'm not quite sure how loud or distinguishable that one word was. Did she hear me? I don't think so. I can start over unnoticed.

Once Around the Sun

Two. She looks at me. Our eyes lock for an instant, and my heart pounds with each step. Great. She did hear me.

One. She is waiting for me to speak, and I'm still counting my steps.

"You're in Barrett's class right?" Really, how could I open this conversation by asking her to confirm a detail of her life? Of course, she's in Barrett's class. That's not a question you ask someone right after you saw her walk out of the classroom. How would I know that she's in that class? She's going to think I'm a creep for sure. Oh well, just keep talking. If I don't act like my comment was odd, she won't think my comment was odd.

"Professor Barrett? Yeah. How about you?" she says with a slight smile on her face, which attracts me to her even more. What am I going to say now? I don't know anything about the class or professor. I'm just in the class across the hall.

"So how'd you do on that last test?" I ask. I hope the class is not one where students only write papers and don't have any tests until the final. I'd be finished already, and I'd have to confess the lie that I'm in the progress of telling. What's the big deal in fabricating a harmless little lie? She might even think my approach is cute, that is, of course, if she ever finds out. Maybe I'll tell her after a couple dates and she knows I'm not an outright liar.

A couple of dates? Don't get ahead of yourself. You don't even know her name, yet.

"Not near as well as I'd hoped. I got a low C. I was really hoping to squeak out a B in the class, but it doesn't look like that's gonna to happen. What about you?" she asked to my relief.

"I did all right. I got a ninety," I said after a slight hesitation. This was the grade I just received in another class, so the number was fresh on my tongue.

"I don't really like it that much. Most of my other classes are a little more interesting," she responds.

"This is probably my favorite class, but I'm an engineering major, so Political Science is a good change of pace from my other classes. What's your major?" I ask. At least I've now told her one truth about myself. I am an engineering major.

She responds, but I don't hear what she said. I was busy trying to figure out how I was going to make it through this lie.

All right, for one thing, don't throw in too many details. You don't want her to know that you're making things up.

No way does she suspect that I'm not in that class. Of the at least two hundred students, she perhaps knows four or five of them. Just go ahead and tell her the truth: that you are stalking her.

I think guys are allowed a certain small window to "stalk" the girl that they want. We have to have the time to work up our courage or at least think of something clever (the latter part is not going so well for me thus far). Additionally, it's not really stalking if the girl likes the attention and thinks my actions are cute, right? On the other hand, I imagine people who might be considered stalkers think that they're doing things in a cute way, but they just don't have the charisma to succeed. That or they just choose the wrong girl to pursue. You can't expect to win over Natalie Portman by spelling "I love you, Natalie" on her lawn with two thousand waffles. The result would probably be tightened security at her mansion and snacks for a month for the guard dogs (not to mention a restraining order). One's girlfriend, on the other hand, might think such a gesture is cute and romantic in an oddly charming way.

I should probably get her name. This has to be the worst pick up attempt ever. Yet, as I look over at her, she gives me a smile and answers the question that was a second from leaving my lips. "I'm sorry. I didn't catch your name. I'm Autumn."

My first instinct is to make a joke before I tell her my name, but all that's coming to my mind is "That's because I didn't throw it your way," but of course I didn't attempt this ridiculously pathetic joke and merely said, "My name is Matt."

This Business of Wood

Sally W. Paradysz

In the silence of dawn, admiring the soft hue of rough-cut native lumber, Addie grabbed her chainsaw from its home by the door. She lingered in the corner of the small barn, dedicated to cant hook, helmet, and chaps. All had stood the test of time. The leather chaps, cracked and worn, were an heirloom from her grandfather and father. They were too heavy for her to wear, but she treasured them for their history. Raising them to her face, she noticed with gratitude that the scents of the past still lingered.

Her new equipment, the stuff of the nineties, was lighter, easier to handle. Her chaps were made, not of leather, but of a cloth designed to break apart and clog the saw blade should it miss its mark and get caught in them.

As she had every decade since her father taught her the trade, she loaded the tools into her tractor and headed for the woods behind the sturdy shed she had built for herself when she was young. Her home, nestled in the Berkshires of Massachusetts, was not far off the historic Mohawk Trail. Those mountains had given her a rich and varied life; one she loved.

She bumped along on her tractor to the edge of the wetlands and the tiny millpond beyond. Once there, she rested for a moment on the large flat rock overhanging the water. Bending carefully forward, she cupped handfuls of chilled water to her mouth. Its spring-fed freshness brought a smile to her face.

Those hands, so like her father's: thick, calloused, and strong. Workers' hands. Three generations of loggers were in her blood, giving her experience, and plenty of stories to remember and share with those who listened. This business of wood, its smell and warmth, had soothed the souls of her family for well over a century.

Her father had taught her well, as had his father before him. But still, she had not been accepted in the world of lumbermen. Respected, yes. Accepted, no. *But that's okay,* she thought. *It's all behind me now.*

Norm hadn't heard her drive up. Crossing her legs Indian style, she watched her brother notch a tree before he cut it down, thinking thirty years back to the accident that had changed their lives.

Felling a tree against the lean, Norm had misjudged its height. It struck Oliver, their younger brother, cutting a tree nearby. Norm threw his saw aside—wounding himself in the process—and ran to Oliver's side, but he was already gone.

Physically, Norm had escaped with a broken wrist and a cut on his face. Emotionally, he'd never been the same.

Every year on the anniversary of the event, still shamed by his mistake, Norm plunged into depression, and she had to watch him.

In the years after Oliver's death, Addie spent hundreds of hours in Lenox with a friend who counseled her through the grief. Norm refused any help, even when he had another accident the following year. He was alone at the time, and forever vague on what happened.

Shaking off the memories, surprised at how heavy they were, Addie stood. "Hey Norm," she yelled, hoping he had his hearing aids in, but assuming he didn't. She circled the pond and walked toward the large pile of cut and stacked logs.

Turning his scarred face toward Addie, he smiled crookedly. "Hey yourself, sis. How are ya this morning?"

They stared at each other for a moment. As Addie drew nearer, she realized he'd aged immensely during these last few years. Norm's stance revealed his bent and twisted body; the result of his accident. Addie was more fortunate, her frame solidly held together by sinewy muscles. Two siblings, both in their seventh decade were about to end three generations of family history.

Noticing that his smile was starting to break under her stare, she set down her equipment and pulled him into an embrace. "We can do this together, Norm. Just like always," she whispered into his ear. "The last day of the lumber business is not the last day of our lives." She stepped back to take another look at his expression. His jaw was clenched, and his eyes glistened in the sunlight.

He nodded, and looked away as he wiped his eyes with his sleeve. "Addie, you look just like Dad today," he said turning back to her. "Is that his old work shirt?"

Looking down at the red-checked plaid, too large for her wiry frame, she felt a smile make its way across her weathered face. "Yes. Stood the test of time, right?"

Norm nodded. "Yup. Dad knew how to pick 'em."

Addie considered her brother's words as they worked, clearing out areas that would make way for newer saplings. Their father had always known how to pick 'em. She remembered his advice about choosing which trees to fell, and which to leave. *Look first at the brushwood, then at the trees. Be selective, and be right, before you cut.*

At noon, as the pungent odor of gas and oil lingered, they headed for the shade of the sugar maples, and lunch. She unwrapped two sandwiches: one baked bean and the other of her meat loaf. Norm unfolded a hunk of fresh baked bread and went to work on some homemade hash with his fork.

Looking over at her brother, her friend, she shook her head. "We are quite the pair of old codgers, that's for sure."

"Yep." He took a bite of bread and looked away.

Finishing their meal, they lay back against the soft earth using their jackets as headrests. The beginning of fall had always been their favorite time of year. They lay side by side, pointing out songbirds in the surrounding forest. How many hours had they spent together? How many tales had they shared?

Watching Norm out of the corner of her eye, she noticed he was wide-eyed and alert. Norm was always game for most anything, never once complaining about the long hours of work.

But it was over.

Over because of a decision Addie made three months ago. She wanted to retire young enough to pursue her love of the arts, especially with Tanglewood and Jacob's Pillow so close by. At sixty-five, she trusted that she still had time for that one passion she had never fulfilled.

She rolled to her side and let her chin rest on the palm of her hand, her elbow propped on the soft moss below. With a pang of regret she contemplated this family history coming to an end. No new generations on the horizon to take their place.

They had all made lives for themselves here in the westernmost part of Massachusetts, supplying the lumber for many homes in the process. She'd realized over the years that her nature was both tender and fierce, like a mother's when it came to these beloved woods. Gentle and powerful; she liked that combination.

"Norm." Her voice sounded loud in the quiet woods. "Remember the story about Gramps and how he broke his leg after it wedged between two logs that slipped off the skids?"

"Yup. He made a splint out of stickers and worked that busted leg for the rest of the day. Then, for the first time in his life, he rode one of the two work horses home holding onto its leather collar for support."

Addie nodded. "Must have hurt like hell."

Norm shuddered and said, "Reminds me of my last accident, as clear as if it happened yesterday. Wouldn't be here today if you hadn't come along."

"Good timing on my part," Addie said softly, not wanting to press Norm for the details he never shared.

He shook his head slowly and looked into the forest. "No Addie, you always kept your mind clear and thoughtful. When I didn't come home on time, you came looking for me. You found me under that large oak, head smashed and limbs broken. As much as you wanted to go out with friends, you always waited until every bit of work was finished, and we were all home safe. I owe you my life."

"I'd better get back to work," she said rolling onto her feet and heading toward her saw. She hoped he had not seen her tears.

Five large oval boulders defined the edges of the cutting area. Their upright position reminded her of Stonehenge. She felt they must have been sacred offerings from earlier Indian tribes. Addie's fingertips traced the layers of mica embedded within. She picked off a piece with her fingernail. Centuries ago these stones had accepted the first dusting of snow in early winter. She offered her own gift of a kiss, from lips to finger, and finger to stone. Looking skyward she smiled and spread her arms wide and whispered, "This is all I have."

Chainsaw in hand, she cut the felled trees into sixteen-inch logs. These pieces would fuel their own woodstoves for many winters to come. As she worked, the whirring blade spit warm chips onto the ground; the small piles marking her progress to the end of each trunk. Norm dropped a dozen more trees, leaving the smaller ones alongside as undamaged as possible, then he topped them and left the brush for animals to hide under in harsh weather.

Addie glanced at Norm every few minutes to make sure he was okay. He had delivered the last load of lumber they would ever cut for others and deposited the last check they would ever earn.

Three hours later, exhausted, she packed her gear into her tractor's front-end loader. "Norm," she said when his saw was quiet, "I'll wait for you tonight near the skids of our sawmill, somewhere around six-thirty. Let me treat you to dinner at The Morgan House in Lee. We'll reminisce on the way; see how many old stories we can tell in the forty-five minutes it takes to get there. I want to look at this day as a celebration, not a death."

"I'll be there," he said, smiling and shrugging his shoulders.

She waved and climbed aboard her Kubota. On the trail back, she thought about her conversation with Norm and the team of horses her grandfather had used years before. It must have been quite a sight: seven brothers plus their father coming out of the woods toward the mill in the late afternoon. When they had time off, they entered the team in "horse draws" at the country fairs, always held in the fall. It was the highlight for each kid in town, and something Oliver had looked forward to every year of his young existence.

Oliver. Addie remembered him laughing at her when she was just fourteen. She'd been using her dad's forklift to load the truck with lumber and snakes had fallen out between the boards, scaring her half to death. Those same stickers her grandfather used to splint his leg held the pieces of lumber apart from each other to dry in the sun. In summer, the snakes loved the heat and slithered between the boards. Oliver heard her yelp and rolled on the ground laughing.

Home again, Addie put her equipment away and headed inside for a well-deserved hot shower. As she toweled dry, the nap of the material scraped across her thin wrinkled skin. She looked at her body with dismay.

"I have gotten old," she said, shaking her head.

Refreshed, she lay back on her bed with her eyes closed and immediately fell into a deep slumber. She had learned to function well on small intervals of sleep, plus the occasional catnap.

She woke a half-hour later to the long shadows of early evening, and, choosing a pair of nice slacks and a light sweater, she dressed and headed for the mill. Once there, she leaned against the skids that her grandfather had made and waited. Norm's truck was missing. He'd likely gone home to shower and change. After all these years, he still didn't like going out in public. As close as they'd become over the decades, she knew he still felt self-conscious, even in her presence. Only in the forest could he relax.

She looked at her watch; it was six forty-five. He probably left the woods late, held back by something he needed to finish. He was known for that.

This Business of Wood

Addie walked over to the silent mill, empty of workers after all these long years. She wrapped her arms against her chest, attempting to hold the memories back. Even so, they flooded in with such force she was compelled to sit for a moment on the metal rail of the log bed. She looked at the gears, handles, and saw. Blades, three feet in diameter. Huge. Some of the fondest memories of her dad were of him sharpening those blades. He would wedge it with a block of wood so the saw wouldn't spin and then hone its tips to perfection with his wide file. They had spent many summer evenings on this labor; father and daughter, working together and sharing their dreams.

A list of words that described the father who so shaped her life ran through her mind: integrity, respect, and devotion. He was a man of strength, both physically and morally. *I miss him terribly*, she thought. *I wish that I could have loved him longer, but I have to trust that my deep love for him was enough.*

She stood and looked at her watch again. An hour had passed. Norm wasn't coming. *I guess he couldn't stand the pain*, she decided as she walked back. She would let him handle this transition in his own way. There would be no judgment from her. She, too, found it difficult to think that the business of wood was over. Wyman's Lumber, the end of an era.

I hope he's okay, she thought, walking into her home to see if he'd left a message.

The red light on the phone's answering machine did not blink.

No longer hungry, she turned off the lights and climbed the stairs to her room. The last blush of evening caught the soft glow of knotty pine, some of the last lumber cut from her father's sawmill back in the early seventies. Yet another reminder of her heritage.

In bed, she doused the light and closed her tired eyes. Beneath their lids, she viewed the tracks of her life, the landscape of them wide and varied, yet constant. Her soul contained both the strength of the walls that surrounded her and the tenderness of the delicate lady slippers in her back yard.

As she rested, wind rattled her window screens and howled through the trees. An approaching storm sounded like the cacophony of a nighttime orchestra warming up.

Addie looked over at the silent phone, sat up, and pulled on a boot.

About the Authors

Courtney Annicchiarico has lived in the Lehigh Valley for the past eight years with her loving husband, their two sons, and their crazy dog, Macs. When she is not writing, she knits badly, bakes, and works to raise Autism awareness.

Jeff Baird is a natural Redhead, a career educator at the secondary and post-graduate level, and a self-proclaimed computer junkie. He has presented at numerous state and national technology conferences and has published in the field of educational technology. He now turns his energies to publishing his humorous memoir, *The World According to a Redhead,* a book about all things Redhead. You can check out his Redhead Profiling blog at jeffbaird.blogspot.com and his website at www.jeffbaird.net

He resides in the Lehigh Valley of Pennsylvania with his wife Mary, a Redheaded wannabe, true Redheaded children, Ashley and Ryan, and their dog Casey, an honorary Redhead.

Carol A. Hanzl Birkas resides in Bethlehem, Pennsylvania with her husband, Gene. She has had several articles published in both newspapers and magazines, and one short story, "Visions of Sugarplum Grandmothers," which appears in *A Christmas Sampler: Sweet, Funny, and Strange Holiday Tales* by the Bethlehem Writers Group. Her greatest achievement is a children's picture book entitled *Christmas Treena,* which debuted during the 2009 Christmas season.

David Chesney is an engineer with the NASA robotics division. He's busy building robots, but hopes to soon return to his favorite pastime: writing novels and screenplays. His story, "Autumn Pursuit," won the 2011 Bethlehem Writers Roundtable Short Story Award.

Once Around the Sun

Bernadette De Courcey was born and raised in Connemara, Ireland, where she grew up listening to the best ghost stories and local folklore. She graduated with an MA in Modern English Literature from the University of Limerick, Ireland, and is currently an English Professor at Keiser University. She enjoys writing creatively, co-editing the *Bethlehem Writers Roundtable*, and sailing.

A. E. Decker is a former doll maker and English as a Second Language tutor who holds degrees in English and history. With her focus on fantasy, she attended the Odyssey Writers' Workshop in 2011. "Dee's" short stories have been published by *Fireside Magazine*, *Beneath Ceaseless Skies*, and *World Weaver Press*. She is currently outlining a fantasy romance novel about magical chocolate. Like all writers, Dee is owned by three cats.

Marianne H. Donley taught mathematics to a variety of students from middle school to university level. She now writes fiction from short stories and quirky murder mysteries to humorous romances fueled by her life as a mom and a teacher. She's a member of Romance Writers of America and its Orange County (CA) chapter and Sisters in Crime. She makes her home in Pennsylvania with her husband and a tank full of multiplying fish.

Katherine Fast, a.k.a. Kat, is in her eighth or ninth life focusing on fiction writing, watercolor, and handwriting analysis. For the past three years, she has been a contributing editor/publisher of Level Best Books with primary responsibility for the design and production of their annual anthology. Her stories have appeared in anthologies and ezines. One of her stories, "The Bonus," won NEWN's Flash Fiction contest in 2007. Her story, "Ava Maria," won the 2013 Bethlehem Writers Roundtable Short Story Award.

About the Authors

Headley Hauser, author of the Genre Series beginning with *Trouble in Taos*, and former host of the critically unclaimed TV show *Headley and the Rug (and Cral)* writes for food. "I've got lots of stuff," he says, "make me an offer! I particularly like Pop Tarts." Links to his work are available on Go Figure Reads (gofigurereads.com). His blog is Just Plain Stupid (headleystupid.blogspot.com). Headley lives in Winston-Salem, NC, but is willing to move if you have a comfortable couch.

Jerome W. McFadden has held various esoteric jobs around the world while supporting his writing addiction, including selling industrial chemicals in Africa, surfboards in Europe, and crayons in Asia. He has twenty years experience in freelance writing for American magazines and newspapers, but is now focusing on fiction. He received the Second Place Bullet Award in June, 2011, for the best crime fiction on the web, has had one of his stories read on the London stage by the UK Liars' League, and has received top mentions in several national short story contests.

Emily P. W. Murphy is a freelance writer and editor who lives in a small town in western Maryland. A native to Pennsylvania, she is a graduate of Lafayette College and member of the Bethlehem Writers Group. Emily is a devoted Red Sox fan and a lifetime member of the Jane Austen Society of North America. You may visit her website at www.emilypwmurphy.com.

Once Around the Sun

Sally W. Paradysz was born, raised, and earned her degree in the Berkshires of New England. She writes memoir and fiction from the cabin she built in the woods of her Bucks County, Pennsylvania, home, and it is from there that she pens a weekly blog for those searching for a breath of calm. As an advocate for the self-empowerment of women, she draws upon her own life experiences bringing the world a message of healing, love, and inspiration. Ordained into the ministry of the Assembly of the Word, founded in Quakertown, PA, Sally has provided spiritual counseling and ministerial assistance for more than two decades. She is the mother of three, grandmother of eight, and is a slave, by choice, to her two flamboyant Maine Coon cats, Kiva and Kodi, who love their life in the woods. Her story, "This Business of Wood," was a finalist in the 2010 Salem (MA) Literary Festival Writing Competition.

Jo Ann Schaffer began reinventing herself in her early sixties. Prior to that, she was an executive assistant to CEOs or a corporate communications editor/manager in such diverse fields as banking, pension trust, international philanthropy, Japanese real estate development, and healthcare. After moving to Bethlehem from Queens, NY, where she had spent most of her life, Jo Ann trained to be a Clinical Hypnotist. Upon retirement, she started her own company, Options Hypnosis. It was also during those early years in Bethlehem that she started to hone her skills as a writer of short fiction, and became a founding member of the Bethlehem Writers Group. She has traveled in six continents, but the UK holds a special place in her heart. Her other interests include reading, yoga, Buddhism, architecture, and technology.

About the Authors

Diane Sismour has written poetry and fiction for over thirty-five years, starting with journalism, children's stories, middle-grade adventures, as well as science fiction and young adult novels. Recently, she has added the Romantic Mystery genre and Teen Historical Horror to the list. Diane is also the founder of Network for the Arts and connects thousands of artists with workshops, events, and publishing news every day. She discusses the Network for the Arts and writing as a guest speaker on radio talk shows all over the country and as a guest author for blogs, newspapers and magazines. She is a member of the Romance Writers of America, the Bethlehem Writers Group, Liberty States Fiction Writers, Bucks County Romance Writer's Chapter, and she is a past vice-president of the Pocono Lehigh Romance Writers.

Paul Weidknecht's work has appeared most recently in *Pisgah Review*, *Clackamas Literary Review*, *James Dickey Review*, *The Quotable*, and *decomP magazinE*. Previous story publications include *Rosebud*, *Shenandoah*, and *The Los Angeles Review*, among others. He read his poem "Nya Sverige" before King Carl XVI Gustaf and Queen Silvia of Sweden during the 375th Anniversary Jubilee in celebration of the landing of the Swedes and Finns at Wilmington, Delaware and was awarded a scholarship to The Norman Mailer Writers Colony. He lives in New Jersey where he has completed a collection of stories, *Fly in a Cube of Amber*. For more, please visit: www.paulweidknecht.com

Once Around the Sun

Carol L. Wright is a former lawyer, adjunct law professor, pre-law advisor, and book editor. She is the author of several articles on law-related topics, and of the book, *The Ultimate Guide to Law School Admission*. She has published several short stories and is currently at work on a murder mystery set in western Massachusetts. She is a life member of Sisters in Crime and of the Jane Austen Society of North America, and is a life-long Red Sox fan. She is married to her college sweetheart and lives in the Lehigh Valley of Pennsylvania. You may visit her website at www.carollwright.com.

Will Wright is enjoying positive reviews for the first book in his Dragon Alliance series, *Cinder,* and for his two collections of his short stories, *Without a Tear* and *Salt for the Journey*, also available as e-books. In addition to Dragon Alliance, Will is preparing to launch a second fantasy series with *Bottle's Queue,* expected in 2014. His work can be found on Go Figure Reads: gofigurereads.com. Will lives in Winston-Salem, NC.

Acknowledgements

Bethlehem Writers Group, LLC, would like to acknowledge the contributions of those who helped to make this book a reality.

We especially wish to thank the esteemed authors Jonathan Maberry and Hank Phillippi Ryan. Mr Maberry served as the judge of the 2012 Bethlehem Writers Roundtable Short Story Award, and selected "Autumn Pursuit" as the first-place winner. Ms. Ryan has offered BWG unflagging support and served as the judge of the 2013 Bethlehem Writers Roundtable Short Story Award competition. She selected "Ava Maria" as the winner. Both of the first-place stories appear in this compilation.

In addition, new BWG members Terrie Daugherty and Ruth Heil (www.thewritebeat.com), despite not having stories in the anthology, gave valuable assistance in copy editing and layout respectively.

No book is ever produced without the cooperation of a large team of talented individuals, and we are most grateful to all those who dedicated countless hours to see this volume through to fruition.

CPSIA information can be obtained at www.ICGtesting.com
Printed in the USA
BVOW07s0806151013

333748BV00001BA/1/P